A Sgt. Windflower mystery

Dangerous Waters

MIKE MARTIN

Also by Mike Martin
in the Sgt. Windflower Mystery Series

Ottawapress and publishing.com
Copyright © Mike Martin 2022
ISBN 978-1-988437-82-8 (book.)
ISBN 978-1-988437-84-2 (e-book)
Printed and bound in Canada
Design and composition: Writers First
Cover based on a photograph by Hunter Martin.

Library and Archives Canada Cataloguing in Publication
Title: Dangerous Waters / Mike Martin. Names: Martin, Mike,
1954- author. Description: Series statement: A Sgt. Windflower mystery
Identifiers: Canadiana (print) 20210218916
Canadiana (ebook) 20210218959
ISBN 978-1-988437-82-8 (softcover)
ISBN 978-1-988437-84-2 (e-book)
Classification: LCC PS8626.A77255 S24 2021
| DDC C813/.6—dc23

DEDICATION

To Joan. Thank you for your love and support. You are my Sheila and I try every day to be a better Windflower to you.

ACKNOWLEDGMENTS

I would like to thank a number of people for their help in getting this book out of my head and onto these pages. That includes beta readers and advisers: Mike MacDonald, Barb Stewart, Robert Way, Denise Zendel, Allister Thompson for his excellent copy editing and Alex Zych for final proofreading.

Chapter One

Eddie Tizzard looked down at the three files on his desk. Three men, all in their early sixties, reported missing from their homes and families in Grand Bank. One, Cedric Skinner, was found floating at the far end of Quidi Vidi Lake in St. John's. The other two, Paddy Slaney and Leo Broderick, were still missing.

He had just finished talking to Leo Broderick's wife. She was doubly distraught, first by the unexplained absence of her husband, then by the death of Cedric Skinner and the disappearance of Paddy Slaney. "What's going on?" she'd asked Tizzard. He had few answers for her or the other women in this small community on the southeast coast of Newfoundland.

"We'll do everything we can," he told Leo Broderick's wife. But truthfully, right now, there wasn't much anything he or anybody else could do to bring her husband back. He only hoped that it wasn't too late.

Tizzard leaned back in his chair and looked out the window. There was snow on the ground and more falling by the hour. Nothing unusual there. February in Newfoundland at the easternmost tip of Canada was cold, wet, and snowy. What was unusual was the fact that this wasn't his chair, and it wasn't his office. He looked down and saw something else that was new: corporal's stripes on his uniform. Two chevrons, to be exact, and an Acting Corporal title to go along with them.

He was acting head of the Grand Bank detachment of the Royal Canadian Mounted Police, the Mounties. He had been a corporal before but was demoted when he had an altercation with a superior officer. But now they needed him, so they gave him back his stripes, at least on a temporary basis until they figured things out. What caused all of this to unfold was the sudden resignation of his old boss, Sergeant Winston Windflower. That's whose chair Tizzard was sitting in as he looked out at the snowy morning in Grand Bank.

Winston Windflower wasn't looking out the window, nor was he thinking about Tizzard or the Mounties this morning. He and his co-worker, Levi Parsons, were nearly done refinishing the hardwood floors at the beautiful old B&B that Windflower and his wife Sheila Hillier owned and co-managed. Levi was a shy and quiet young man who had somehow built a friendship with the much older Windflower, and under his tutelage, had been working at the B&B for a couple of years now. He was even taking hotel and hospitality classes to learn the management skills he needed to help run the B&B.

But today the skills he needed were more of the manual labour type. They had already sanded and buffed the floors over the weekend, and now they were applying a new coat of stain. Tomorrow, they would start on the finish, and three coats of that later they would have perfect-looking hardwood floors to welcome their first dinner guests.

The B&B had been closed for over a year since the pandemic, and they were using this time, and Windflower had lots of it, to fix up the place before what they hoped would be a stellar tourist season. It had better be, thought Windflower. They would soon be without any steady income when his last few cheques from the RCMP dried up. Sheila had lots of business ideas cooking, but none were ready to provide them with the finances they would like to support their lifestyle and two small children.

Levi went off to clean their brushes while Windflower poured himself a coffee in the kitchen and walked upstairs. He went to the small veranda on the second floor and opened the doors. The cool, fresh air flooded in, aided by the ever-present wind. He stared out, past the lighthouse and what was left of downtown Grand Bank, into the vastness of the ocean. It always calmed him to have this view, and today was no exception. He paused for a few moments, gave thanks for the view and the beautiful day, and went downstairs.

He went out the back door of the B&B so as not to disturb the good work they had done so far on the hardwood floors. He was going to head home when he saw a familiar face waving at him from across the street. Herb Stoodley was the co-owner of the Mug-Up café, the best and only diner in Grand Bank. Herb and his wife Moira were also self-adopted grandparents to Windflower's two children.

Stella was a bright and curious five-year-old and Amelia Louise was a two-and-half-year-old whirlwind.

Herb and Windflower had hit it off from near the beginning when Windflower was first assigned to Grand Bank. They shared a love of the law, with Herb being a former Crown attorney, and under his tutelage Windflower was learning to share his love of classical music as well. The latest offering that Herb had provided was a version of Rachmaninoff's Piano Concerto No. 2 recorded by the Boston Symphony Orchestra. Windflower liked listening to classical music when he went on his weekly runs on Sunday morning with Amelia Louise on his back. This piece was perfect, thought Windflower as he thought about the swirling of the instruments and the haunting piano that pulled you back in.

"Morning, Herb," said Windflower.

"How are ya, b'y?" asked Stoodley. "You bored yet?"

"The B&B is keeping me going right now," said Windflower. "Although I have to say that it's hard to drive past the office without stopping in. My car just naturally wants to turn into the parking lot."

"It may be like that for a while," said Herb. "How's Sheila and the girls?"

"They're all well," said Windflower. "Sheila's working on getting some financing for some of her projects, and the girls are great. Stella is getting figure skating lessons in Marystown, and Amelia Louise is as rambunctious as ever."

"They're both so much fun," said Herb. "Moira is knitting new hats for them, but don't tell them, it's a surprise."

"They love surprises," said Windflower. "Anyway, I gotta run. Sheila needs the car to pick up some groceries. We'll see you soon. Oh, and thanks for the Rachmaninoff."

"Glad you liked it," said Herb. "It's one of my favourites. When you're ready, I have another one for you."

"Thanks, Herb," said Windflower as he waved goodbye to Herb and drove slowly home. He paused by the RCMP detachment, just for a moment. It looked busy, he thought, with one car pulling in and another leaving. With a small pang of something that might

3

be regret, he passed by and headed for home. Sheila and Amelia Louise were glad to see him. Sheila, especially. She kissed him on the cheek and took the car keys from his hand. "I'll see you soon," she said. "There's soup on the stove."

The other one who was pleased that he was home was Lady, his Collie and four-legged ally. There was another pet in the house, Molly the cat. But Molly did not move from her basket in the kitchen, even when Lady started her happy dance around Windflower and Amelia Louise. Windflower looked over at her once and thought he could see her peeking, but she gave no indication that she could care one way or another that the so-called master of the house was home.

She and Windflower had a like-hate relationship. He tried to like her, but she clearly showed him only disdain. "Never mind," said Windflower, mostly to himself as he looked around at the random display of toys in the living room. He understood immediately why Sheila needed to get out. Fast. Amelia Louise was adorable, but she was also a nonstop Energizer Bunny. Before she could loop Windflower into her next game, he preempted her with an offer of soup and grilled cheese sandwiches.

They went to the kitchen, and he lifted her up so she could see the pea soup in the pot on the stove.

"Pea soup," he said. "My favourite."

"My favrit, too," said Amelia Louise.

She helped him get the sandwiches ready. Helping consisted of her eating a slice of cheese and telling him a story that really had no beginning and clearly no end. Windflower knew this game and played along by nodding at what he thought were the most important moments in his daughter's monologue. He put the sandwiches on the frying pan, and while they were cooking, he took up a bowl of soup for her to cool as they were waiting.

When the sandwiches were done, he put her in her chair and tried feeding her the soup. That lasted about three spoonful's and then she grabbed the spoon from his hands. There would soon be soup everywhere, but Windflower would clean that up later. He gave Amelia Louise part of her sandwich and sat to enjoy his soup.

The pea soup was excellent, and he savoured every drop of the thick and creamy broth with flecks of salt meat and chunks of carrot and turnip. He was just finishing up when Sheila came in with her bags of groceries. He helped her put the things away, cleaned up Amelia Louise and the kitchen and then got everybody, including Lady, ready for a walk around the neighbourhood. With Amelia Louise in her wagon and Lady on her leash, they walked down their street and then headed down to the wharf.

As Windflower and most of his family were enjoying walking around Grand Bank this snowy afternoon, Eddie Tizzard was on the phone with his new supervisor, Inspector Bill Ford. Ford was actually acting, like Tizzard. He had almost retired but was pressed back into service when the previous inspector, Ron Quigley, took a promotion in Ottawa.

"I'm sorry, Eddie, but we haven't got a body to spare over here either," said Ford. "We've got two active drug investigations underway and a hit-and-run that needs to be looked into as well. We're just getting by in Marystown as it is."

"There's no way I can do justice to this case by myself," said Tizzard. "And we're getting tons of pressure. Not just from the families of the men who are missing, but throughout the community. We need to figure this thing out."

"Well, do your best for now," said Ford. "I'll call up the line to see if we can't get you another body somewhere."

"Thank you, Inspector," said Tizzard wearily. He hung up and went to the back to get himself a snack. His dad always said never to try to think on an empty stomach. He quoted Albert Einstein to him once: "An empty stomach is not a good political adviser." Good advice thought Tizzard as he poked around in the fridge and found a piece of leftover pizza that he popped into the microwave. He sat to enjoy his pizza when his cell phone rang.

It was Constable Rick Smithson, the youngest member of his RCMP team.

"Hey, what's up?" asked Tizzard.

"There's a body," said Smithson. "I'm down by the brook, closer to the dam. I got waved down as I was coming back from Fortune. Roy Saunders found him. He was out walking his dog."

"Do we know who it is?" asked Tizzard.

5

"Roy says it's Leo Broderick," said Smithson. "I've called the paramedics."

"Okay," said Tizzard. "I'll be right over."

Chapter Two

Windflower and Sheila walked along the waterfront in Grand Bank and stared out at the large white lighthouse with "Grand Bank" in big red lettering along the side. The light snow fluttering in the air gave it a mystical look, and both laughed at Amelia Louise trying to catch snowflakes on her tongue.

"How's your business planning going?" asked Windflower.

"It's good, but it takes time," said Sheila. "The arts co-op is moving its way through Tourism, and I think the development corporation is finally onboard. And I'm meeting with the IT guy at the council, Reg Shears, later this week to set up our website and electronic storefront for the mittens."

"That's a great idea," said Windflower. "The mittens."

"Well, we're not the only ones, but ever since that book came out about the history and tradition of the 'Saltwater Mittens,' everybody wants them. Once we get that moving, we'll be able to add quilts and all sorts of home-made goods," said Sheila. "You done any more thinking about what you want to do?"

"I'm okay with the B&B for now," said Windflower. "I needed a break."

"Well, there's no rush," said Sheila. "Once we get to the summer, the B&B will keep us all busy. And I kinda like having you around more."

"Me too," said Windflower. "I could certainly get used to this lifestyle."

Amelia Louise was getting a little cranky, and the snow was getting a little heavier, so Sheila and Windflower walked around the corner and passed by the B&B as they walked home. The lights were on and the magnificent old lady glistened in the snow. They were admiring their place when an RCMP cruiser came roaring past them with its lights flashing and siren blaring.

Windflower and Sheila involuntarily jumped back but were still close enough to see a serious and clearly determined Eddie Tizzard race by.

"Looks like something's up," said Windflower after the police vehicle had passed.

"Do you miss it?" asked Sheila.

"Not really," said Windflower. "I'm curious, but it feels like it's not my problem anymore."

"That would be correct," said Sheila. "Let's get her home before she falls asleep in the wagon." She pointed to a slumping Amelia Louise.

"Good plan," said Windflower. "I might have a little nap, too."

Somebody who was definitely not having a nap today was Eddie Tizzard. He had arrived on the scene to find the paramedics and the volunteer fire department already there. As he was coming closer, he also saw the distinctive black sedan of Doctor Vijay Sanjay, the unofficial coroner for the area. He pulled up and walked over to Smithson, who was standing beside the doctor. He nodded to Smithson.

"Hey, Doc. What do you think?" asked Tizzard.

"Other than he is dead and has been for at least a day or so, it's still unclear as to how this man died," said Sanjay. "No visible wounds. Might be a heart attack. Who knows? I'll take him back to the clinic and take a closer look if that's okay?"

"Do you have what you need from here?" Tizzard asked Smithson.

"I've got pictures, and there doesn't appear to be any more evidence around here," said Smithson. "I'll double-check the extended perimeter before we leave."

"Okay, Doc. You're good to go," said Tizzard. "Let me know as soon as you have anything."

"I have to do my examination," said Sanjay. "'You can't cross the sea merely by standing and staring at the water.'"

"I know, I know," said Tizzard. "And before you tell me that 'the butterfly counts not months but moments, and has time enough,' we will need to move quickly. The community is already shaken."

"I understand, my young friend," said Sanjay. "I will move expeditiously. How is your old boss doing?"

"He's probably relaxing right now," said Tizzard with a sigh.

That would be correct. Winston Windflower had successfully gotten his youngest daughter to sleep and was settling in nicely for what he hoped would be a restful and peaceful siesta in his bedroom.

He fell asleep easily and quickly, but soon after, he woke up in a dream. This hadn't happened in while. Not since he left work with the RCMP. But being awake in a dream wasn't new for him. His whole family, led by his grandfather, were dream weavers. That meant that they sought to interpret the messages received in their dreams and even practiced trying to stay alert during a dream, so they didn't miss anything.

Windflower had been tutored by his late Auntie Marie and his Uncle Frank. They were both master dream weavers, and he had spent some time learning the craft back home in Pink Lake, Alberta, where his Cree First Nation reserve was located. Not all his people, or even all Indigenous people, were able to interpret dreams, even though many had a strong sense that the dream world might be as real as the one in which they walked. But his family could, and they had passed this knowledge on to him.

One of the first techniques his auntie had taught him was to look for his hands whenever he found himself dreaming. That allowed him to be more present and to really experience what was happening around him. He looked for his hands, and when he found them, he started to be more fully awake inside his dream. He could see that he was in a large, open meadow surrounded by forest on all sides.

It was summertime, and wildflowers were blowing everywhere by a light breeze that felt warm on his cheeks. It felt like he was completely enclosed within the meadow, but suddenly he saw rustling, and a rabbit hopped out of the trees and came right up to him.

Windflower was used to animals appearing in his dreams. His Uncle Frank had told him that the animals were intermediaries between the human and dream worlds. They often carried messages back and forth. The other thing that was almost always true was that the animals over here could talk. Windflower decided to check this out with his new rabbit friend.

"Good day, Rabbit," he said. "Have you got a message for me?"

"Don't waste any time, do you?" said the rabbit. "That's good, since I'm in a hurry." The rabbit reached into his fur and looked like he was going to pull something out.

"It's not a watch," said the rabbit, reading Windflower's mind. "You forgot that I can see your thinking."

Windflower said nothing and tried his best not to think anything. He waited for the rabbit to show him what she had.

It was a small wooden box, beautifully carved with a lid that had some sort of mysterious drawings on top.

"What is it?" asked Windflower.

"It's an abundance box," said the rabbit.

"What does that mean?" asked Windflower.

The rabbit said nothing else but lifted the lid of the box. Windflower leaned over, and as the box opened there was a brilliant light that emanated from inside that filled the world all round him. He blinked, and when he opened his eyes, he could hear Amelia Louise singing on the baby monitor next to his bed. He shook himself awake and went to see her.

As he was walking out of his bedroom, he saw it on the dresser on Sheila's side of the bed. It was the same box from his dream. He stared at it and picked it up. With great trepidation, he opened it very slowly. He was expecting the blast of light again, and he really hoped to be able to see what was inside. But there was no light and only a couple of pairs of Sheila's earrings inside. He didn't have time for further examination. Amelia Louise was calling his name now, repeatedly. He would ask Sheila about the box later.

Chapter Three

Tizzard left Smithson to double-check the scene for evidence and drove back to the detachment. Betsy Molloy, the long-time administrative assistant, was waiting for him.

"They're already calling," she said, holding several yellow slips in her hand. "Was it really Leo Broderick?"

"Yes," said Tizzard. "You'll have to tell the media to wait. We'll try and have a statement for them a little later. I have to call Ford in Marystown first."

"His poor wife," said Betsy.

"I'll have to go see her, too," said Tizzard. "I'll call Carrie, I mean Constable Evanchuk, and ask her to come with me." Evanchuk was the third member of the RCMP team and Tizzard's life partner. She was also the mother of Tizzard's pride and joy, little six-month-old Hughie, who she was likely tending to right at this moment.

"That's a good idea," said Betsy. She went back to her desk, where all the lights on her phone were blinking. Tizzard went to his office and called Bill Ford.

"We'll need someone to confirm the deceased," said Ford.

"I'm going to see his wife, I guess widow, right after this call. Will you put out the statement from over there?" asked Tizzard.

"Send me the details, and we'll look after that. But you will probably have to do a press conference. I can come over for that," said Ford.

"That's great," said Tizzard. "But this is going to set this place on fire. I need help."

"I'll call Ron Quigley," said Ford. "He might be able to put in a word for us with Halifax or help us get somebody. Any idea on cause of death?"

"Nope," said Tizzard. "Doc Sanjay is going to have a look at the body as soon as he can."

"Okay, keep me posted," said Ford.

Tizzard sat back in his chair and looked out the window again. The snow was still coming down. He buzzed Betsy on the intercom. "Betsy, what's the weather forecast?"

"Snow," said Betsy. "They said it's going to snow on and off for next day or so. With a chance of drifting and blowing snow as the wind picks up later today."

Great, thought Tizzard. A dead man, another man missing and a storm on the way. And it was only Monday.

Meanwhile, Bill Ford had problems of his own. His regional operations at Marystown were severely stretched, and he was barely keeping his head above water. He knew that Tizzard was right about the situation in Grand Bank. It could explode very quickly, especially once word got out about the second missing man who was also found dead. He found Ron Quigley's cell phone number.

"Bill, nice to hear from you," said Ron. "Are you coming up to Ottawa for a visit?"

"Sorry, Ron," said Ford. "It's not a social call."

"That's a mess," said Quigley when he heard about the body that was just found in Grand Bank. "But I'm not sure what I can do about it."

"We need somebody in here who can deal with this, professionally and sensitively," said Ford. "That's not me, and it's not Eddie Tizzard."

"It might be Winston Windflower," said Quigley.

"He's gone," said Ford.

"Not exactly," said Quigley. "He's still on leave while he uses up all that overtime he accumulated."

"He won't come back," said Ford. "He's done."

"Do you have a better suggestion?" asked Quigley.

"No," said Ford.

"I'll give him a call. The worst he can do is to say no," said Quigley.

That was exactly what Windflower said when Quigley finally reached him.

"What part of no don't you understand?" asked Windflower.

"I know you're out, but will you just consider this? As a special request from me and Bill Ford. Eddie can't manage this, and you know it. They're running out of options," said Quigley.

Windflower stayed silent for more than a moment. "I will think about it," he said. "But only as a favour to you and Bill. And if I do it, it will be a one-shot deal. Got it?"

"Got it," said Quigley. "'Go to your bosom: Knock there and ask your heart what it doth know.'"

"Don't try to trick me with quotes," said Windflower. "How 'sharper than a serpent's tooth' is an ungrateful old boss."

"That's harsh," said Quigley. "'Give thy thoughts no tongue.'"

"Bye, Ron," said Windflower. "I'll go talk to Sheila and walk my dog. I'll let you know tomorrow. But it may be no."

"'Modest doubt is called the beacon of the wise,'" said Quigley.

Windflower tried to think of another quote to come back with, but Quigley had hung up.

"Who was that?" asked Sheila.

"Ron Quigley," said Windflower.

"How is he doing in Ottawa?" asked Sheila.

"It wasn't that type of call," said Windflower. Sheila looked at him quizzically. "Let's talk tonight after supper when the kids are in bed."

Shelia started to ask more questions, but the school bus pulled up in front of their house, and Stella ran in with her knapsack.

"Let's have some snacks," said Windflower, and he went to the kitchen, cut up an apple and got a bunch of carrots and put them on a plate. He added a couple of oatmeal raisin cookies that were, of course, the first things picked by his daughters.

"I tried," he said to Sheila in mock protest.

Sheila laughed and took a carrot stick. "We'll talk later."

Back at the RCMP detachment, Eddie Tizzard was trying to talk to two women who had come in to demand that the RCMP take action on what they called "a bloody disgrace."

13

Tizzard didn't disagree with them, but he couldn't say that. Instead, he sat and listened to them harangue him and condemn the RCMP in very colourful language. Finally, Betsy came to rescue him, and he managed to escape his office.

"Media Relations in Marystown called and asked me to set up the press conference for tomorrow morning. Is ten o'clock okay for you?" she asked once they were out of earshot of the two women.

"Fine," said Tizzard.

"And Doc Sanjay called," said Betsy.

"I'll call him from the boardroom," said Tizzard. "If you could help me get rid of, I mean deal with the two ladies in my office."

Betsy smiled. "They'll be gone when you're done your call."

Tizzard could have kissed Betsy at this point but settled for thanking her profusely and almost raced to the boardroom to call Sanjay.

"What have you got for me, Doc?" asked Tizzard. "I hope you have some good news."

"I'm not sure that what I have qualifies as good news under the circumstances," said the doctor. "But I've appeared to locate at least the source of his demise."

"What do you mean?" asked Tizzard.

"He has a large round, red area at the base of his neck," said Sanjay. "I would surmise that he was infected with some toxic substance."

"Poison?" asked Tizzard. "Like an injection."

"Not just a needle. Some other form of injection," said the doctor. "The hole is much larger than a simple injection and probably delivered with some force, judging by the size of the hole."

"Like it was shot?" asked Tizzard.

"That would do it," said Sanjay.

"What was the substance?" asked Tizzard.

"That, my young friend, will have to wait for analysis," said Sanjay.

"Okay," said Tizzard. "Thanks, Doc. Let me know when you have anything else."

Tizzard hung up with the doctor and sat puzzled for a few minutes. That was a lot to process. The dead man was likely interfered with, most likely murdered. And he had no idea why. No suspects, no evident motive and no witnesses. And no weapon other than a suggestion that he may have been poisoned by an unknown substance, maybe fired from a gun of some sort.

He had no idea of even where to begin. But then he remembered that this was the second man from Grand Bank who was missing and found dead. Maybe they could help him in St. John's. At least that was an option and better than anything else he could come up with right now.

Chapter Four

After their snack, Windflower took Lady and the girls out to the backyard to play in the still-falling snow. It was a very pleasant and fun-filled hour, and everyone was in great spirits when they went back inside. Sheila had taken out some hamburger patties to thaw and was just finishing off an apple pie that she put into the oven.

"Dessert?" asked Windflower after he'd helped the girls get their snowsuits off and laid them out to dry.

"Be ready when the burgers are done," said Sheila. "I got the laundry washed too. I was hoping to put it on the line, but I guess that's not happening."

Windflower looked out the window. "No, I guess not. But it's pretty beautiful."

He didn't have much more time to chat with Sheila as the girls captured him for their latest game. He had to play the abominable snowman while Stella was Yukon Cornelius and Amelia Louise was Rudolf the Red-Nosed Reindeer. They had been playing this game since watching the movie a dozen times since Christmas and never seemed to tire of it. Windflower didn't mind too much, especially since today nobody was playing the elf who wanted to be a dentist.

When the girls tired of the games, Windflower snuck away and started up the barbeque. He and Lady went out on the deck and watched the steady snowfall as the burgers sizzled on the grill. Sheila had made some peas and carrots and a handful of French fries for everybody that the girls happily dipped into their little pools of ketchup. It was a happy and contented family scene. Windflower stopped for a moment to smile at Sheila and be grateful for his good luck.

Eddie Tizzard wasn't feeling as special right now. He had to do more, but what?

He took out the three files, laid them on his desk and stared at them. There must be some connection with all of them, but what? They knew each other, but everyone in Grand Bank knew everybody else. They were all United Church, but that was the predominant denomination in town. They were all roughly the same age, married and worked at some form of manual labour. That was pretty common too. But what else?

"Well, two of them are dead," he said out loud to himself. "Maybe I can start there."

He picked up the Skinner file and opened it. Cedric, a.k.a. Sid Skinner, age fifty-eight. He started reading the report from the local cops, the constabulary. He went right to the end and found a name. Detective Ernie Wicks. He called the RNC in St. John's.

"Can I speak to Detective Wicks? It's Corporal Eddie Tizzard, Grand Bank RCMP."

A few moments later, another voice came on the line. "Wicks."

"Detective, it's Eddie Tizzard from Grand Bank RCMP. I'm calling you about Cedric Skinner. The guy that was found at Quidi Vidi."

"What about him?" asked Wicks. "Pretty open-and-shut case. His body was found at the far end of the lake, down near the gut. No visible wounds or signs of a struggle."

"Was there an autopsy?" asked Tizzard.

"I don't think so," said Wicks. "Let me pull up his file." A few seconds later he added, "I don't see anything. Like I said, this was an easy case to close. Besides, we don't have the manpower to follow every wild goose chase. What's this about, anyway?"

"We found another missing man," said Tizzard. "In Grand Bank. This time it looks like he may have been poisoned, but we're still trying to figure that out. And we've got a third man missing, too."

"I can send you the file," said Wicks. "Not sure what else we can do from our end."

"Send me the file. Here's my email," said Tizzard. He hung up and watched his monitor until the email with the attachment appeared. He opened it and sent it to the printer at Betsy's station. He was pulling the paper out of the printer when his phone rang.

"Are you coming home soon?" asked Carrie.

"You didn't hear yet? We found Leo Broderick's body up on the trail," said Tizzard.

"Oh my God," said Carrie.

"Can you come with me to see his family?" asked Tizzard.

"Your dad is here. I'll get him to watch Hughie, and I'll be right over," said Carrie.

Ten minutes later, Tizzard and Evanchuk were knocking on the door of a well-kept bungalow on Hickman Street. When the woman opened the door and saw the Mounties, she almost fainted on the spot. She looked in their eyes for good news, but then her heart sank when that was not forthcoming.

Afterward, the two police officers sat quietly in Tizzard's car. Finally, he turned it on and drove back to the detachment. When they got there, Smithson was writing up his report.

"Anything?" asked Tizzard.

"Nothing else at the scene," said Smithson. "What did Doc Sanjay say?"

"He thinks he may have been poisoned somehow," said Tizzard. "But no idea what until we get toxicology reports and nothing on how it was administered, other than it wasn't a simple injection."

"Like shot from a gun?" asked Evanchuk.

"Or a blowgun?" added Smithson.

Tizzard looked at him. "Really? A blowgun. That's what you got?"

"We don't know anything yet," said Evanchuk.

"True," said Tizzard.

"Anyway, why don't you both go home? I'm going to do a bit more digging," said Tizzard. Smithson nodded and left. Carrie stayed behind.

"Go home and have your supper. Your dad was making fried cod," said Carrie. "It's my shift tonight anyway."

"I'll have supper and come right back," said Tizzard. "Then you can go and tuck Hughie in before he goes down for the night. I

18

have to try to figure this out or at least have a plan. This community is depending on us."

Carrie kissed him and pushed him out the door. "I'll see you later."

While Tizzard was heading home, Windflower was cleaning up the dishes as Sheila gave the girls their bath. When he was done, he grabbed Lady and her leash and took her out for her final walk. It was a quick and snowy trip around their neighbourhood, and after cleaning her up the best he could, Windflower made it back upstairs for story time. Tonight, he was reading with Stella.

"Reading with" was a good description because Stella's reading was really improving. Today she had picked one of their favourites, *Crocodiles Need Kisses Too*. It was an easy and fun book to read out loud, with a rhyming text about slithery and slimy and not very huggable creatures. Of course, they all needed and deserved kisses. It showed that everybody is lovable, just because, and that was a good lesson and a whole lot of fun to read.

"That was a great job, Stella," said Windflower.

"Thank you, Daddy," replied a beaming Stella.

He gave her a kiss goodnight and turned out her light. As he was walking out of her room, he heard the phone ring. Just a few times. Sheila must have picked it up, he thought as he went back downstairs.

"Who was on the phone?" asked Windflower as he sat down beside Sheila.

"It was one of the women from the church. She called to tell me that there's a special meeting tomorrow night to talk about Sid Skinner and Leo Broderick and the other man who's still missing. They asked me, as former mayor, to chair the meeting."

"It sounds serious," said Windflower.

"The women are scared," said Sheila. "Can't say as I blame them. She was also asked to talk to me about something else."

"What?" asked Windflower.

"If I could persuade you to come back to the RCMP," said Sheila.

"What did you tell her?" asked Windflower.

"That I would talk to you and see what you thought. But that you would have to make that decision," said Sheila. "What do you think?"

Chapter Five

When Eddie Tizzard got home, his dad, Richard, was trying to clean up his grandson and the mess that he'd made with his supper. Eddie reached over, plucked Hughie out of his highchair and wiped his face. That gave Richard time to clean off the chair and warm a bottle of milk in the microwave. He handed the bottle to Eddie, who checked it first and then plopped it into Hughie's waiting mouth.

"Let me fry up a piece of fish for you," said Richard, and he went to the fridge and pulled out a large cod fillet. He turned the burner on and got the pan with the oil and fried pork rinds called scrunchions nice and hot. When it was sizzling, he took the cod and coated it in flour and laid it in the skillet. Five minutes on each side and it was done, just as little Hughie was finishing his bottle. Eddie laid him in his chair on the floor beside him and sat at the table.

"This is a very nice piece of fish," said Eddie as he started to tuck into his cod and a large helping of mashed potatoes.

"King of the sea," said his father. "Once it was so plentiful that you could throw your net out of the boat and pull it back in full of fish. That's not so long ago, either."

Eddie had heard this story a hundred times but never tired of hearing his dad talk about something he loved.

His father continued. "Even before the white men came, the first people of this area, the Beothuk, were fishing the waters off the coast. When the Europeans started coming in the fifteenth and sixteenth centuries, they scared them off and forced them inland. Many believe that's a major factor why the Beothuk are extinct today."

"That's a sad story," said Eddie as he forked another delicious piece of cod sprinkled with scrunchions into his mouth.

"Sad but true," said Richard. "They don't teach much of that history in schools. What we hear about is John Cabot lowering baskets from his ship in 1497 and pulling them back in full to the brim."

"Wasn't the first fishery a salt cod fishery?" asked Eddie, playing his part in the saga.

"When the French, Spanish and Portuguese fleets started coming, they salted their fish on board their ships, and it wasn't dried until they got back home," said Richard. "The English fished closer to shore and dried their fish on land and then salted it. That was the beginning of the English settlement of Newfoundland."

"That's a long time," said Eddie.

"Yes," said his dad. "There was the Banks fishery, which was based right here in Grand Bank, and then when refrigeration came along there was onshore processing capacity. It lasted right up until the 1950s. That's when the factory fishing began with super trawlers that dragged up everything off the bottom of the ocean. It was also the beginning of the end. By the early 1990s the industry collapsed, and they imposed the moratorium on the cod fishery."

"But it's coming back, right?" asked Eddie, finishing up his supper.

"Yes, but very slowly," said Richard. "At least we can catch a few in the food fishery. It would be a shame not to have some cod fish."

"Thank god," said Eddie. "Thank you for a delicious meal." He picked up his son and swung him over his head. Hughie squealed with delight. Eddie handed the baby to his dad.

"Are you okay with looking after Hughie for a few minutes?" asked Eddie. "I have to get back to work."

"Yes, my son. Hughie and I will get along fine. At least until he needs his mother again. But he is a great joy to me. Doc Sanjay says that 'every child is a message that God is not discouraged of man.'"

"I think that's Tagore," said Eddie. "The famous Bengali poet."

"He might have gotten it from Doc Sanjay," said Richard.

Eddie kissed Hughie on the cheek and waved goodbye to them both as he headed back to work.

As Eddie Tizzard was driving back to work, he could hardly see the road. That was because the wind had picked up, and now it was blowing snow everywhere. That wasn't good, he thought. His second thought was to phone Marystown to get a report on the weather and the highways.

While Tizzard was getting his weather report, Windflower and Sheila were deep into their conversation about the push, or maybe it was a pull, to get him back on the job with the RCMP.

"I know they need help, but I just left," said Windflower.

"For many good reasons," said Sheila.

"Exactly," said Windflower. "I sympathize with Eddie and the crew, but I have a feeling that this is just a hook to get me back in there."

"Well, you certainly don't have to do it," said Sheila. "But it sounds like a lot of people are upset about what's going on around here and with the Mounties, too."

Windflower shrugged. "I'm going to take the dog out for a walk."

He grabbed Lady's leash and put on his winter coat and boots. That was a good plan, because as soon as he opened his front door, a gust blew a heavy drift of snow right into his hallway. He pushed his way out, and Lady followed close behind as they jumped the growing mound of snow at the end of the driveway and started walking down the middle of the street.

The plow had been around earlier, so that made walking around their neighbourhood a little easier. But when they got to the end of their street and turned down towards the water, the wind almost picked up man and dog and carried them off. That was a signal to both Windflower and Lady to turn around and skedaddle home.

He dried Lady off and filled both her and Molly's bowl before turning out the lights and heading upstairs, where Sheila was comfortably ensconced, propped up in bed with her book.

"I'm not a heartless old coot, you know," he said as he sidled up beside Sheila.

"I know," said Sheila. "I don't judge you."

"But others will," said Windflower.

"That might be true," said Sheila. "But only you know what is right for you. What does your heart tell you?"

"Ron Quigley suggested the same thing," said Windflower. "It doesn't feel right for me. At least not right now. 'This above all; to thine own self be true.'" He reached over and kissed Shelia, and despite everything on his mind, he was soon fast asleep and didn't hear a thing until he felt Sheila move in the morning.

Chapter Six

Sheila had the radio on when Windflower came down, and the girls were sitting at the kitchen table eating their cereal. He heard the last of the announcement about the schools.

"No school today, Daddy," said Stella.

"No school," said Amelia Louise, not wanting to be outdone by her older sister.

One look out the window was enough to know why. It was blowing wildly, and Windflower could see that there were already drifts across the road in front of his house and up into his driveway.

He went to Sheila, kissed her on top of her head and grabbed a cup of coffee.

"There won't be much moving anywhere today," he said. "What's the forecast?"

"It's going to keep going all day and maybe even overnight," said Sheila. "We're okay. We've got everything we need. I just didn't plan on a snow day."

"It's a snow day," said Stella.

"Schnow day," said Amelia Louise.

Soon, both were chanting "snow day" and marching around the house. Windflower laughed at their antics and then realized they would have them all day.

"I'm going outside for a minute," he said.

"In this?" asked Sheila.

"I need it," said Windflower. He put on his parka and grabbed his smudging kit from the porch. He pushed open the back door, and Lady squeezed out in front of him. He cleared off a small portion of the deck while the dog waded through the deep snow to find an appropriate place for her morning routine.

Smudging was something that Windflower tried to do daily if he had time. It allowed him to connect with his Indigenous spirituality, and it also brought him a sense of peace and comfort that he certainly could use today. Windflower mixed up his sacred herbs, a pinch each of cedar, sage, sweetgrass and tobacco. He put them into an abalone shell and lit them with a wooden match. Once it started to smoke, he used a large feather to waft the smoke from the medicines over all parts of his body.

He passed the smoke over his head and eyes to help him see and think clearly. He did the same near his heart to keep it pure, and under the soles of his feet to help him walk a straight path. When he was finished smudging, he laid his bowl down and said his morning prayers. Praying was just as an important part of his morning ritual as smudging.

His first prayers were always ones of gratitude, and he had learned that the more he was grateful, the more he received. He also said a silent prayer for his ancestors. That included his parents, long dead, and his Auntie Marie who had passed not long ago. He prayed as well for his immediate family, and this morning he also said a prayer for his former colleagues at the RCMP. They would have a very busy day.

Windflower was right about that. Tizzard had gotten a couple of hours sleep but was back into the office before it got light. Carrie was on her way in as soon as she could get Hughie dropped off, and Smithson was picking up Betsy to bring in her in, too. It was an all-hands-on-deck kind of day. Betsy would put the emergency plan into effect, and everyone would have a job to keep them busy as the rest of Grand Bank hunkered down to wait out the storm.

There was always something unusual that happened during a snowstorm; sometimes a baby decided to be born a little early or an elderly person thought they were having a heart attack, or the power went out, leaving the whole community a little cold and a little scared. Tizzard hoped that the power would stay on, but like most things, and especially the weather, he had little control over that.

He called over to Marystown to talk with Bill Ford and get an update on the weather and the roads.

"The weather isn't expected to improve until late tonight," said Ford. "The roads are basically impassable. I guess we'll have to postpone the media event."

"That's fine by me," said Tizzard. "Have the Highways closed the road yet?"

"The word just came in," said Ford. "We'll look after this end if you can take one more run to make sure nobody is stuck out there. The plow went through after midnight and didn't report anything."

"Okay. I'll go with Smithson to do the final run, and let me know when it's all clear," said Tizzard. He hung up and looked out the window. Or tried to. Then he saw lights coming toward the building and went out to meet Smithson and Betsy.

Betsy got herself set up quickly at the front and was already plugged into the emergency network when Tizzard followed Smithson out the door.

"Be careful," called Betsy.

Tizzard waved and climbed into his Jeep. They would travel in a convoy with Smithson coming about five minutes after him in his cruiser. Tizzard made slow and steady progress on the highway, thinking that it was a good thing that there was no other traffic on the road, since he could hardly see a thing. But as he moved into the barren area past the second Garnish turnoff, he saw it. It wasn't hard to miss.

A passenger van was sitting in the ditch with its lights blinking. Tizzard radioed to Smithson to warn him, parked his Jeep and ran towards the other vehicle.

After breakfast, Windflower was playing a card game with the girls while Sheila did the laundry. There was a knock on their door, and he went to check who could be out on a day like this. It was Levi Parsons, his young helper from the B&B, bundled up like a mummy with a plastic bag in his hands.

"Levi, what are you doing out on a day like this?" asked Windflower.

"My dad wanted me to drop off these fish," said Levi. "Said you might like to have some. He got his quota on the weekend."

"That is so kind of him," said Windflower. "Tell him thank you."

"Okay," said Levi. "See ya tomorrow."

"Bye," said Windflower. He and the girls watched Levi trek back through the snow in the driveway and then disappear into the snow.

"Who was at the door?" asked Sheila as she came upstairs with a basket of folded laundry.

"It was Levi," said Windflower. "And he brought us two beautiful fish," he added, holding up one of the cod fish for everyone to see.

"Beautiful," said Sheila. "You can make us a nice fish supper. And we can freeze the other one for later."

"And we can play Go Fish with a real fish," said Stella.

Both girls thought that was the most hilarious thing ever. Once they stopped rolling around the floor, Stella got out the Go Fish cards and handed them to Windflower.

"I'll put this away while you have your fun," said Sheila, laughing.

Windflower smiled wryly and retook his seat in the living room.

Back out on the highway, Eddie Tizzard wasn't having nearly as much fun as Windflower. There were six people in the van, German tourists who had been travelling all over the province as a winter wilderness adventure. They'd already been out to the west coast to visit Gros Morne, and now they were planning on a short trip to the French territory of Saint-Pierre that was located a ferry ride away from Fortune, Grand Bank's sister community.

But they hadn't planned on a snowstorm, and since they spoke enough English to get by but not enough to understand the weather reports, they had totally misjudged the storm and the very real risk to them. This all came out in jumbled pieces of English as Tizzard tried to get their information. Finally, he gave up and just pointed. Four of them to come with him and the other two with Smithson.

They seemed reluctant to leave all their stuff behind, but Tizzard held up one finger and pointed to the vehicles. They got that message, and each grabbed a small bag and their laptops and expensive-looking camera equipment and got into the vehicles as directed. Tizzard radioed in to Betsy, who would relay the information to Marystown. They would have to look after securing

28

the rest of the highway. Tizzard and Smithson had a full load to take back to Grand Bank.

Chapter Seven

Tizzard and Smithson brought their human cargo with their supplies back to the detachment. Betsy made sure they were comfortable in the boardroom with a pot of tea and the last of her Christmas cookies. They looked pretty happy in there, thought Tizzard. For now.

He called Betsy back to the front. "I guess we'll need to put them into our food plan. Is the Mug-Up open?"

"Not to the public, but I called Herb, and he said they would make us a couple of trays of sandwiches and a pot of soup," said Betsy.

"Let's see if he can look after our friends, too," said Tizzard. "But they can't stay here tonight. Is the motel open?"

"I think they're closed for the season. Just like the B&B," said Betsy. "But I can call over."

"Okay," said Tizzard. "Let me know what you find out."

He went to the back to check on the Germans and saw Smithson talking to them. In German. They looked like they were sharing a great story, and Tizzard waited until the end before he pulled his colleague aside.

"You speak German?" he asked.

"Not very well," said Smithson. "But I did a gap year in Europe and ended up dating a German girl for a while."

"But you know enough to understand them? What the heck were they thinking?" asked Tizzard.

"They have been lost all over the world," said Smithson. "They just expect that someone will find them."

"Interesting," said Tizzard. Although crazy was what he was thinking.

"Oh, and they're hungry, if there's any food," said Smithson.

"Great," said Tizzard. "Now we're supposed to be running a B&B."

Smithson just shrugged. But that gave Tizzard an idea. He phoned Windflower.

Windflower was glad of the break in his nonstop action with his daughters. He extricated himself from the blanket fort that the girls had erected in the living room and grabbed his cell phone.

"Hello," he said as he walked into the kitchen and sat at the table.

"Hey, Sarge. It's me," said Tizzard.

"Good morning, Eddie, how's things going over at the shop?" asked Windflower.

"It's really busy, especially with the storm and everything," said Tizzard. "We need your help."

"I don't know," said Windflower. "Ron Quigley called me already. I'm not sure I want to come back."

"Not that kind of help," said Tizzard. "We rescued half a dozen German tourists, and they need a place to stay tonight. I was wondering about the B&B. I know it's closed, but could you open just for tonight? We're kinda stuck over here."

Windflower thought for a moment. "Let me talk to Sheila and see what she thinks. I'll call you back."

"Who was on the phone?" asked Sheila as she came in from the living room.

"We might have guests for the B&B," said Windflower.

"In this storm?" asked Sheila.

"Because of this storm," said Windflower. He told her about the Germans and Tizzard's request.

"Why not?" said Sheila. "Can you pick up Beulah and bring her over to help get the rooms ready? I'm sure she'd be happy to help out. I'm not sure what we can do about food, though."

"I'll call Herb and see if he can help out," said Windflower. "We'll bring the girls over with us and have a night out at the B&B." Sheila called Beulah Stokes, their long-time housekeeper at the inn, and Windflower called Tizzard.

"Okay," he said. "We're on. Give us a couple of hours to get everything ready. I'm going to call Herb Stoodley about food."

"Already looked after," said Tizzard. "And thank you very much. This is a great help."

"No problem," said Windflower. "I was already going stir crazy being locked in with the girls."

Sheila came back into the kitchen. "Beulah's ready if you can go pick her up," she said.

"Better yet, I'll get the Mounties to look after that," said Windflower. While Sheila got the girls all dressed up in their snowsuits, Windflower called Tizzard back.

"Can you send someone over to Beulah's house to pick her up?" he asked. "We'll need her to help get the rooms ready at the B&B."

"No problem," said Tizzard. He was going to send Smithson over, but when he looked back in the lunchroom, his younger colleague was engaged in what looked like a heavy conversation. He shouted out that he was going out for a few minutes and left.

The snow was really piling up now, and Tizzard was glad he had his all-wheel-drive Jeep to get him through. He pulled up in front of Beulah's house and went to the door to help her get out and into his vehicle. He was driving along the main road when he saw a familiar dog and two large figures walking along, pulling along a toboggan.

Tizzard rolled down his window when he got close. "Kind of a hard day for a stroll about town," he said.

Windflower and Sheila laughed. "The best kind, b'y," said Windflower. They continued trudging along while Tizzard went ahead to the B&B.

Tizzard helped everyone get safely into the inn after pretending to fall into a snow drift while bringing the girls in. They thought it was great fun and were still laughing when Tizzard headed back to the detachment.

When he got back, Smithson and his new German friends were playing cards. Tizzard had to pull Smithson out and asked him to explain to their guests that he had arranged accommodation for them at the B&B for the night. They were very happy about this, and all came to thank him and shake his hand.

"No problem," said Tizzard. "How do you say that in German?" he asked Smithson.

"Kein problem," said Smithson.

"Kein problem," repeated Tizzard, and all the Germans applauded.

"How do you say get back to work?" asked Tizzard.

Smithson half-smiled and followed Tizzard out into the main office.

"Take a tour around town and make sure everything looks okay," said Tizzard.

Chapter Eight

Sheila and Beulah got busy getting the guest rooms ready for their German visitors while Windflower set the girls up with a puzzle in the kitchen. That kept them busy as he reorganized the dining room and set things up for supper that evening. Sheila had brought both of their cod with them, along with some fat pork to fry it in. He looked out the window of the B&B and saw a light on at the café across the way. He called over.

"Winston how are you, b'y?" asked Herb. "I didn't expect it, but we're kinda busy today."

"Us, too," said Windflower. "Eddie Tizzard asked us to open up the B&B for our unexpected visitors."

"Great," said Herb. "I'm just making up an extra couple of trays of sandwiches for them."

"I was thinking about making some fish for supper," said Windflower. "Have you got any veggies over there?"

"We've got lots of potatoes and probably some carrots and turnips," said Stoodley. "Do you think you have enough fish for that crew? I think I might have a couple of cod fish in the freezer. Maybe even a bag of shrimp if you're interested."

"I'll take all of it," said Windflower. "This'll work out great. I can look after supper tonight if you'll do breakfast in the morning."

"Perfect," said Herb. "I'll be over soon."

Windflower smiled to himself when he thought of the delicious meal he was going to cook tonight. That brief moment of joy gave way to alarm when he heard Lady's yelp from the kitchen. When he got there, the girls had started wrapping the Collie in newspaper, using a roll of masking tape to try to keep it on the dog.

"What are you doing?" asked Windflower as he started to pull the paper and tape off Lady.

"We were making a mummy," said Stella.

"A mummy," said Amelia Louise. "Like the Gypshuns."

34

Sheila came into the kitchen as Windflower was finishing his clean-up job. She looked at him quizzically. "Don't ask," he said.

"Okay," said Sheila. "We're ready for our guests."

"Excellent," said Windflower. "I'll call Eddie."

Tizzard was more than happy to hear from Windflower, and he and Carrie, who'd arrived a little after Smithson left, loaded their visitors up and drove them to the B&B. Windflower and Sheila showed their guests to their rooms while the two Mounties went back to the detachment. They had just arrived when the lights flickered, dimmed and finally went out.

The emergency generator kicked in shortly afterward. That was reassuring to Tizzard, but it was also a sign that they would have an interesting evening ahead of them in Grand Bank. He was right. The calls started coming in shortly after the power went out. Smithson and Carrie helped Betsy answer the phone calls, which were mostly from people who wanted to tell them that the power was out. And to find out when it would be back on.

That's what Tizzard was trying to find out as well. But there was not much news from NL Power and little help from Marystown either. He called everyone together in the lunchroom that had been vacated by their German guests.

"Nothing yet from the power people except to say that there are outages all over the region," said Tizzard. "Looks like we're on our own. What are you hearing on the calls?"

"Mostly people looking for information," said Carrie. Smithson nodded in agreement.

"Folks want to know how long this is going to last," said Betsy. "Many people have generators, but the ones that don't are worried about what happens overnight."

"I guess we need a contingency plan," said Tizzard. "Can we set up an emergency shelter?"

"We had one over at the high school when we had the hurricane a few years back," said Betsy. "They had back-up generators, and the town council brought in a few more. And they have a kitchen. They used to teach home economics years ago."

"Now it's called Family Studies," said Smithson. "I didn't take it, but they had it at my high school."

"Of course, you would know what it's called," said Tizzard. "More importantly, they have a kitchen. Betsy, can you call the council office and see if we can set up at the high school?"

Betsy left to check that out while all three of the RCMP officers went back to answer the blinking phone lines. Tizzard could hear Carrie offering what comfort she could to her caller, and he tried the same.

"It's going to be okay," he said to the old lady on the other end of his call.

"But we got no heat, b'y, and mister wants his supper," said the lady.

"Maybe the power will come back on by then," said Tizzard. "If not, call us back and we'll look after you."

Reassured by Tizzard's promises, the old lady hung up. Before he could make another commitment that he wasn't sure he could keep, Betsy came in to rescue him.

"The council is sending someone over to open the school," said Betsy. "They will turn on the emergency power, and they have space heaters for the gym. They also have an emergency supply of sleeping bags and blankets in storage that they are bringing over."

"Perfect," said Tizzard. "Now we have to tell people about our plan. Put out a quick notice to all the media and tell them I'll talk to them if they need a sound bite. Then put your telephone tree into operation."

Betsy beamed at that last order. A few years ago, under the direction of her former boss, Windflower, she had put her networking skills to work establishing a very effective community connection program. Betsy, who knew everybody in town and most of their business, had about twenty regular contacts she would phone with a message. They, in turn, would reach out to their list, and within an hour or two most of Grand Bank had the news they needed.

"We'll need to tell everyone that the gym at the high school will be available for overnight tonight and that we'll have a light supper around six o'clock. We'll need volunteers for food prep and serving and a couple of drivers with all-wheel-drive vehicles to pick people up," said Tizzard.

Betsy smiled again at Tizzard and went to put her plan into effect. He called Smithson in and gave him the job of coordinating the drivers, while Carrie would be the greeter at the gym. That way she could bring Hughie with her as she got the mostly older folks organized. There would be no shortage of volunteer grandparents happy to look after their baby for a while.

Tizzard took on the job of organizing the food. He called the manager of the supermarket at home, and he agreed to make a donation to the cause if Tizzard could have somebody pick it up. Then he called Warren's and asked what extra meat they might have. They had a back-up generator, too. But the local grocer and meat market couldn't keep all their supplies frozen for long. Tizzard managed to get a couple of boxes of cut-up chicken and a few bags of frozen peas and carrots.

"Sounds like we're having chicken stew for supper tonight," he said to Betsy as she came back in with a short report on her activities.

"That's great," said Betsy. "I'll pass that along to Anne and Mildred, who've agreed to organize the cooking. They're ready to go when we can pick them up."

"Okay," said Tizzard. "Smithson is organizing the rest of the driving, and I can pick up our cooks."

"And I thought you could just record a clip," said Betsy. "Just a few words about tonight that I could send to the radio stations."

"Super," said Tizzard.

"I have the message here," said Betsy, handing him a sheet of paper.

"Of course you do," said Tizzard. He followed Betsy out to the front, put her headphones on and recorded the message. Afterward, he drove around to pick up his cooks and took them over to the high school.

Chapter Nine

Windflower and Sheila and Beulah were all busy at the B&B as well. Moira Stoodley had come over with some more supplies, and she took the girls back with her to the Mug-Up to make some cookies for dessert. She called an hour later to ask if they could stay for supper with the Stoodleys. That was perfect for Windflower and Sheila.

The German visitors were up in their rooms. Probably having a nap, thought Windflower. For a brief moment he envied them, but he quickly snapped out of that when he heard one of them come into the kitchen. The man with a bushy red beard motioned, and Windflower interpreted that to be that he was looking for something to drink.

He offered coffee or tea or soft drinks, but the young visitor shook his head. "Wir möchten etwas bier, bitte," he said a little softly.

Windflower understood two words. Beer and please. "Let me have a look," he said. He went to the storage room at the back of the kitchen and returned with a twelve-pack of Quidi Vidi Honey Brown Ale. "Local beer," he said. "From St. John's."

"Danke," said the young man with a broad smile. "Danke schön," he said again when Windflower handed him the case.

"Supper is at six," said Windflower.

"Danke," said the German one more time as he left with his precious cargo. Windflower wasn't sure the man understood anything he just said, but they would smell the fish once he started cooking. That would bring them looking for their supper.

Beulah and Sheila scoured the dining room and set out fresh place settings while Windflower started making a shrimp salad. That, along with the fried cod and vegetables, would make a great meal. Plus, Beulah had brought two of her famous cheesecakes with her, the ones that were so popular at the Mug-Up. A perfect dessert, thought Windflower.

Sheila came in to peel the veggies while he got out all ingredients for the shrimp salad. He'd found a great recipe that wasn't heavy on the mayo, like some others he'd had, and got to work cleaning and deveining the crustaceans. Once that was done, he tossed them in oil, applied a heavy hand of salt and pepper and put them on a large baking sheet, which he placed in the oven.

He zested a lemon and got some light mayonnaise and Dijon mustard and put it in a bowl. He diced a red onion and some celery, and when the shrimp was done, he added some dill and tossed the whole mixture together. He put it in the fridge to serve on a bed of romaine lettuce when the rest of supper was ready.

Sheila had the vegetables boiling, so he took out all the cod and laid it on a large plate. He patted the fillets dry and left them to dry some more while he chopped up the fat back pork for his scrunchions. Scrunchions were a great medium for frying cod, and they also made a perfect accompaniment to pour over the top of the fish when it was done.

When the oil was super hot, he dipped pieces of cod in flour and laid them into the sizzling cast iron skillet. He sprinkled a little salt, a lot of black pepper and a good sprinkle of cayenne pepper over the fish as it was frying, about five minutes on each side until it was golden brown. Sheila got the vegetables ready while he finished off the rest of the fish and laid his shrimp salad on the romaine lettuce.

He went to the edge of the stairs and called out to his guests. "Supper's ready."

When there was no answer, he called again. Still no reply.

"Try essenszeit," said Beulah, who was standing nearby.

"Essenszeit," he yelled.

He didn't receive an immediate reply, but then he heard a stamping of feet and what sounded like a herd of cattle coming down the stairs.

"You speak German?" asked Windflower.

"My cousin married a German," said Beulah.

Windflower wanted to ask her more, but he had to get the fish up and plated. He laid the fish on the plates, and Sheila added the vegetables. Beulah carried out the shrimp salad to a crew of young Germans who looked like they were starved. By the time Windflower got back with the wine, they were already about halfway through the shrimp salad and were murmuring pleasant sounds that Windflower didn't need a translator to know meant that they liked their supper.

He and Sheila and Beulah had an abbreviated version of the meal back in the kitchen. When they were done, Windflower and Sheila cleared the tables while Beulah sliced up the two versions of the cheesecakes. They were offering coffee and tea along with dessert when the lights flickered and came back on. Everyone cheered, especially the Germans, and one of them scooted upstairs and came back with a bottle of schnapps.

People cheered at the high school as well. Nobody there was happier than Eddie Tizzard. He had not been relishing the idea of babysitting the eighty people who had crammed into the gym, expecting to spend the night. Now, they were warm, fed and could be driven home. Tizzard finished off his own bowl of chicken stew, grabbed a couple of cookies from the trays and trays of desserts that people had dropped off, and started organizing the rides home.

Betsy, and the ladies she had organized, were pretty happy too, since they finally got to sit and enjoy their meal as well. Tizzard gave her a wave as he pulled Smithson and Carrie aside to get the transportation system going. He went out to the doorway for some privacy and to get a breath of air from the hot, sticky gym.

"It's stopped snowing," he exclaimed.

"That's great," said Smithson. "Do you want me to do a quick run around town to make sure there's no obstacles or anything?"

"That would be good," said Tizzard, and Smithson grabbed his coat and took off.

"I'm going to drop Hughie off at Margaret's," said Carrie. "I'll be back in a few minutes, too."

Tizzard stayed near the door and helped Carrie get the baby into the car seat and then watched as they drove off. He was smiling to himself as he walked back into the kitchen at the back of the gym.

"You're pretty happy," said Betsy when she saw him.

"Why wouldn't I be?" asked Tizzard. "The best way to cheer yourself up is to try to cheer somebody else up. That's what my dad always says, anyway."

"Good motto," said Betsy. "We'll start getting this place cleaned up."

"I'm going to get people home," said Tizzard.

Three hours later Tizzard turned off the lights in the gym and went back to the detachment. He had sent Smithson home, and Carrie was long gone. He sat alone by himself in Windflower's old office and put his feet up on the desk. Despite his best efforts to stay awake, he was soon fast asleep.

He woke in a dream. At least he thought it was a dream. He almost never dreamed, and when he did, he couldn't remember it. This time he tried to pay more attention. He'd heard Windflower talk about dreaming one time with his Uncle Frank. How you could wake yourself up in your dreams. How did they do that again? Something about your hands, but what was it? He looked down at his hands, and it was like everything got brighter. Then he realized his dream was in vivid colours. That never happened. But man, was it beautiful.

When he looked around a little more, he saw that it was summertime, and he was walking along the T at L'Anse au Loup. Like most people in Grand Bank, Tizzard loved the T. It was a narrow strip of land that was crossed by a little peninsula forming the distinct shape that gave the place its name. The tides came in and out here, and Tizzard loved walking along the areas of the bog when the tide was out. It was like discovering a whole new world.

It was also a magical place in the summer with wildflowers sprouting up all along the oceanside, and so many different birds that called and chased each other from one end of the beach to the other. Tizzard was walking along enjoying the sun on his back and the beautifully fresh breeze coming in off the Atlantic Ocean. He thought he was alone, and then he saw him standing there, down near the end of the T where the harp seals played in the large rocks near the shore. He was coming towards Tizzard.

Tizzard thought he recognized him but couldn't place him.

The man put out his hand to Tizzard. "I'm Sid Skinner."

Tizzard shook the man's hand. It felt cold and clammy. When he looked closer, he could see the man didn't look very good either. He had a greyish tinge and looked like, well, a corpse.

"That's right," said Skinner. "I'm dead."

"Did you drown?" asked Tizzard. "What happened to you?"

"That's a long story," said Skinner. "Life is full of surprises. Some good and some bad."

Tizzard had a million more questions, but the man kind of melted into the ground beneath his feet. And then he was gone and Tizzard was standing on the beach at the T at L'Anse au Loup. He couldn't wait to talk to Windflower about his dream. If only he could remember. That was when he woke up with the phone ringing in his ears.

"Tizzard. Grand Bank RCMP."

"Morning, Corporal. It's Ray Shears from Highways. Just wanted to let you know we've reopened your route. Do you want us to take the barriers down?"

"Yes, thank you," said Tizzard, feeling groggy and trying to bring himself back into reality. "What time is it?"

"It's just after four in the morning," said Shears. "Everything okay over there?"

"Everything's fine," said Tizzard. "Thanks again for your help."

Tizzard walked to the back and put on a fresh pot of coffee.

"Did that dream really happen?" he said out loud. He rummaged around the fridge and found the remains of the sandwich tray from yesterday. He had a lot of thinking to do, but that was always better on a full stomach.

Chapter Ten

Windflower and Sheila had finished up late, too. He had picked up the girls and got Sheila and them home before driving Beulah to her house.

"That was a great meal tonight," said Windflower. "Thanks for all your help."

"No problem," said Beulah. "I'm happy to help out."

"Plus, you got to practice your German," said Windflower as he came up to her house.

"Yes, but they all use slang now, so I couldn't follow everything they said," said Beulah. She paused before getting out of the car.

Windflower looked at her. "Is there something else?"

"Well, I don't know if I should be saying anything," said Betsy. "I'm not sure I completely understood, you know."

"Did you hear something?" asked Windflower.

"I thought I heard two of them talking about picking up a package," said Beulah.

"That's not unusual," said Windflower. "They might be going to Walmart."

"Not that kind of package. They said they were meeting Adam in Saint-Pierre," said Beulah. "If they had nothing to hide, then why were they whispering?"

"I don't know," said Windflower. "But thank you for telling me."

Beulah thanked him for the ride and trudged through the snow to her house. When she got to the door, she waved back at Windflower to let him know she was okay. He waved back and drove to the B&B. Levi Parsons was arriving as he pulled up in front.

Windflower rolled down the window. "You okay for the night?" he asked.

"No worries," said Levi.

"I think our guests are probably gone to bed for the night. But if there's any problems you call, okay?"

Levi nodded and went into the B&B.

Windflower looked at the old inn, now all lit up and filled with guests. She's a beauty, he thought. With that pleasant thing in mind, he turned around and headed for home.

Everyone in the Windflower household slept well that night, but none better than Windflower himself, who fell asleep thinking about a day well spent and didn't stir until Stella woke him in the morning.

Tizzard stayed at the RCMP offices until Smithson came in to take over. Then he dragged himself home, and while going to bed would have been the best option, playing with his son was even better. Hughie had been fed and changed, and once he and his dad were completely tuckered out, he fell asleep quickly in his crib with Eddie Tizzard not far behind in his own bed.

Tizzard was deep in sleep when he thought he heard ringing. He realized it was his phone. "Good morning, Corporal," said Betsy. "I hope I didn't get you up. I know you were here all night."

"No worries," said Tizzard groggily. "What's up?"

"Well, we still need to do the media conference," said Betsy. "Inspector Ford called and wanted to know if you could do it at one today."

"Sure, that's fine," said Tizzard, checking his phone for the time. "I'll be over in an hour or so." He hung up and heard a wonderful sound coming from his son's bedroom. It was his dad playing with little Hughie, singing him a song that he remembered from his own childhood. Then he smelled something that was even more wonderful. There was bacon frying in the kitchen.

Two great incentives to jump out of bed to go see who was having the most fun. It was clearly his dad, Richard Tizzard. He said a quick good morning to Richard, gave Hughie a kiss on the top of his head and went to see Carrie in the kitchen.

"Oh my god, that smells great," he said as he came up behind to give her a hug.

"Bacon. The surest way to a man's heart," said Carrie. "This will be ready in a few minutes."

Tizzard tried to steal a piece of bacon from the frying pan and got slapped back with a spatula. "Why don't you stop messing with the cook and go get cleaned up?" said Carrie.

Chastened, he hurried to the bathroom and had a quick shower and shave. When he came out, Carrie was dishing up.

"This is so great," said Eddie. "Bacon, scrambled eggs and my favourite people."

"Probably in that order, too," said Carrie as she fed Hughie while the adults ate.

"You know, 'The secret of success in life is to eat what you like and let the food fight it out inside,'" said Richard.

"That's very good, Dad," said Eddie. "Did you make that up yourself?"

"I wish I had," said his father. "Mark Twain."

"I love Mark Twain," said Eddie, reaching for a piece of homemade toast and smearing it with strawberry jam. As he did, Hughie started to cry.

"I think he wants some," said Eddie, looking to Carrie for direction.

"Give him a little piece," she said. "He's been eating the puréed veggies for a while now, might as well see if he likes it."

Eddie tried to gingerly hand a very small piece of toast over to Hughie in his highchair, but the baby grabbed it from his hand and stuffed it in his mouth.

"Just like his father," said Richard.

Eddie smiled and watched as Carrie took Hughie out of his chair and cleaned him up. He dropped his plate in the sink and started to do the dishes.

"You go on," said Richard. "I'll clean up here. You've got a busy day ahead, I'm sure."

"Thanks, Dad," said Eddie. He gave Carrie and Hughie a kiss. "I'll see you in a while."

"See you soon," said Carrie. She went to the window with the baby to watch him leave.

Tizzard looked back and waved. "I'm a lucky man," he said out loud to himself. What was it that Windflower used to say? Then he remembered. "I bear a charmed life." I do indeed, he thought as he drove his Jeep over the piled-up snow in his driveway. Richard would get the snowblower out later to clean that up. He had bigger fish to fry, dealing with the media and trying to explain to them about an investigation that he, and they, knew was going nowhere.

Chapter Eleven

Windflower didn't have as much on his plate today. Maybe help out with the guests at the B&B. And that suited him just fine. Sheila was already getting Stella dressed and ready for school when he came out of the bedroom. He and Amelia Louise went downstairs to get breakfast started. This morning it would be simple, fruit and cereal. Amelia Louise helped him set the table and in return got her Rice Krispies and banana first. A distinction she was quick to point out to her sister when she came down with Sheila.

Windflower put the coffee on to brew and went to let Lady out into the back. He tried to, anyway. But he couldn't push the door open with the snow drifted up against it. He grabbed his parka, and he and Lady went out the front door and circled around to the back, where he shovelled out that entrance while Lady performed her morning ritual.

He finished off the walkway at the front with Lady by his side. He could look after the driveway later with Amelia Louise. Now, he needed a cup of coffee.

Sheila poured him a cup while he got his own bowl of cereal and sat at the table with his daughters. Stella was babbling about some project she was going to work on at school, and her little sister was trying to keep up.

"Mila got projex, too," she said. "Right, Mommy?"

"Yes, you have daycare this afternoon," said Sheila. "And I think you have crafts again."

Amelia Louise beamed broadly at her mother's comments and almost smirked at her sister. Stella sighed and stoically continued to talk about her schoolwork.

"You have anything today?" asked Windflower.

"I have a meeting with a couple of angel investors from St. John's," said Sheila. "Online, of course."

"What's that?" asked Windflower.

"They're people who put up some seed money for new projects," said Sheila. "Usually, they take a portion of the company in return for start-up funding."

"Aren't you worried about that? Like them taking over your company?" asked Windflower.

"Not really," said Sheila. "I'm trying to set it up as a cooperative, not-for-profit deal. They'll get a share of the profits, but it could be quite a while before we have that kind of money. More important to get this off on the ground, and at the front end it's all about advertising and generating interest. That's where their money can help."

Windflower nodded and finished his cereal. They all kind of jumped when they heard a large noise from outside. The girls ran to the window in the living room to see the snowplow go by.

"Let's go, Stella. We need to get ready for school," said Sheila. "Will you make her lunch?"

"Sure," said Windflower. Amelia Louise helped him load the dishwasher, and then he had to make her a lunch, too, when he started making Stella's lunch bag for school. "But I can make your lunch later," said Windflower.

"No," said Amelia Louise defiantly. "Mila want samwich."

"Okay, okay," said Windflower, and he packed two lunch bags, one he handed to Stella when she came down and one that Amelia Louise put in the fridge after proudly displaying it to her sister. Stella just sighed again, put on her knapsack and went to the door to wait for the bus.

After Stella had gotten safely off to school, Windflower sat in the living room with Sheila and had the last cup of coffee.

"How about you?" asked Sheila. "Plans for today?"

"Well, me and Amelia Louise have to clean up that mess outside," he said. "Then I thought I'd check in with Levi to see how our guests are doing. And once we get cleaned up again, we can get back to work on the floors. We might have to scrape off the last layer we put on and start over. But I've got lots of time for that."

"You do indeed," said Sheila. "I have to say that it's nice having you around more. She really enjoys it, too."

Amelia Louise had come over and climbed up onto Windflower's lap.

"Are you ready to go shovel some snow?" he asked.

She was, and so was Lady, who was more than eager to get outside. Molly the cat just looked at the three of them as they headed out into the cold and snow as the craziest creatures she'd ever seen. She curled up on top of the couch to watch and pity them.

An hour later, all three of them came back in a little tired and more than a little wet, but all very happy. The two humans were also very pleased with the hot chocolate that Sheila had made. Lady was more than happy with her Milk Bone treat. Even though Molly had done no work at all, she was happy with her treat that she successfully cadged from Windflower.

He was just finishing his hot chocolate when his phone pinged. He checked his text messages.

"Who is it?" asked Sheila.

"Levi," said Windflower. "He said our German friends are getting ready to leave. A tow truck just brought their van, and they're packing up. I told him I'd be over later to help clean up."

"I'll call Beulah to see if she can come, too," said Sheila.

Smithson was arriving at the detachment just as Eddie Tizzard was pulling in.

"The highway is all clear," he said to Tizzard. "I passed the tow truck with the Germans' van on the way in. They were dropping it off over at the B&B."

Tizzard nodded and went inside, where Betsy handed him a draft media statement.

"Thanks, Betsy," he said. "I'll take a look."

A few minutes later the media started arriving, and Tizzard could hear them tromp down the hallway outside his office to the boardroom at the back, where the media conference was being held. He waited until it was quiet and went to give the release back to Betsy with his suggestions. The only real change he had made was to strike out the line about having no suspects at this point. That might be true, but he didn't want to admit it publicly and take the heat from the media. The statement would simply say that the RCMP had a number of leads they were following up on. Almost true, thought Tizzard as he watched Betsy rapidly make the change and then print out the copies to hand out.

As she was finishing, he saw Bill Ford arriving. He grabbed two copies from Betsy and went to meet him.

"Morning," said Ford.

"Good morning," said Tizzard. "We haven't got much to give them." He handed Ford a copy of the statement.

"The investigation is continuing," said Ford.

"I was thinking that we could say we are working with the Constabulary in St. John's on the first case," said Tizzard. "That is true, although they have closed the case."

"Did we get the autopsy report into the first man?" asked Ford.

"Skinner," said Tizzard. "They didn't do one. Said they assumed he drowned and didn't have the resources to follow up."

"So, let's announce that we're going to do it here," said Ford. "I'm assuming Doc Sanjay can do it."

"I guess so," said Tizzard. "But won't we tick off the guys in St. John's?"

"I'll deal with that," said Ford. "Let's see how it goes, and if we get stuck, you can make that announcement."

Tizzard nodded and led Ford down the hallway, where the cameras captured them walking into the crowded boardroom.

The event did not go well, and about halfway through Bill Ford gave him the nod.

"We do have one announcement to make," said Tizzard. "We will be exhuming the body of the late Mister Skinner and performing an autopsy to determine the exact cause of death."

There was a murmur through the room, and reporters started yelling questions.

"Does that mean you think that Sid Skinner was murdered?" asked one of the reporters in front.

"All possibilities are on the table," said Bill Ford. "Thank you, ladies and gentlemen." He led Tizzard out of the room and into his office.

Chapter Twelve

Ford, said, "You better phone Sanjay and get him on this."

Tizzard was about to do that when Betsy knocked on his door.

"I've got Rob Skinner on the phone. He's asking questions about what he just heard on the radio," said Betsy.

"That was fast," said Tizzard.

"I guess they carried it live," said Betsy. "It's big news around here. What should I tell him?"

"Can you talk to him?" asked Tizzard. "I don't think I can do that this morning. I'll call Doc Sanjay, and you deal with Skinner's family."

"Okay," said Ford. "We'll have to get their permission anyway."

"If you come with me, you can take the call at my desk," said Betsy.

Ford went along with Betsy while Tizzard phoned the doctor. Sanjay was more than happy to help. That was the last smooth thing that happened to Tizzard that day.

He had just finished with Sanjay when Smithson burst into his office.

"They found a man out on the highway. Snowplow operator found him," said Smithson breathlessly.

"Dead, I assume?" said Tizzard. "Where was it?"

"Closer to Marystown," said Smithson.

"So, it's their case," said Tizzard hopefully.

"Sorry," said Smithson. "It's on our side of the line. They'll hold the scene for us, though."

"I bet they will," said Tizzard. "Let me talk to Ford about it before you go rushing off. Any other details?"

"Yeah," said Smithson. "The dead guy is a German national. That's what his passport says. "Uwe Meeir, age twenty-eight," he read from his paper.

"Here's something you can do. Go see if our German friends at the B&B know this guy."

Smithson drove to the B&B as Windflower was arriving with Beulah.

"What are you doing here?" asked Windflower.

"I'm looking for our visitors," said Smithson.

"They're gone," said Levi Parsons, who opened the door to the inn to let Beulah in. "I got them breakfast sandwiches and coffee from across the road, and they paid their bill and took off. Headed for Saint-Pierre, I think."

Smithson looked at his watch. "They'll be gone by now if the ferry is on schedule. But I'll go to Fortune and check."

Levi went back inside, and Windflower followed Smithson to his cruiser.

"What's going on?" he asked.

"They found a body out on the highway," said Smithson. "A German."

Windflower raised an eyebrow. Smithson hesitated, as if he was unsure about telling Windflower anything more.

"It's me, Smithson," said Windflower. "Is he connected to our guests?"

"We don't know yet," said Smithson. "Anyway, I've got to get to Fortune." He jumped in his cruiser and raced off. Windflower went back into the B&B.

Beulah already had her coat off and was filling up a bucket with soap and hot water in the kitchen to start the cleaning. She started in the dining room. Windflower went to help Levi take off the bedding from the rooms upstairs.

"Everything quiet last night?" he asked.

"Yeah, they stayed up for a while watching TV, but not a peep after midnight," said Levi. "Then, this morning they ate their breakfast, and when their van came, they loaded up and left."

"Did you hear them talking about anything?" asked Windflower.

"They were speaking German," said Levi. "The only words I picked up were 'Danke' and 'Adam,' whoever that is."

Windflower nodded and grabbed an armful of sheets and brought them downstairs. Levi followed behind, and they loaded up the industrial washer in the basement. Levi went to help Beulah, and Windflower stayed behind, hearing the motor of the washing machine turn around. His mind was turning, too. Despite himself, he was curious to know what was going on with the dead man who turned up on the highway and what exactly these Germans were doing here in the middle of winter. Not normally tourist time.

But then he shook himself and walked back upstairs to help the B&B staff. Solving murders wasn't his job anymore.

But it clearly was Eddie Tizzard's. He had managed to convince Bill Ford to take the case of the man found on the highway, but that still left him with two active cases, plus a missing man. And a community ready to string him up if he couldn't come up with some answers. Bill Ford headed back to Marystown after talking to the Skinner folks, and Tizzard sat brooding in his office.

He was already tired, and it wasn't even noon. What was it his dad said about times like this? Oh yeah, he felt like he'd been ridden hard and put away wet. The only thing that cheered him was the thought of a coffee and a snack at the Mug-Up. He passed quickly by Betsy, who waved at him with a stack of phone messages, and then got into his Jeep for the short drive to the café.

He opened the door to an almost full house but found a seat at the small table in the back corner.

Herb Stoodley came over with a cup of coffee. "Are you in hiding?"

"Witness protection program," said Tizzard. "But it's not so bad that a nice raisin tea biscuit couldn't make it better."

"Coming right up," said Stoodley.

Tizzard could feel all the eyes in the café staring at him, but he pretended not to notice. Herb was back soon after with his hot tea biscuit and a little pat of butter. He was putting the butter on his steaming snack when a friendly face came into the café.

Windflower saw Tizzard in the corner and waved. He came over a few minutes later after talking to Herb and getting his own cup of coffee.

"Morning, Eddie," said Windflower. "You look like you had a hard night."

"Morning, Sarge," said Tizzard. "And it looks like a worse morning."

"I'm not a sergeant anymore, Eddie. You can call me Winston now," said Windflower.

Tizzard thought about that for a second. "Nah, I think you'll always be Sarge to me. If that's okay with you."

"Fine with me," said Windflower as Herb came by with Windflower's own raisin tea biscuit.

Not much was said between the men as they savoured their snack. Once they had finished, Herb took away their plates and refilled their coffee cups.

"Do you want to talk?" asked Windflower. "About work, I mean. You don't have to if you feel uncomfortable about it. Smithson looked like a deer in the headlights when I asked him about the man out on the highway."

Tizzard didn't need time to think about that. He was soon spilling all the information he had about the two cases and the autopsy that Sanjay was going to perform. "Any suggestions?" he asked.

Now it was Windflower's turn to think. He had offered to listen but wasn't really planning on getting involved. He tried to be careful. "I think you're doing a lot of things right. But I might make two suggestions if you're interested."

"I'm all ears," said Tizzard.

"First, I might look for connections between the two dead men," said Windflower. "This is a small community, and everyone knows everybody else to some degree. But did they do anything together? Put the third man, the missing one, in the mix, too. Did they go to church? Were they involved in the Lions or the Masons? Did they golf out at Grande Meadows?"

"That's good," said Tizzard. "I could check with their families."

"That would be good," said Windflower. "Cause that's my second point. You need to show the community that you have an active case. That you are doing your job to protect them."

"I heard there's a big meeting tonight to talk about this," said Tizzard. "Should I go?"

"Not unless you're invited," said Windflower. "Unless you have anything concrete to tell them. Do you?"

Tizzard shook his head.

"Then have someone monitor the meeting and report back to you. Maybe your dad," said Windflower.

"He'd love that," said Tizzard. "Undercover, like."

"Something like that," said Windflower. "And while you're doing your investigation with the family, get Smithson to start asking the other men in the community about the victims. People love to talk, and maybe he'll pick up something that the families don't know about."

"That's really good," said Tizzard. "You're really good at this, you know. Maybe you should rethink your decision and come back."

"Nice try, Eddie," said Windflower. "'All the world's a stage, and all the men and women merely players: they have their exits and their entrances.' I have made my exit. But you can buy my coffee and tea biscuit, thank you very much."

"Okay, you can't blame a man for trying," said Tizzard.

"And one more piece of advice," said Windflower as he went to the cash to pay. "'When in doubt, tell the truth.'"

"Shakespeare?" asked Tizzard as he followed Windflower out of the café.

"I think I first heard it from your dad, Richard Tizzard," said Windflower. "But he probably stole it from Mark Twain." He waited for Tizzard's stunned reaction and then started to laugh.

They were both still laughing as Windflower walked back over to the B&B and Tizzard made the slow drive back to work.

Chapter Thirteen

Betsy didn't bother trying to hand him any messages this time. She stood across the hallway, blocking the entrance to his office.

"You have to sign these forms for Doctor Sanjay to start the autopsy request process. And you have to get a family member to sign the bottom one," said Betsy.

"Can you call his brother, Rob, and ask him to come over?" said Tizzard as he signed the top form. "Is that it?"

"Inspector Ford called," said Betsy. "And there's a dozen media requests for follow-up from this morning."

"Nothing more to add right now," said Tizzard. "Tell them we'll get back to them when we have more information. I'll call the inspector."

"There's something very interesting about our dead guy," said Ford over the phone. "All the folks at HQ are asking about him."

"What are they looking for?" asked Tizzard.

"I guess there was going to be a big meetup of a couple of networks. From Germany and the Netherlands, and even some Americans," said Ford. "They couldn't figure out where the meeting was going to be held. Europe is definitely too hot, and most of them couldn't get into the States. Our drug guy wanted to know if we saw or heard anything suspicious in our neck of the woods."

"Besides a vanload of German tourists in the middle of winter?" asked Tizzard.

"Are they still here?" asked Ford. "Can you confirm that?"

"Let me ask Smithson," said Tizzard. "He's just coming back in."

"What's going on at the B&B?" asked Tizzard.

"The Germans are gone. On the ferry to Saint-Pierre. I confirmed it with the ferry terminal," said Smithson.

"No longer here," said Tizzard to Ford. "Gone to Saint-Pierre."

"Okay. I'll pass it along," said Ford.

"How did your visit with Rob Skinner go?" he asked before Ford hung up.

"He was pretty upset," said Ford. "Can't say as I blame him."

"Thanks," said Tizzard. He wasn't surprised, but that didn't make him relish a visit from that angry man later today when he came to sign the form. But maybe he could follow Windflower's advice and see what he could find out about the late Sid Skinner, the guy who showed up in his dream.

He was still thinking about that when he realized Smithson had continued to stand in the doorway of his office.

"Good," said Tizzard. "I've got a job for you." He explained how he wanted the younger officer to find out all he could about the three men in their case. If there was anything weird or different about them and if they had anything in common.

"So, basically a snoop," said Smithson.

"Think of it more of an investigative reporter," said Tizzard. "It might be interesting to find out more about the people in your community, Smithson."

"They won't talk to me," said Smithson.

"That's your challenge," said Tizzard. "Find a way to connect to them and then get them to feel important by telling you what they know. Tell them that you are sworn to secrecy. You'd get fired if you told anybody their secrets."

"I'll try," Smithson said finally.

"You'll be great," said Tizzard. "People love talking about other people, especially other people's problems."

Smithson went away, still looking a bit unsure about this latest request, but Tizzard knew he would give it a good shot. He wasn't worried at all about the next person on his list.

"Yes, b'y, I'll do that," said Richard Tizzard. "I'll be your undercover informant at the meeting tonight."

"Just don't tell anybody that you're working for the RCMP," said his son. "Not even your buddy Jarge. You can tell him afterward. Okay?"

"Yes, Corporal," said his father. "We have to be careful with state secrets. I heard that Mark Twain once said, 'two people can keep a secret if one of them is dead.'"

"That's a good one, Dad," said Eddie Tizzard. "I'll see you later."

Tizzard had just finished talking to his father when Betsy came in, followed closely by a large, burly man that she introduced as Rob Skinner.

"Take a seat, please," said Tizzard.

"I'll just stand," said Skinner. "Too many people sitting around on their arses over here already."

This should be good, thought Tizzard.

While Tizzard was talking to Sid Skinner's brother, Windflower was driving Levi and Beulah home. All of them were too tired to do any more work today, and Levi and Windflower would go back to the B&B in the morning to get back at the floors. After dropping off his staff, Windflower went directly home where Sheila was set up on the computer in the living room on a Zoom call.

He went to the kitchen and made himself a sandwich that he ate while listening to the radio call-in program on CBC. Then he went upstairs to find his book. It was the new Donna Leon mystery, *Trace Elements*. It was part of a murder mystery series that Windflower had been reading for years. He loved the protagonist, Commissario Guido Brunetti, and the setting for the stories in Venice, Italy. That was on his long bucket list of places to see. Maybe he could talk Sheila into taking a trip with him this year.

As he was leaving with his book under his arm, he saw the box again on the dresser. What was it that the rabbit had called it in his dream? Oh yeah, an abundance box. He was still thinking about that when he came downstairs. Sheila was winding up her call.

"Some tea?" he asked.

"That would be grand," said Sheila.

Windflower made the tea and brought out a tray with a plate of cookies as well. "Might as well have dessert, too. How'd your call go?"

"Great, I think," said Sheila. "The people I talked to seemed interested, and now they're going to see if they can find the individual investors we need."

"That's super," said Windflower, grabbing a hermit cookie off the plate.

"How did it go at the B&B? I assume you're not doing the floors today," said Sheila.

"Nah, Levi was tired from working the night shift."

"And he had to twist your arm to get a day off work?" teased Sheila.

"I was a bit tired today, too," said Windflower. "Anyway, our guests are gone. They had their van towed in and are off to Saint-Pierre."

"That's strange, isn't it? To come here and visit Saint-Pierre in the middle of winter. Don't you think?"

"It is strange," said Windflower. He paused and thought about whether he wanted to tell Sheila about something else that was strange: seeing that little box in his dream and then having it show up on her nightstand. He decided to jump in.

"You know that box on your nightstand. The one with the fancy lettering…" he started.

"What about it?" she asked.

Now he had to tell her. At least part of it.

"I just noticed it," he said. "It's beautiful. Where did you get it?"

"I've had it for a while," she said. "I think I got it at that craft shop in Cashel's Cove. What's so special about it?"

"I saw it first in a dream," he admitted. "I think it's an abundance box."

"What does that mean?"

"I'm not really sure," said Windflower, a little sheepishly. "A rabbit told me that. When it opened the box in my dream, a blinding flash of light came out."

Sheila started laughing. She tried not to but couldn't help herself. Soon she was laughing so hard that Lady came in from the kitchen to see if she was okay.

Windflower took his book and started walking upstairs.

"Wait, I'm sorry, Winston. Winston," called Sheila.

"I'm going to read my book," said Windflower, feigning disappointment. "That's the last time I share my deep secrets with you."

He thought he could hear Sheila still laughing as he lay on their bed and opened his book. He read a few pages but could feel his eyes droop. Before he knew it, he was out cold. And before he knew anything else, he woke up with the rabbit from his last dream right in his face.

"They never understand," said the rabbit.

Windflower sat up. Then he realized he was in bed and that there was a talking rabbit in front of him. It took him a minute to get his thoughts together. "What is an abundance box?" he asked.

The rabbit pulled the box out of his fur. "You mean this box?" The rabbit slowly opened the box, and Windflower saw the brilliant light emanating from the box again. He also heard a mystical music, like chimes.

"That's just my sound effects," said the rabbit with a laugh. The animal found that so funny, it started rolling around on the bed. Windflower tried to grab it to slow it down, but it hopped away and stared at him. "No touching."

"Okay, okay," said Windflower. "Tell me about the box."

"Abundance is what we create in our lives," said the rabbit. "It is also what we create in our minds. What we can imagine, we can create. Think about what you would like in your life, and you can have it."

"It's as simple as that?" asked Windflower. "So, why do we need the box?"

"Well, I don't need the box, but you do. Humans, that is," said the rabbit. "You need to be reminded that you have been given all that you need and that in order to keep it you have to be grateful."

"What if I want different things?" asked Windflower.

"You mean more than a good life, good friends, a great partner and two beautiful children?" asked the rabbit.

"No, I want all that, but I want more, too," said Windflower.

"Be careful of that other G-word," said the rabbit. "What you are not grateful for will slip away, and all you'll have left is greed. Wanting more."

Windflower didn't have a good response to that, so he stayed silent.

"One more thing about abundance," said the rabbit. "Although this may be lost on you. You have to give it away to keep it."

"What does that mean?"

But the rabbit curled up in a ball and refused to answer. When he went to touch the rabbit, it kind of melted in his hands, and when he woke up he was rubbing the soft, velvety edge of Amelia Louise's baby blanket. He shook himself awake and went back downstairs to see Sheila.

Chapter Fourteen

Somebody who wished he could have a nap today was Eddie Tizzard. But he had to deal with Rob Skinner. After listening to his complaints for fifteen minutes, he finally got to ask him some questions about his brother.

"Sid was a simple guy," said Rob Skinner. "He liked going trouting and trying to get a moose in the fall. He loved his four-wheeler and heading off into the bush by himself to get a bucket of berries."

Tizzard could see the brother getting more emotional and almost tearing up as he talked more about his sibling. He had learned from watching Windflower interview people that this was a very vulnerable time for the person being interviewed but also a great opportunity to gather important information. He probed gently.

"Did your brother have any troubles you know about? How were things at home?"

"Best kind, b'y," as far as I know," said Rob Skinner. "We weren't as close as we have been in earlier days. I guess we all got too busy living our lives."

"He sounds like a nice man," said Tizzard. "Did he have any bad habits. Drink too much, smoke weed?"

Rob Skinner laughed. "Sid was the last guy you'd think about with drugs. Yes, he'd have a few rum and cokes sitting around his garage. But nothing serious."

"What did he do in his spare time?" asked Tizzard.

"He worked a lot, so he didn't have much of that," said the brother. "Every time I went over to visit, the missus would be sitting up in the living room watching TV and Sid would be in the basement on the computer."

"What was he doing on the computer?" asked Tizzard.

"Beats me," said Rob Skinner. "That's not my thing. I don't even know how to turn it on. I asked him one time what he was up to down there all the time."

"What did he say?" asked Tizzard.

"Said he was doing research," said the brother. "I laughed at him at that. He didn't even have his high school."

"Who did he hang around with?"

"Sid was a bit of a loner," said Rob Skinner. "He would be polite with people, but like I said, he would rather be off in the woods on his bike as anything."

"Did he have any enemies? Anybody who might want to hurt him?" asked Tizzard.

"No, b'y," said the other man. "That's what's so hard for the family. There was no reason for anybody to hurt Sid. I still can't believe he's gone." He looked like he might even cry. "Is that it?"

"You've been a big help," said Tizzard.

Rob Skinner signed the release form and left the office shortly afterward.

Tizzard sat in his chair and thought about what he had just heard about the late Sid Skinner. Not much, really. But most people are like that, he thought. We only see the tip of the iceberg, and most of us is hidden underneath the surface. What was under Sid Skinner's surface, and how would he find that?

All that thinking made him hungry. He was about to go to the back to get a snack when the phone rang. It was Bill Ford.

"Inspector. How can I help you?" asked Tizzard.

"I like that attitude, Eddie," said Ford. "Keep it up and you'll go far in this man's RCMP."

"Thank you, boss," said Tizzard.

"The Drug guys are driving me crazy," said Ford. "They want to know who the Germans were that were just in Grand Bank."

"I don't know them personally," said Tizzard.

"Can you find out any of their names?" asked Ford. "They registered at the B&B. Maybe they have a record."

"I'll get Smithson to check it out," said Tizzard. "Why are they so excited?"

"Not really sure," said Ford. "But they might be connected to something bigger. Way beyond my pay grade."

"Okay. I'll let you know if I hear anything."

Tizzard called Smithson. "Do you know the names of the German guys who were here?"

"Just their first names," said Smithson. "Why?"

"The big boys in Ottawa are interested," said Tizzard. "Can you see if their names are on the registration at the B&B?"

"I can check the van registration, too," said Smithson. "I'm pretty sure it's a rental."

"Good idea," said Tizzard. "Keep trying to find out what you can about Sid Skinner. Okay?"

"I'm trying," said Smithson. "People want to talk. Very quietly, but they all want to talk. Mostly they are trying to pump me for information."

"Then give them something," said Tizzard.

"Like what?" asked Smithson.

"Tell them we think the cases are connected and we're trying to find the missing link," said Tizzard.

"That's good," said Smithson. "I'll try it out after I run over to the B&B."

"Oh, and I thought of something else you can do," said Tizzard. "Can you go over to Sid Skinner's house and have a look at his computer? I'll call his brother and clear it with him. He said that Sid was always on it. What was he doing?"

"Got it," said Smithson.

Tizzard hung up and went to the lunchroom before anybody else could call. He was rummaging around in the fridge when Carrie came in with two Tupperware containers.

"What is that?" asked Tizzard.

"My supper and your lunch. If you want it," said Carrie.

Tizzard opened his container. "Chili. God bless you, Carrie."

"You owe me. Again," said Carrie. "What's been going on around here?"

Tizzard put his chili in the microwave. "Where do I start?"

He told Carrie about his morning, and she gave him a long stare after he was finished.

"What's that about?" he asked.

"Why didn't you ask me to snoop around, too?" she said. "Everybody else gets to do it. And besides, no older man is going to talk to Smithson, no matter how many cups of coffee he buys them. Me, on the other hand…"

"You know what, you're right," said Tizzard. "I'll pull Smithson off that and let you take over. Remember, we're looking for links between them or anything unusual. Anything at all. I'm desperate now."

"We should be," said Carrie. "I hear there's another storm brewing for this meeting tonight. They may be over here with pitchforks and torches."

Tizzard finished his lunch and went back to his office. The rest of the afternoon sped past, and just before five he left the building and went home to relieve his dad, who was on babysitting detail this afternoon. At least he had the evening with Hughie to look forward to. That put a smile on his face that lasted long after his dad went home to change for the meeting.

Windflower's afternoon had been quiet, too. He had picked up Amelia Louise from daycare, and they waited in the driveway for the school bus to drop Stella off. After she and her sister had a snack, Windflower took all of them for a ride around town on the toboggan with Lady happily tagging along on her leash. He even took them near the B&B, where there was a short hill that ran down towards the wharf. After a couple of rides, the girls begged for more, but Windflower had had enough. As they were leaving, he saw Smithson drive by the inn, slow down and then drive off again. He tried to get his attention, but the young officer seemed very intent on getting away as fast as he could.

Windflower lugged his little family home, and while the girls watched TV, he got supper ready. That was pretty easy, since Sheila had already put the macaroni and cheese in the oven. He sliced some vegetables and put them on a plate and made a little salad. He also put a loaf of garlic bread wrapped in tinfoil into the oven. His stomach churned overtime as the smells of the casserole and the garlic bread filled the kitchen.

Sheila came down just in time to sit at the table for supper.

"You look very nice tonight," said Windflower. She had put on a nice black dress and wore her mother's pearl necklace.

"I'm wearing my power necklace," she said. "I have a feeling I'll need it. I've been getting texts all day from people. They're pretty upset."

"I don't blame them," said Windflower. "They don't know what's happened to those men, and they're probably worried about their own people. But they have to trust the process. 'Our doubts are traitors and make us lose the good we oft might win by fearing to attempt.'"

"True," said Sheila. "But they have some reason to doubt the effectiveness of the police to protect them, given what's happened so far. 'Modest doubt is called the beacon of the wise.'"

"Touché," said Windflower, finishing up his second helping. "Tea?"

"No, I better get going," said Sheila. "Are you going to be okay with these two?"

Stella and Amelia Louise had started throwing small bits of garlic bread overboard, and Lady and Molly were scrambling to pick them up.

Windflower laughed, cleaned both girls' hands and banished them to the living room with a promise of dessert. "I'll be fine," he said. "I think I have the easier job tonight."

Chapter Fifteen

Eddie Tizzard was thinking the same thing as he took little Hughie out of the bath and put on his pajamas as the baby squirmed and giggled. He warmed up a bottle of milk and fed him while he watched the news on TV. He just caught the end of the big story, the one where he was a featured player. There he was, standing alongside Bill Ford, looking exactly as he felt: like a deer in the headlights. At the end the reporter looked directly into the camera. "It looks like the RCMP have no answers for a community that is part in mourning and part in dread for what may happen next."

He clicked the TV off. Hughie was starting to doze on the bottle, and Tizzard shook him a little and got him to burp before taking him into his crib and laying him in, hopefully for the evening. He was about to get himself some dessert when his cell phone rang.

"Sorry to bother you at home, but I thought you'd want my report," said Smithson.

"Shoot," said Tizzard, taking a tub of ice cream out of the freezer and sitting at the kitchen table with a large spoon. That was the kind of day it was.

"So, I couldn't get anything from the B&B. It was all closed up. But I went to the ferry terminal in Fortune and found their rental vehicle," said Smithson.

"And?" asked Tizzard, taking a large scoop of ice cream.

"And I opened it and checked it for prints. I ran them through the system, and one name in particular popped out," said Smithson.

"Spill the beans," said Tizzard, growing impatient with the younger officer's attempt to string his story out.

"That name was Gerhard Müller. It's a pretty common German name, but this Gerhard Müller is pretty special. In a bad kind of way," said Smithson.

"What do you mean?" asked Tizzard, taking another scoop of ice cream.

"His name almost jumped off the screen," said Smithson. "He's wanted everywhere across Europe. The Dutch think he is the mastermind of a meth and ecstasy network that's supplying most of Europe and is seeking to expand into the United States. There are messages waiting for you from Interpol and our HQ. What do you want me to do?"

Tizzard closed the tub of ice cream and thought for a moment. "I'll call Bill Ford," he said.

"Okay," said Smithson. "I'm just going over to the Skinner house to take a look at the computer. Do you want me to do anything else?"

"That'll be good," said Tizzard. "You stick with the computer stuff and let me know if you find anything. And you're off the hook for looking for information about our victims. I've got Evanchuk on that. Maybe more flies with honey than vinegar."

Smithson didn't sound upset about this change of assignment at all. In fact, he sounded relieved as he said goodnight. At least one person was happy with me, thought Tizzard. Let's see what Inspector Ford has to say. He called his number in Marystown.

Windflower had finally got the girls settled down and in bed. He listened for more activity, but the coast seemed clear. He made himself a pot of tea and grabbed a couple of cookies. He sat in the living room and watched a repeat of the suppertime news. He saw an uncomfortable Eddie Tizzard and then Bill Ford trying to explain the situation to a skeptical reporter. Next up was a shot of the meeting hall, which was rapidly filling up.

The reporter managed to grab a couple of the women who were going inside and asked them what they were feeling and what they hoped to get out of the meeting.

"It's awful," said one woman. "Everybody's scared and nobody has information."

Another woman expressed much the same concern. "It's about time dat the RCMP get off their high horses and tell the people what exactly dey is going to do about dis. It's shameful."

As his old friend, Ron Quigley used to say, "I think we'll mark her down as undecided." Windflower chuckled to himself about this, but he knew, more than most, that this situation could not continue. He was finishing off his last cookie when the phone rang.

He thought it was Sheila saying that she was on her way home. But it was Ron Quigley.

"Ron. I was just thinking about you," said Windflower. "I'm making the wild guess that this is not a social call. But you know what, Ron? I think I miss you."

"That's nice, Winston," said Quigley. "'There is flattery in friendship.' I miss you, too. But I actually have a business proposition for you."

"That's interesting," said Windflower. "Tell me more. And remember, 'no legacy is as rich as honesty.'"

Quigley laughed. "I know you don't want to officially come back onboard. But how about a contract?"

"How would that work, and what would I have to do?" asked Windflower.

"You would be an outside supplier to the RCMP with a specific project, and you would report directly to me," said Quigley.

"I like the last part," said Windflower. "I don't want any part of RCMP politics. But what's the project?"

"At least you didn't say no right away," said Quigley. "We just had a person of interest to the Drug Squad pop up in Newfoundland. Grand Bank, to be specific."

"In Grand Bank?" said Windflower. "Who is it?"

"Gerhard Müller," said Quigley. "You know him?"

"He might be one of our German guests," said Windflower. "But they're gone to Saint-Pierre. Left this morning."

"But they'll be back," said Quigley. "And we think they're bringing a lot of stuff back with them."

"From Saint-Pierre?" asked Windflower. "There's not much over there. Some nice restaurants. But not much else."

"There's an international airport," said Quigley. "With daily direct flights from Paris."

"Assuming I would undertake work related to this case, what would my role be?" asked Windflower.

"Does that mean you're interested?" asked Quigley.

"I'm interested in finding more about what the risks might be to me in any operation involving an international drug smuggling ring," said Windflower.

"Killing is not really their thing. But they will have arms," said Quigley. "It's not without danger. But I'm asking you to do surveillance at this point. We can't get anybody down there fast enough, and I can't ask the Grand Bank office. They have their own problems. The good news is that we have somebody in Saint-Pierre."

"One of the Germans," said Windflower.

"That's why I want you," said Quigley. "You can think ahead. We've got somebody on the inside, but they have to be really, really careful. They will contact you and pass along what they see and hear. That is, if you're interested."

"Let me talk to Sheila. She'll be home within the hour. I'll call you back," said Windflower. "I hope you're not leading me astray, Ron."

"You know how to do this stuff, Winston," said Quigley. "'Things done well and with a care exempt themselves from fear.'"

"Yeah, right," said Windflower. "'The devil can cite Scripture for his purpose.' I'll call you back."

Windflower could feel a little tingling at the base of his spine. Was that adrenaline, thinking about working on a case? Or a niggling fear creeping back up. He didn't have much more time to gauge that sensation as Sheila opened the door and collapsed on the couch beside him.

"You have to help them," was the first thing she said.

Richard Tizzard said much the same to his son when he got back from the meeting.

"It was a combination of anger and fear all mixed up in a nasty broth," he said. "I've never seen people as upset as tonight. The women were the worst. I'd be very surprised if they're not out banging on your detachment door first thing in the morning. You have to do something."

Eddie Tizzard looked at his dad, then slowly walked into the kitchen and put the kettle on to boil. When the water was steaming, he made the tea and brought out two mugs to the living room. "Okay," he said. "Tell me everything."

An hour later, after hearing a virtual blow-by-blow account of the meeting, Eddie was spared more torture by the baby monitor that alerted him that Hughie was awake and not happy about something. His dad took his leave while Eddie changed the baby and warmed up the remainder of his bottle. Thankfully, that was enough to get Hughie to start dozing off.

Chapter Sixteen

Across town, Windflower had listened patiently to Sheila's account of the community gathering. When she was done, he told her about his call with Ron Quigley.

"Are you going to do it?" she asked.

"I wanted to talk to you first," said Windflower.

"Sounds like you're leaning in that direction," said Sheila. "Is it dangerous?"

"It might be, but I'm not going to directly interact with the bad guys," said Windflower.

"Will you have to travel?"

"Not very far," said Windflower. "Maybe to Saint-Pierre."

"If you're going over, I want to come," said Sheila. "I want to get some perfume, and maybe they might have some new clothes in the shops."

"Sounds like you're leaning towards it now."

Sheila laughed. "I wish you'd get involved with the case here in Grand Bank. But I understand. I just want you to be safe and come home every night. You were starting to go stir crazy doing nothing anyway."

"I was working on the B&B," protested Windflower.

"We used to call that a make-work project," said Sheila. "Levi can probably handle that job on his own. If not, his dad, Jerimiah, would be happy to help."

"So, you are giving me the green light?"

"More like a flashing yellow," said Sheila. "I'd say try it out. You might like doing contract work."

"Okay," said Windflower. "I'm going to call Ron back and then walk the dog."

"I'll see you upstairs," said Sheila.

As Windflower was calling Ron Quigley, Eddie Tizzard was crawling into bed. He was exhausted. Mentally, emotionally and physically. He fell asleep quickly. But that peaceful state didn't last. He found himself in another dream.

This time he "woke up" standing on the wharf in Grand Bank on a very foggy morning. About the only thing he could see was the flashing white light on top of the lighthouse. There was nobody else on the wharf, which was unusual at any time of day in this seaside town. There wasn't even a sea gull or two or three flying around. That wasn't just unusual. It was weird.

Tizzard could feel the sea breeze on his face, and even though it was cool, it felt refreshing at the same time. He was enjoying the peace and tranquility of this scene when he felt a wave wash up over the wharf, and it absolutely drenched him. He stood there sputtering and spitting out salt water when he heard what he thought was laughter. He opened his eyes and saw a very large and very fat harp seal sitting in front of him on the wharf.

He just stared at the seal for a minute until the seal stopped laughing.

"Can't you talk?" asked the seal.

"You can talk?" said Tizzard.

"Duh?" said the seal. "It's me, Sid."

"Sid?" asked Tizzard. Then he realized who or what the seal might be. "Sid Skinner? You're a seal?"

"You can be anything you want over here," said the seal. "I like swimming, and it lets me visit back home. At least in the water."

"That's cool," said Tizzard, thinking that he might be a little crazy chatting with a talking seal.

"What's crazy about that?" asked the seal. "I can see your thinking over here. It's one of the other benefits. Although I'm not sure it's a benefit all the time."

"Why are you here?" asked Tizzard. "In my dream?"

"It may be your dream, but this is all I have now," said the seal. "I want you to give a message to my wife. Tell her I love her. Will you do that?"

Tizzard felt he had no choice but to nod. "Before you go, can you tell me what happened to you?"

"I drowned in a lake," said the seal.

"I don't think so, and we're going to dig up your body to find out. Another guy got poisoned," said Tizzard.

The seal kind of sighed. "You can have that body," he said finally. "I like this one just fine, although I think I'll switch to a rabbit for the summer. I hear they have more fun if you know what I mean." With that, the seal started laughing again.

"Can you tell me anything else?"

"I know, I know," said the seal. "The women are going to string you up."

"Well?" asked Tizzard. "Please."

"Forty-nine times out of fifty, nobody will call your bluff," said the seal.

"What does that mean?"

"Sometimes you gotta take a risk," said the seal. "Now, I've got some swimming to do." With another giant splash, the seal jumped off the wharf and into the water. What seemed like half the ocean washed over Eddie Tizzard as he stood there and watched the seal disappear into the fog.

He woke up in bed drenched to the bone, although the sheets all around him were perfectly dry. He lay in bed, wondering if that really happened. When he ran his tongue over his lips, he could taste salt water.

Quigley had been very happy with Windflower's decision, although Winston wasn't as sure himself as he took Lady for her nightly constitutional. The night was cool but comfortable, and the night sky was completely full. Windflower gazed up to find the most popular constellations as Lady explored previous canine visits to the snowbanks along the way. They went all over town, passing by the B&B before making the turn for home.

Windflower filled the pets' bowls and went upstairs to find Sheila asleep and gently snoring. He moved her over a little and slid in beside her. Instinctively, she reached for him, and he cuddled closer. Soon he was drifting off into a beautifully calm sleep. But like Eddie Tizzard in his little house over the way, Windflower also found himself inside a dream.

He found his hands first and then started looking around. He was trying to see if that rabbit would show up again. He had been thinking about questions to ask it. But no rabbit today. In fact, no

74

animals at all. That was strange, thought Windflower as he surveyed the landscape of this dream. It appeared to be a desert, although Windflower had never been in one. He'd only seen them in pictures or on TV.

But it was a desert, all right. That became really clear when he felt the wind pick up and the pricks of sand on his cheeks. Soon, he was in the middle of what must be a sandstorm. The sand was hitting all parts of his body now, like a needle poking him everywhere. His hands did little to slow down the relentless attack on his face, and in desperation he lay on the ground and covered his head with his arms.

He closed his eyes, and when he opened them, he expected to be buried under a mountain of sand. Instead, he peered around and saw a beam of light coming from one corner of his eye. He got to his knees and crawled towards the light. As he got closer, he could see a cave, and inside the cave was a fire. Someone was sitting next to it.

"So, you made it," said the person next to the fire.

Windflower recognized the voice. It was his Auntie Marie, who had passed some time ago but had appeared in his dreams several times since.

"Auntie Marie, it is so nice to see you," said Windflower. "What are you doing here?"

"You mean in this cave under the sand? Or in your dream?" asked Auntie Marie. "I'll answer the cave question first. I always wanted to travel the world. Now I can," she said. "We're under a pyramid. Pretty cool, eh?"

"It is," said Windflower. "I'm glad that you are happy. But why are you here in my dream? I mean I'm really glad to see you…"

"You called me," said Auntie Marie. When Windflower gave her a puzzled look, she added more. "At least your subconscious called me. Your spirit. That's the voice I listen to now."

Windflower smiled and nodded.

"Come and sit and have some stew," said Auntie Marie. "We have no moose meat over here. It's considered bad form. You never know who it might be." She started laughing and could hardly keep her hands still as she scooped up a bowl for Windflower from a pot hanging over the fire.

He cradled the bowl in his hands, savouring the aroma first and then sipping the broth. "Oh my god," he said. "This is heavenly."

His aunt laughed. "That's the point." She handed him a fork to spear out a tender carrot and sat back to watch him enjoy his stew. When he was finished, he passed the empty bowl back to her.

"That was incredible," he said. "Thank you for that. But I'm guessing you have more to give me than a bowl of stew."

Auntie Marie smiled. "Your insides are unsettled. Once again you are being pulled back into the past, and you have to decide if it will be your future."

"What should I do?" asked Windflower.

"Focus on today," said his aunt. "It is a gift. That's why we call it the present. Tomorrow will look after itself."

Windflower had many more questions to ask his aunt, but as he started to speak the sand started whipping up again, and soon he and everything around him was lost in a cloud of dust. He closed his eyes, and when he opened them, he was awake in his bed with Sheila. He lay there for a minute until his breath came back to normal. Then he slowly drifted back to sleep.

Chapter Seventeen

Eddie Tizzard stirred and tried to get up, but his tired body weighed him down. He felt Carrie get up and go to Hughie. She brought him back to bed with her a few minutes later. She changed and fed the baby while Eddie watched with great pleasure. When she was done, she passed Hughie over to him.

"I'm having my shower," she said. "Maybe you can make us some coffee."

Tizzard tucked Hughie under his arm and carried him downstairs, where he put the coffee on and checked the weather. Clear and cool, he thought as he surveyed their front yard and the street in front of their house. He turned on the radio but quickly shut it off when they started playing excerpts of last night's meeting. He grabbed a banana and gave Hughie a little piece to gnaw on.

Carrie came down a little while later and they both played with the baby and had their coffee.

"I hear it was an awful meeting," said Carrie.

"It's not good," said Tizzard. "We have to get something, anything, moving on this. Once we get Skinner's body back from St. John's, we should be able to start seeing if there's a pattern."

"They have to be connected. Somehow," said Carrie. "The place is too small for them not to know each other and to have them go missing, and two turning up dead is more than a coincidence."

"That's your job now," said Tizzard. "Find the connection." He sat quietly for a moment enjoying his coffee and the time with Carrie and his son. Then he spoke again. "Do you believe in dreams?"

"What do you mean?" asked Carrie.

Tizzard paused for another moment, trying to decide how to open this conversation without appearing to be a raving lunatic. He decided on a soft approach. "You ever have dreams that seem really real? Even if they're far-fetched?"

"Like what?" asked Carrie.

Now he was stuck. He could dive in or hold back. One more pause, and he jumped right in. "I had a dream, and Sid Skinner was in it," he blurted out.

"The dead guy?" asked Carrie.

"Yes," said Tizzard. "I actually had two dreams with him in them. The first was kind of normal, except that he was dead. The other one, last night... He was a seal."

"Like a seal that swims around in the water?" asked Carrie.

"Yeah," said Tizzard. "Except the seal, Sid, could talk."

"What did you have for supper?" asked Carrie. When Tizzard looked a little crestfallen, she added, "I'm sorry, couldn't resist. What did the seal say?"

"You don't think I'm crazy?"

"That's a different matter," said Carrie. "We had all kinds of people with strange beliefs back around Estevan. Travelling evangelists who could breathe fire and claimed to walk on water. Flat-earth people. It was the prairies, after all. My dad always said that people could believe whatever they wanted as long as we didn't have to follow them. So, what did Sid the seal have to say for himself?"

"He said something about forty-nine times out of fifty you might be able to get away with a bluff, and that you gotta take a risk sometimes," said Tizzard. "What do you think that means?"

"I have no idea," said Carrie. "I think the person who's having the dream gets to interpret it. It's your subconscious. What does it mean to you?"

"I don't know," said Tizzard. "Maybe I should talk to Windflower about it. His family are dream weavers or something."

"That's a good idea," said Carrie. "He's hanging around the B&B these days. I saw him when I was driving by."

Tizzard nodded.

"Was there anything else you wanted to tell me about your dreams?" asked Carrie.

"Sid asked me to tell his wife he loved her," said Tizzard.

"Are you going to do it?"

"I don't think I have a choice," said Tizzard. "How could I refuse a talking seal?"

Windflower woke early and got up before Sheila. He checked in on the girls, but they were sleeping as well. He crept downstairs and shushed Lady when she came near. He put on the coffee and went out in the back with Lady. He also brought with him a pipe this morning. Not any pipe, but a ceremonial pipe that had been gifted to him by his Auntie Marie.

She had explained to him before she died that the pipe was one way she used to connect with her ancestors. When she passed, she had left instructions with his Uncle Frank to pass it along to Windflower. He felt honoured by this gift and tried to treat it with the reverence it deserved. He took it out of the blanket it had been wrapped in and cradled it in his hands. It had a beautiful long wooden stem and catlinite, or pipestone bowl.

He put a small amount of tobacco in it and lit the pipe. He took a couple of puffs to get it started and then let the smoke curl and waft around him in the cold morning air. Then he waited. After a few minutes, the air around him grew warm, and there came a beam of light that grew and grew until he felt like he was surrounded by light.

It was like nothing existed besides him and this great light until he started to make out shapes in the near distance. He stood and walked towards the figures that were seated around a large, blazing fire. He recognized his grandfather first, with his long white hair and ceremonial headdress that he only put on for special occasions. Then he saw his mother and father on the other side of the fire talking to his Auntie Marie. He tried to get closer, but it was like they were in a bubble and he couldn't break through. He called out to them, but they couldn't hear him either.

Sooner than he would have liked, the bubble started to evaporate, and within seconds he was standing alone in his backyard. He wasn't exactly alone. Lady was sitting in front of him, staring up at him to see if he was okay.

"I'm okay, girl. Let's go in."

He was pouring his first cup of coffee for the morning when he heard the pitter-patter on the stairs. It was Stella.

"Good morning," said Windflower.

"Good morning, Daddy," said Stella, sitting on a chair across from him. He noticed her staring at him.

"Can I you get you something? Juice?" he asked.

"Daddy, why were you smoking outside?" asked Stella. "I saw you out the window. At school, the teacher says smoking is bad."

"I wasn't really smoking," said Windflower. "I was using Auntie Marie's pipe as part of a ceremony."

"What's cerrymonny?"

"You know how I smudge sometimes with my medicines and smudge bowl," said Windflower.

Stella nodded. "That's when you make the smoke go all over you. Don't you choke?"

Windflower laughed. "It's not that much smoke." He tried another approach with his daughter. "You know how you go to church with Mommy, and they say prayers and stuff?"

"And sing songs," said Stella.

"And sing songs. It's kind of like that for me," said Windflower as he heard larger steps come down the stairs.

"What are you talking about?" asked Sheila.

"Daddy was smoking in the backyard," said Stella.

Windflower just shook his head and got Sheila a cup of coffee. After breakfast and clean-up, Windflower walked over to the B&B to see Levi. Sheila was right. Levi didn't have any problem continuing with the floor work on his own. In fact, he looked more than a little relieved not to have Windflower hanging over his shoulder.

Windflower was going to head over to the RCMP detachment to pick up some files that Ron Quigley had promised to send last night, but the lights and aroma coming from the Mug-Up were too great to resist. He was walking across the street when he saw an RCMP Jeep barrelling down on him. He jumped back. Then he saw it was Eddie Tizzard.

"I'm so sorry," said Tizzard, jumping out of his vehicle.

"Slow down, man," said Windflower. "You almost gave me a heart attack."

"I'll buy you a coffee to make up for it," said Tizzard.

Windflower had to laugh at the hangdog look on the young officer's face. "And a tea biscuit."

"Done," said Tizzard, jumping back in his Jeep and wheeling it into the last parking spot near the café.

Chapter Eighteen

The café was humming this morning, and Windflower and Tizzard got their coffee and tea biscuits to go. They stood at the front and greeted people while Herb and Moira appeared briefly to take or deliver orders. They sat in Tizzard's Jeep, and he drove them down to the wharf, where they watched the seagulls circle the fish plant looking for their own breakfast.

"I'm coming back to work," said Windflower. "Well, partially, on a contract."

"That's great news," said Tizzard. "We're drowning. I'm so glad you decided to come back."

"It's not that kind of deal," said Windflower. "I'm on a special assignment, working with Ron Quigley and the National Drug Squad."

"Oh," said Tizzard, sounding disappointed. "The Germans?"

"Yeah," said Windflower. "How'd you know about that?"

"Smithson found their van and got some prints. When he put them in the system, the alarm bells started ringing," said Tizzard. "So, what are you going to be doing?"

"I don't know yet," said Windflower. "I'm their eyes over here for now. I guess all of that will be revealed." He looked over at Tizzard and could see the weariness in his eyes and the stress in his body. "I won't be working directly with you," he added. "But there's no reason why I can't be helpful to you. Like if you want to run things by me or something."

"That would be great," said Tizzard, brightening considerably. Fifteen minutes later he had given Windflower a summary of what he knew about the case and what he didn't. The latter was much longer.

"I still think you're on the right track to look for a connection. There has to be one. Maybe the autopsy will help with that," said Windflower.

"I should go see Doc Sanjay," said Tizzard. "But I can drop you off home if you want."

"I'm going to the detachment," said Windflower. "Quigley is sending me some stuff."

"I'll drop you there," said Tizzard. "I'm really happy you're back. But someone else will be super happy about it."

"I'm not back, exactly," said Windflower. Although he knew who Tizzard was talking about.

Betsy Molloy was more than happy when she saw Windflower walk in the door of the detachment.

"Oh, my God, I hoped it was true," said Betsy. And before Windflower could do anything to prevent it, she had her arms wrapped around him and enveloped him in a tight hug. "I'm so glad you're back. I heard a rumour, but I didn't want to get my hopes up. But it's you and you're here in the flesh."

"I'm not really back," said Windflower. "I'm only on a contract working with Ron Quigley in Ottawa."

"That's why all that stuff came in for you from him," said Betsy. "But what do you mean you're not back? You're here, aren't you?"

"I'm here, but only working on one project with Ron," said Windflower.

"So, you don't want your office back?" asked Betsy, looking puzzled.

"No," said Windflower. "I'll take what Ron sent and be on my way. I may drop in from time to time, but I won't need an office."

"Oh," said Betsy. "Well, you'll get to visit, and that'll be nice. Maybe you'll change your mind and come back full-time." She marched off to get the papers, looking pretty pleased with herself at that pleasant thought.

"And maybe I won't," said Windflower very quietly to himself. But he had to admit that he felt pretty good himself to be back in these familiar surroundings. He took a look around Betsy's area at the front and walked back to his old office. Tizzard hadn't changed it much. Except for Hughie's picture on the desk instead of Amelia Louise and Stella, it was pretty much the same.

He came back to the front and noticed his name had been taken off the board and there was only an empty slot next to the place where his messages used to be. It hadn't been that long since he'd been gone, and yet it felt like forever. He came back to reality when he saw Betsy coming back with a large file folder. Betsy handed him the folder. "Here you go, Sergeant," she said. "Oh, I guess you're not my sergeant anymore."

"Thank you, Betsy," said Windflower and went to the back to read the file.

Eddie Tizzard was thinking about his old sergeant, too, as he drove to see Doctor Sanjay. He hoped that he would come back, but by the sounds of it, that wouldn't happen. He also wondered if he should have told him about his dreams. Maybe Windflower could have helped Tizzard understand them. There might be time for that now, since he was going to be around more.

That gave Tizzard a smile as he parked by the side of the clinic and walked down the hallway to Sanjay's office. It took him quite a while to get there, since everybody in the waiting area wanted to say hello, and Tizzard was happy to oblige. This was the best part of his job, and he was enjoying it quite a bit. Until one older lady started haranguing him about the missing men. He made a quick exit and escaped to Sanjay's small office at the back.

"Good morning, my young friend," said Sanjay. "How's she going b'y?" Sanjay had been around these parts forever, and he loved slipping in a bit of the local lingo.

Tizzard was happy to play along. "She's going great, b'y. How's it going with you, me old trout?"

Sanjay laughed and clapped him on the shoulder. "Come in, come in. I have some news for you."

"We haven't got Skinner's body yet?" asked Tizzard.

"No, but it's on its way," said Sanjay. "That's not my news. I think I know what killed Leo Broderick."

"What?" asked Tizzard.

"Venezuelan tree frog poison," said Sanjay. "There are these small frogs that have enough poison in them to kill ten grown men. The poison is called batrachotoxin. It causes paralysis and death when it enters the bloodstream, even in minuscule amounts. My friend at the lab in St. John's found the poison and is confirming it with the FBI lab right now."

"You've got to be kidding me," said Tizzard. "Some kind of exotic frog poison? Here in Grand Bank?"

"My friend is a well-respected expert in poison control and identification," said the doctor. "He said that there have been a number of cases where this particular poison has been found in the United States. Apparently, the Colombian cartels like to use it. It is one of their signal assassination marks."

"That's too much, Doc," said Tizzard. "Colombian drug dealers and tree frog poison."

"If that's what the science is, we have to go with it," said Sanjay. "My lab friend will be back to us as soon as he hears back from the American lab."

"So, assuming all of this is correct, did these South Americans bring up blow guns with them, too?" asked Tizzard.

"They may have, if in fact it was South Americans," said the doctor. "But the media reports say that whoever was administering this poison in the States was using a modified pellet gun."

"Lots of those around here," said Tizzard. "Okay, thanks, Doc. Let me know when Skinner's body gets here and if you have any more news."

"I will," said Sanjay. "Oh, I hear that your sergeant may be coming back. Any truth to that?"

"News travels fast," said Tizzard. "He's back, but only on a contract to help Ron Quigley in Ottawa. Not in our shop."

"That's too bad," said the doctor. "You could probably use some help."

Tizzard nodded, left the doctor's office, and snuck out the back door to escape more attention. He walked around the back of the building, trying to clear his head, which had just been given a good shaking up with the visit to Doctor Sanjay. There was no way he was telling anybody that a man had been killed in their little community by Colombian drug dealers using some Venezuelan tree frog poison. But what if it was true?

He was still muddled when he got back to the office and Betsy handed him his messages. Every single one, but one, was from the media. The last was from Bill Ford.

"Sergeant Windflower is in the small boardroom," she said. "He said not to use sergeant, but I'm still hoping he comes back, aren't you?"

Tizzard nodded, smiled at Betsy, and went to see Windflower.

Chapter Nineteen

Windflower said, "Good morning, Corporal, I hope you don't mind if I hang around in here for a while. Quigley is going to call, and I want to have all the papers laid out so I can follow along on his briefing."

"No worries," said Tizzard. "Listen, I know I'm in over my head," he said. "I'm barely a corporal again, and now we got two dead guys and another missing, and everyone from the media to little old ladies at the clinic are yelling at me. I'm trying, but I can't seem to get anywhere."

"I'm not coming back to take over," said Windflower. "That's not going to happen. If it was, Marguerite Slaney would have been the final nail in that coffin. But I can help when I'm not working for Quigley. What did Sanjay say?"

Tizzard smiled. "First, let's get a snack."

Windflower laughed. "That sounds just like you, Eddie."

"You know what my dad says," said Tizzard. "Life is uncertain. Always eat dessert first. I think there's some of Betsy's date squares still left in the fridge."

Windflower laughed again and followed Tizzard to the coffee room in back. This felt more than familiar. It was like coming home, thought Windflower as Tizzard put the tin of squares on the table and got them both a cup of coffee.

Tizzard ran through everything again, but when he got to the latest news from Doctor Sanjay about the tree frog poison, he looked defeated.

"That is certainly strange," said Windflower. "And I might not share that too widely. But if Doc Sanjay says the guy was poisoned, that's all you really need to know right now. Plus, the Skinner autopsy will tell you if he's on the right track. Focus in on what you can do, which is trying to find the connections and why anybody might want to harm these men."

Tizzard nodded and finished off the last of the date squares. Then, he stopped talking. For more than a minute. Windflower let the silence sit and then finally spoke up. "Is there anything else?"

"I've been having some dreams," said Tizzard. "I know you have dreams sometimes. Do animals ever appear in your dreams?"

"Sure," said Windflower. "There's animals in many of my dreams. My Auntie Marie used to say that animals can bring us messages from the other side."

"Do they ever, like, talk to you?" asked Tizzard.

"Sometimes," said Windflower. "I thought it was really weird, but in my family it happens all the time. At least, that's what Auntie Marie and Uncle Frank taught me."

"Did you ever have a talking seal?" asked Tizzard.

"You know, I think I did one time," said Windflower. "I don't remember much about that dream, except that the seal kept laughing at me."

"Really?" asked Tizzard. "Mine did, too. Except that my seal said he was somebody."

"Who?" asked Windflower.

"Sid Skinner, the dead guy," said Tizzard.

"What did he say?" asked Windflower. "That's the really important part."

"Well, Sid actually came to me in my dreams twice," said Tizzard. "But only once as a seal," he added. "The first time he just looked like a drowned dead man. He said something about life being full of surprises. But he slipped away before I could ask any more about that."

"What did the seal say?" said Windflower. "Sometimes the messages from animals are clearer in our dreams."

"Sid, I mean the seal, said the women in town were going to string me up," said Tizzard.

"Some truth in that," said Windflower, trying to lighten the mood. But Tizzard only grimaced.

"I think he also said that I had to take a risk," said Tizzard. "What does that mean?"

"I don't know," said Windflower. "You'll have to ask the seal. If he comes back in another dream. Did he say anything else?"

"He said to tell his wife that he loved her," said Tizzard. "Should I do that?"

"I guess you have to," said Windflower. "But you don't have to tell her that a talking seal told you this in a dream. You can find a way to tell her that you know Sid loved her. That will be enough."

"That's great, Sarge," said Tizzard. "I mean Winston."

"Hey, Sarge," said Smithson, who walked in as Tizzard was finished speaking. "You're back."

"No," said Windflower, for the third time that morning explaining what he was doing in the RCMP offices.

"Anyway, I've got an update on Sid Skinner's computer," said Smithson.

Windflower stood to leave, but Tizzard indicated he should stay. "He's an advisor on the case now. Go ahead, Smithson. What did you find out?"

"Sid Skinner spent a lot of time on his computer, according to his wife," said Smithson. "But there was no browsing history."

"None at all?" asked Tizzard. "Could he have erased it?"

"Yes, but it would still show up when I checked," said Smithson. "But there was nothing. Nothing on his hard drive either. That's less unusual. People put stuff in the cloud these days anyway."

"So, you can't tell what Skinner was doing on the computer?" asked Tizzard.

"I didn't say that," said Smithson. "When a computer is that clean, it is either not being used or there's something else going on."

"I think he's talking about the dark web or something," said Windflower. "We had somebody using that a few years ago to smuggle drugs. We found out that it was pretty common, especially in Canada."

"Is that what Sid Skinner was doing?" asked Tizzard. "Dealing drugs?"

"Maybe," said Smithson. "All his Internet activity is encrypted. I've managed to break into some of it, but there's a lot more there that I'll have to dig into. I did find something really interesting, though." He paused as if for effect.

Tizzard looked at him, and his eyes started to bulge. "Spill it, Smithson."

"Okay, okay," said Smithson. "Sid Skinner has a bitcoin account. With four hundred bitcoins in it."

"Is that a lot?" asked Windflower.

"Each bitcoin is worth about fifty thousand dollars," said Smithson. "US dollars."

"That's a couple of million bucks," said Tizzard. "What was he doing to generate that kind of money?"

"That's what I hope to find out when I go through his computer tonight," said Smithson.

"Okay," said Tizzard. "Let me know what you find out."

Smithson went off with a box containing what appeared to be Sid Skinner's computer and headed for the back storage area that he used as his techie zone.

"Thanks for listening to me," said Tizzard after Smithson had left. "And for not thinking I'm crazy."

"Well, you are crazy, Eddie," said Windflower, laughing again. "Just take it one step at a time and things will work out."

"It just seems overwhelming," said Tizzard. "What's that quote? Something about problems coming in a battalion."

"'When sorrows come, they come not single spies. But in battalions,'" said Windflower. "You'll figure it out. You're a good man, Eddie, and a good cop."

"Thanks, Sarge," said Tizzard.

"Now, I've got to go through this paperwork before Quigley calls," said Windflower.

He had in fact just finished sifting through the last of the documents in the file folder when his cell phone rang.

"Good morning, Winston. How are you?" asked Quigley.

"I'm well, Ron," said Windflower. "But our young friend, Tizzard, thinks that 'hell is empty and all the devils are here.'"

"You could help him, you know," said Quigley.

"I'm on an assignment, remember," said Windflower. "With you."

"That's why I called," said Quigley, switching gears. "You have a look at the files? Anything stands out?"

"Other than the largest meth and ecstasy organization in Europe is looking to expand to North America, not much," said Windflower. "But why are they coming over? I'm assuming they want to target the American market; they can't be too interested in Canada."

"Exactly," said Quigley. "They are trying to get into the US because the market is so big. The Americans produce a lot, especially meth, but it's cheaper to produce ecstasy in bulk. And the Germans have perfected that. They have labs in Germany, Holland and France and are now expanding into Eastern Europe, where costs are even lower. By the way, the name of our job is called Project Adam."

"Adam. That name rings a bell," said Windflower.

"It's a nickname for ecstasy in Germany," said Quigley. "Where did you hear the name?"

"I think the Germans at the B&B were talking about Adam," said Windflower. "Beulah thought it was somebody they were meeting in Saint-Pierre."

"I guess she was right," said Quigley.

"So, what exactly do you want me to do?" asked Windflower.

"We think that they are going to try to bring back a shipment through Newfoundland and then down into the United States by boat," said Quigley. "Our guy on the inside will let us know what is happening, and you watch and report back to me. He will call you to make a connection as well."

"Okay," said Windflower. "So, I wait to hear from him?"

"That's it for now," said Quigley. "But anything could go wrong at any time with these guys, so be ready. You can get a service weapon from Tizzard. Tell him Bill Ford will authorize it. But, and this is very important, Winston, do not engage. Got it?"

"I got it, boss," said Windflower. "I think I'll pass on the weapon for now. I actually like not having one around. And I'll wait to hear more from you or our friend on Saint-Pierre. 'All the world's a stage,' and I am but a player."

"You never know my friend," said Quigley. "'Some are born great, some achieve greatness and some have greatness thrust upon them.'"

Windflower tried to think up one more quote to match Quigley, but he was gone. He packed up his files, said goodbye to Tizzard and managed to escape without a hug from Betsy, who was tied up on the phone. Time to go home to see Sheila and maybe even get a bite of lunch. This was a good life, he thought. Then he felt the first of many large, wet snowflakes hit his face. Around here, that was almost never a good sign.

Chapter Twenty

When he got home and checked the weather on his phone, that thought proved to be correct.

"Another storm is on the way," he said to Sheila as Amelia Louise ran to him and jumped in his arms and Lady circled his feet.

"Well, we're not going anywhere," said Sheila. "Although those two are ready to go outside. Take them for a walk, and I'll organize lunch."

Windflower bundled up Amelia Louise and put her in the wagon. With Lady on the leash beside them, they had a great stroll around town. They walked down by the wharf and then back up by the Mug-Up, which was full of lunchtime customers. Windflower noticed Jerimiah Parsons' pick-up out in front of the B&B but didn't see any sign of Levi or his dad. Maybe they were at lunch, too.

All the thought of people eating lunch gave Windflower an appetite too, and he raced home with Lady happily running beside the wagon and Amelia Louise waving hello to everyone they passed.

When he opened the door, he felt almost weak at the aroma coming out of the kitchen.

"That smells gorgeous," said Windflower. "Fish chowder? My favourite."

"Everything's your favourite," said Sheila, ladling up a large bowl for him.

"Everyting," said Amelia Louise, happy that her dad was in trouble and not her. Sheila gave her a smaller bowl that she had already cooled a little.

Windflower took a piece of baguette from the basket that Sheila had put on the table and dipped it into his soup. He tasted it and oohed and aahed. "Missus Hillier, that is the best fish chowder ever. How do you make it so good?"

"I'm glad you like it," said Sheila. "It's my mother's recipe."

"I like that it's thinner than most chowders you get in a restaurant. But still creamy," said Windflower, scooping up a brimming spoonful of broth and fish and vegetables.

"Mom always said to keep the flour to a minimum," said Sheila. "She said she wanted to taste the fish, not eat a bowl of flour."

"Did you use salt fish?" asked Windflower. "It is delicious."

"Yes," said Sheila. "I soaked it overnight like my mom would do. The other secret is to boil your potatoes and carrots with celery to give them more flavour. But that's the last secret I can give you, or I'll have to kill you."

"I'll be grateful for life if you'll just give me another small bowl," said Windflower. Sheila laughed and refilled his bowl.

"So, how did it feel to be back in the detachment?" she asked.

"It felt really good," said Windflower. "Really familiar. And everyone was so nice. Especially Betsy."

"She loves you," said Sheila. "Although I can't see why."

"Very funny," said Windflower. "I'll clean up if you want a little break."

"Great," said Sheila. "Our little one will likely have a nap, and then I can get some of my work done." She took Amelia Louise out to read her a story while Windflower cleaned up. He was just turning on the dishwasher when his cell phone rang. "Unknown number" came up on the screen. That usually meant somebody from the police world. He walked onto the back porch and said hello.

"Windflower, it's Roger Grimsby. Although you might remember me as Hans. Bushy red beard. From the B&B," said the person on the other end of the line. "Although I was speaking German at the time. I thought you might be RCMP."

"Used to be," said Windflower. "Are you still on Saint-Pierre?"

"I'm calling to give you a heads-up. HQ knows this, but there's a shipment moving out tomorrow," said Grimsby. "Müller is flying back to Europe, and I'm supposed to go with him."

"I thought you were coming back with the shipment," said Windflower.

"Change of plans," said Grimsby. "You will have to take over as point person until they can get their crew down from HQ. Listen, I gotta go."

With that, Grimsby was gone, and Windflower was left holding the phone. Maybe holding the bag might be more appropriate, he thought.

"Everything okay?" asked Sheila as she noticed the puzzled look on his face when he came into the living room.

"I think so," said Windflower. "You want me to take her up?"

Sheila handed a wiggling Amelia Louise to him. "She may or may not go. Maybe try another story."

"Mila wants a story," announced Amelia Louise.

"Okay, princess," said Windflower.

"Mila a pwincess," said Amelia Louise as Windflower carried her upstairs.

He got her to pick out a book. She came back with three and they settled on two.

The first was called *Catch That Chicken*. It was about a young girl in an African village who is an expert at catching chickens. But one day she loses that special ability and can't chase the chickens anymore. Amelia Louise loved this story and how the young girl, Lami, finally figures out how to fix her problem. The second book was a new one, one that Windflower hadn't seen before.

"Did you and Mommy go to the library?" he asked.

"Lieberry," said Amelia Louise, nodding.

The second book was *Corduroy*, about a little stuffed bear who lives in a store. He hopes that someone will buy him and take him home. But he has a missing button, and people don't seem to want a stuffed animal that's missing a button. Corduroy starts looking around the store at night for a button, but in the end, he's adopted and loved for just the way he is. Windflower loved that story, and so did Amelia Louise, who started drooping on the last page of the book.

He tucked her in and went back his own bedroom to call Ron Quigley. If they wanted him to do something, he'd need more direction than the brief conversation with the Grimsby guy. No answer, so he left a message and went downstairs to see Sheila.

Eddie Tizzard was talking to Bill Ford when an excited Smithson ran into his office.

"It's not drugs," he said. "Well, I don't think he was selling drugs."

"Can I call you right back?" Tizzard asked Bill Ford and hung up.

"What are you talking about?" asked Tizzard.

"Sid Skinner wasn't selling drugs," said Smithson. "I don't know for sure, but I think he may have been laundering money. There's lots of interactions between him and Swiss bank accounts and with unknown entities in Albania, the Cayman Islands and Pakistan. They are amongst some of highest-ranked countries when it comes to money-laundering."

When Tizzard looked at him quizzically, he added, "I looked it up online."

"I don't understand," said Tizzard.

"It looks like Skinner might have been taking money and turning it into bitcoin," said Smithson.

"Who was he doing that for?" asked Tizzard.

"That's not clear," said Smithson. "It could be anybody from rich people trying to avoid paying taxes or businesses trying to hide money or gangs involved in illegal activity."

"But can't they trace who is buying or selling the bitcoin?" asked Tizzard.

"That's a really good question," said Smithson. "They can trace some of the bitcoin activity, but I guess what they do is set up one account and then start splitting it off into fake accounts on the dark web in encrypted form."

"How do you know all of this?" asked Tizzard. "Never mind, you looked it up. Great work. Now, look up the contact for Commercial Crime in Ottawa. You'll need to talk to them to see what they think. Do you have everything you need from Skinner's computer now?"

"Yes. I've made a copy of everything and stored it on an external drive," said Smithson.

"Okay," said Tizzard. "I'm going to drop it off back at his house. Let me know what the HQ people have to say."

Smithson went off to find the Commercial Crime info while Tizzard brought the box with the computer out to his car. He drove to Sid Skinner's house. His old house, thought Tizzard. He wanted to drop off the computer personally because he needed to see if Skinner's wife could tell him anything about her late husband's online dealings. Did he have any extra money all of a sudden? And he still had the promise to keep to Sid or the seal, whatever that was.

Mildred Skinner was sweeping the first of the snow off her front porch when Tizzard pulled up in front of her neat little bungalow. He could see her instinctively flinch when she saw the RCMP Jeep. He smiled and walked up the driveway.

"Good morning, ma'am, it looks like we're going to get some more snow," said Tizzard.

"Yes. It looks that way," said the woman.

"I came to bring back the computer," said Tizzard. "Do you have a few minutes?"

"It seems like all I have these days is time," said Mildred Skinner. "Come in. I'll put the kettle on."

Tizzard laid the box with the computer in it in the hallway, and while she made tea, he had a quick look around the living room. Not much unusual there. A picture of Sid and Mildred celebrating some anniversary and a scattering of other pictures of grandchildren in various sporting and school activities. An assortment of knickknacks and one more picture of a sunburnt Sid Skinner and his wife on what looked like an ocean-going fishing boat, probably in the Caribbean.

"That was Cuba. Last year," said the woman when she saw Tizzard looking at the picture. She laid a tray on the table with a teapot, two cups, milk, and a plate of what looked like home-made cookies.

"That must have been nice," said Tizzard.

"Oh my God, it was so hot," said Mildred. "I thought I was going to die. But Sid always wanted to go deep-sea fishing, and it was nice to be away and not have to cook for a few days." She poured them both a cup of tea and sat on the couch. Tizzard sat in a chair across from her and took an oatmeal raisin cookie when she offered.

"These are so good," he said after taking a bite of the cookie.

"They were Sid's favourites," said the woman, seeming to choke up a little. She recovered and looked directly at Tizzard. "Was there something you wanted to ask me about?"

"Yes, ma'am," said Tizzard. "I know I've expressed my sympathies before, but being here I can feel how much he's missed. I can also feel how much he must have loved you." That actually felt really uncomfortable for Tizzard to say, and so was the next few seconds as Mildred Skinner processed what he'd said.

"We were very happy," said the woman. "I think that makes his passing even harder. But thank you for saying that." She dabbed at her eyes with a Kleenex.

"I didn't mean to upset you," said Tizzard.

"There's not much that can upset me any more than what's already happened," said Mildred.

Tizzard nodded. "I wanted to ask you about your husband's finances," he started. "If you don't mind talking about that. It might help to know if you or he were having any trouble in that regard."

"No, b'y," said the woman. "We didn't have much, but we didn't have any worries. We owns the house, and other than spoiling the grandchildren we didn't have a lot to spend money on."

"The trip to Cuba?" asked Tizzard.

"I paid that with my old-age pension," said Mildred. "I'm a little older than Sid. When I turned sixty-five, I just put it in the bank, and then when I had enough, I told Sid to book the tickets."

"Did he ever talk to you about money?" asked Tizzard.

"He just said not to worry about it," said Mildred. "He paid the bills, and if I needed something, like the new dishwasher, he told me to go ahead and buy it."

"What did he do for money?" asked Tizzard, taking another cookie when she offered it.

"He had his pension from the fish plant, which wasn't much, but then he had the Canada Pension and the old age one, too. Why are you asking about money anyway?"

Tizzard tried to ignore that question for now. "I hear your husband spent a lot of time on the computer. Do you know what he did?"

"He was always playing card games when I went down there," said Mildred. "I think he just liked looking at the news and pictures and stuff. You didn't answer my other question, Corporal."

Now Tizzard was kind of trapped, with little wriggle room. He thought about what his dad had said one time about telling the truth. It was a Mark Twain quote. 'If you tell the truth you don't have to remember anything.' He decided to tell the truth.

"When we took a look at your husband's computer, we found some signs that he might be involved in something that involved a lot of money," said Tizzard.

"Are you saying that Sid did something wrong?" asked the woman. "He never did a bad thing in his life. I been with him almost forty years."

"We're not sure he did either," said Tizzard. "But if we are right, then somebody hurt your husband and maybe others. That's what we're trying to find out."

He looked at the woman, but her eyes said she was gone back into her grief. She started to cry softly, and Tizzard knew there was little he could say to comfort her. He thanked her for her time and left as quickly and quietly as he could.

Chapter Twenty-one

Outside, he took a couple of deep breaths, stood next to his Jeep and watched the now-heavy snow swirl around him. Sometimes he hated this job, he thought. He got in his Jeep and drove back to the detachment. When he arrived, Carrie was comforting a very distraught Betsy Molloy.

"What's going on?" he asked.

Betsy was sobbing now. Through her crying she tried to speak but only got more upset. "There's a rumour that they're going to close the RCMP in Grand Bank," said Carrie.

"They can't do that, can they?" asked the weeping Betsy.

Another moment of harsh truth for Tizzard. "I don't know," he said. "But let me see what I can find out." He went to his office and phoned the town council office.

"People are upset, and I don't blame them," said Mayor Jacqueline Wilson. "We've been talking to them about improving services. But they don't seem interested. Now they are planning to shut the Grand Bank detachment."

"Who have you been talking to?" asked Tizzard. "We haven't heard anything."

"Well, you better get on top of it," said the mayor. "These discussions were initiated out of Halifax and have been going on for a while. The latest developments around here just brought them out into the open."

"They started the discussions. Who?" asked Tizzard.

"Superintendent Majesky in Halifax," said Mayor Wilson. "They said they were thinking about closing the Grand Bank Detachment because of costs and only having a one-person station. Most of the services would be provided out of Marystown. We just found out this morning that they intend to go ahead. We'll fight it, but by the sounds of it they've made up their minds."

Tizzard was stunned. He hung up and sat in his chair for a moment, trying to process what he'd just heard. He got up and closed the door to his office. He didn't want Betsy or even Carrie to get to him before he had more information. He called Bill Ford in Marystown.

"I just heard the report on the radio," said Ford.

"Did you know anything about this?" asked Tizzard. "About closing our detachment?"

"Majesky called me a couple of weeks ago to say that because of budget reductions they were looking at a range of options for this region. He asked me not to say anything until they reached a decision," said Ford.

"You knew about this and didn't tell us, tell me?" asked Tizzard.

"I told Majesky that it was a stupid idea to try to serve the whole area out of Marystown," said Ford. "I never thought they would actually go through with it."

"Can I have Majesky's number?" asked Tizzard.

"Are you sure you want to do that?" asked Ford.

"I'm sure," said Tizzard.

"Here's the number," said Ford. "But wait a few minutes before you call. Okay?"

"Okay," said Tizzard and hung up. He sat in his chair, stewing for about a minute. Then he realized he was only getting more upset by waiting. He called Superintendent Wally Majesky in Halifax.

As Tizzard was making his call, Sheila got a call, too. Windflower heard her talking as he was getting Amelia, who'd woken from her nap. She looked a little shaken when he walked into the living room.

"They're closing the RCMP detachment," she said.

"Where?" asked Windflower. "In Grand Bank? They can't do that."

"They can, and apparently they are," said Sheila. "That was Jacqui Wilson on the phone. She wants me to help organize a campaign to get them to change their minds."

"But how will it work with no police presence here?" asked Windflower.

"They are going to have one person assigned here and provide all other services out of Marystown," said Sheila. "The contract was up at the end of the year, and there is a clause that allows either side to back away. We never thought that the RCMP would be the ones to walk away."

"Who's making this decision?" asked Windflower. "It can't be local."

"Superintendent Majesky in Halifax," said Sheila. "You know him. Can you talk to him?"

"I know Majesky, but I'm not sure he's going to listen to me," said Windflower. "I'm not even on the Force anymore."

"Well, find out what you can," said Sheila. "We have to figure out a way to get them to change their minds."

"I wonder how they're taking the news over at the office," said Windflower.

"It can't be good," said Sheila. "Betsy would be the most upset. This really is her life. And Carrie and Eddie will have to figure something out quickly."

"Yeah, they will be both be transferred, and not likely to the same place," said Windflower. "I'll pop over to see Eddie in the morning."

"And I'll phone Carrie," said Sheila. "Let's have them over for supper as soon we can."

They were right about the office. Everybody was really upset when Tizzard came out to report on his phone calls.

"Bill Ford said the decision was being made in Halifax. He'd heard rumblings but never thought this would happen," said Tizzard. "So, I phoned Superintendent Majesky in Halifax. He said they are in discussions with the town and have given the necessary notices to pull out of Grand Bank."

Betsy sighed loudly at those last couple of words. "He did say that there would be one officer left here and that we could decide among ourselves who that would be. He also said that Betsy's job was safe for as long as she stayed. Then they would eliminate the position."

"That's good news," said Carrie, who still had her arm around Betsy's shoulder.

102

"Not if all of you are going to be gone," said Betsy, and she started crying again. "It won't be the same."

Tizzard felt exactly the same way, and together they tried to console Betsy. At least she had stopped crying when they left her in the front and went back to Tizzard's office.

"That certainly is a shock," said Carrie as she closed the door behind her. "What are we going to do? What are our options?"

"Phew," said Tizzard, exhaling loudly. "I don't know. We should talk to Smithson and see what he thinks. But if both of us transfer out, we'll be split up for sure. At least for a year or two. Or I could just quit."

"Well, don't go there yet. It's too easy to just give up. Especially with everything else going on here," said Carrie.

"I guess one of us could try to stay and the other go on leave," said Tizzard. "I can still take paternity leave, and that would give us a few more months to come up with a plan."

"That's not a bad idea," said Carrie. "Would buy us some time."

"But let's not get too far ahead of ourselves on this," said Tizzard. "'All good things arrive unto them that wait—and don't die in the meantime.'"

"Is that your dad again?" asked Carrie.

"He probably stole it from Mark Twain. That's his favourite these days," said Tizzard.

There was a knock on the door.

"Come in," said Tizzard.

"What's going on?" asked Smithson. "Why is Betsy so upset?"

"Come in and sit down," said Tizzard. "We'll fill you in."

After hearing the news, Smithson looked surprisingly relaxed.

"You're not upset?" asked Carrie.

"Not really," said Smithson. "I was hoping to get back to the mainland to be closer to my family. This might actually work out for me. What about you guys? What are you going to do?"

"We don't know yet," said Tizzard. "We'll play it by ear for now. But one thing is sure. If we want to have the public on our side, we better get something moving on our case."

"I had an idea," said Smithson. "Maybe while we're waiting for HQ to get more info on Skinner's computer, we could check if any of the others were involved in any online activity as well."

Tizzard filled Carrie in on Smithson's discovery and his visit to Skinner's wife.

"I think that's a great idea to check the other computers," said Carrie. "I was visiting with the guys down at the wharf, and they said that Sid Skinner told them he had a retirement plan. Something like a Registered Retirement Savings Plan scheme that they could all invest in. They thought it was more of a scam than a scheme. But I wonder if Broderick and Slaney might have taken him up?"

"That's a possibility worth checking out," said Tizzard. Smithson stood to leave. "Before you go, I want to talk to all of you," he added. "Go get Betsy."

When Smithson came back with Betsy, Tizzard gave her his chair and stood in front of all of them. "I know things haven't been easy around here for the last while. We've taken a fair bit of unfriendly fire. Most of it deserved. Now, we have this new development. No one knows how this will play out, but I want us to stay united, be a team as we move forward."

He had all their complete attention now.

"We'll have lots of eyes on us, but let's be strong and professional and do our jobs. Bigger minds than ours will make the ultimate decisions; we don't control that. Let's do a great job with the things that we do control and let the chips fall where they may. Are you with me?"

Smithson nodded, Carrie had a couple of tears leak out, and Betsy jumped to her feet to give Tizzard one of her famous hugs. "Yes, b'y, let's do it," she said.

After Smithson and Betsy had left, Carrie came and gave Eddie her own special hug. "That was amazing," she said. "I know you doubt yourself sometimes, but I think you got this leadership thing. I love you."

"I love you, too," said Tizzard. "All this speechifying has made me hungry. Have we got any snacks left?"

Chapter Twenty-two

Windflower and Amelia Louise waited in the window for Stella's school bus. The snow was still coming down, but it looked to Windflower like it might be letting up a little. That would be good. He checked his phone and confirmed the good news. The snow was going to ease up for now. But as always, there was a dark weather cloud on the horizon around this part of the world. "Major Storm Coming this Weekend" was the headline on the weather app. He tried to think of a Shakespeare quote about worry, but all he could come up with was "be just and fear not."

That was good enough for now. He closed his phone and tried to block the weather news out of his mind. That was easy enough to do as Amelia Louise jumped off the couch and ran to the door to greet her sister. Windflower and Lady were close behind. After snacks, Windflower took the girls and Lady out to the backyard to help build a snowman. He was corrected by Stella, who pronounced their sad-looking creature a snow person. Sheila came to the door to admire their handiwork and passed out carrots, one each for the girls to eat and one to put on as a nose for their snow creation. Windflower added a couple of stones for eyes, and while it wasn't the best-looking snow person ever, it was theirs and the girls were exceedingly proud.

All of them were also exceedingly happy to come back inside and get hot chocolate with marshmallows from Sheila as a reward for their hard work. Windflower was sipping his drink and laughing at the girls talking about how great their snow person was when his cell phone rang. He went in the kitchen to take it.

"The game is afoot," said Quigley.

"I always thought that was Sherlock Holmes," said Windflower.

"Nope, King Henry IV Part I, published about 1600," said Quigley. "Although Sherlock Holmes did say those words at the beginning of *The Adventure of the Abbey Grange*. Perhaps in other books, too."

"Thanks for the modern literature lesson and for calling me back. So, Grimsby said there's a shipment coming tomorrow and that somehow, I'm the point person now. What's going on?"

"We received that information, too," said Quigley. "But there's been another twist. We've lost contact with Grimsby."

"That can't be good," said Windflower.

"No, but there's another source in Saint-Pierre," said Quigley. "An American from the DEA. He called in to his handlers, and apparently Müller and his crew are suspicious that something is up. They've postponed the shipment for a day and are waiting there to see if anything happens."

"What do you want me to do?" asked Windflower.

"We need you to go over there and make contact with the American. Then, see if you can find out what happened to Grimsby. Can you do that?"

"I guess so," said Windflower.

"Maybe go over as a tourist. Take Sheila. Have fun," said Quigley.

"Maybe I should get you to talk to Sheila. Tell her how much fun it might be to go risk our necks with a bunch of cutthroat dope dealers from Europe," said Windflower.

"Listen. The risk is very low, and they already know you from the B&B. If you see any of them, tell them you're over to pick up some wines and liqueurs for the business," said Quigley. "I'll talk to Sheila if you want."

"That was a rhetorical question," said Windflower. "Let me think about this, and I'll call you back."

Sheila loved the idea. All of it.

"I can get Linda to look after Amelia Louise, and Moira would love to have the girls for supper. She can pick them both up here when Stella gets home tomorrow," said Sheila.

"Aren't you worried about being in danger?"

"Are you?" asked Sheila. "If you're not, I'm not. I'm so ready for an adventure. I'll have to work all night putting together the plan for Jacqui and the council about the RCMP stuff, but it'll be worth it. I'm so happy I could dance." Soon, Sheila and both the girls, along with Lady, were doing an impromptu dance in the middle of the living room. Windflower laughed and went to call Quigley while Molly stared at the spectacle for another few seconds before slinking off to the kitchen behind him.

He was sure he heard her sigh as he called Ron Quigley.

"That's great news," said Quigley. "I told you Sheila was more adventurous than you thought. 'Boldness be your friend.'"

"I don't know about that," said Windflower. "'The fool doth think he is wise, but the wise man knows himself to be a fool.'"

"Which are you?" asked Quigley.

"I guess we'll find out," said Windflower. "So, what are my directions?"

"Your man is Roberto Anderssen. He has your number and will call tonight when he can. He and the rest of Müller's crew are at the Hotel Saint-Pierre. Find out what he knows about Grimsby and if he knows what the new plan is. Call me anytime," said Quigley. "'Some have greatness thrust upon them.'"

"You keep saying that," said Windflower. "I guess, 'it is not in the stars to hold our destiny but in ourselves.'"

After hanging up with Quigley, he walked out to the back door and looked out into the darkening sky. He thought about Ron Quigley and how long they had known each other and when they had first started sharing Shakespeare quotes back and forth. It had to be back in RCMP training college in Regina a long time ago. Over the years, they had stayed in touch, and Quigley, who was originally from St. John's, ended up as his boss in Marystown a few years ago. He was now in Ottawa, obviously working with the Drug Squad in some capacity, and Windflower was back working for him.

An interesting turn of events, thought Windflower as the moon came into sight through the clouds. The moon always reminded him of his mother and Auntie Marie, both of whom talked a lot about Grandmother Moon. He had learned that Grandmother Moon was one of the three spirits placed by the Great Spirit to watch over the children of Earth. Auntie Marie said that she could help you with your dreams and visions. Grandmother Moon was a powerful force that ruled over the waters on the earth, and Windflower said a silent prayer for his late mother and aunt and asked Grandmother Moon to watch over his family as well.

Back in his community in Pink Lake, they had a name for all thirteen moons in the Cree cycle. In January, the full moon was called the Frost Exploding Moon, when the trees would crackle from the cold and the really cold winter weather would begin. Here in Newfoundland, nearer the ocean, it would be more likely called the Snow Exploding Moon because while it didn't get too cold, they got a lot of snow. Although, tonight, it thankfully looked like they would be spared the great snowfall that had been forecast.

He went back to the living room, where Sheila was already making the plans for tomorrow's trip.

"What time does the ferry leave in the morning?" he asked as Stella and Amelia Louise tackled him and pulled him to the ground.

"Good news," said Sheila. "They've got a new boat, and they want to try it out before tourist season. We can leave at ten and come back at 5:00 p.m., otherwise we'd have to stay overnight."

"Well, that would be fun," said Windflower, extricating himself from a dual wrestle hold by his daughters. "But that would mean we'd have to arrange overnight babysitting."

"Not on a school night," said Sheila. "But it's too bad because the shops are closed between noon and two, so that's prime shopping time I'll be missing. We'll just have to have a long lunch then. This is so great. An adventure."

"Can we go on this venture?" asked Stella.

"No, sweetie," said Windflower. "You have to go to school."

"Mila don't have to go to skool," said Amelia Louise.

"I'll bring you back presents," said Sheila. "And both of you will have an adventure, too. You're going to Grandma Moira's for supper tomorrow night."

"I love pwesents," said Amelia Louise.

"I love ventures," said Stella.

"It's settled then," said Windflower, finally getting to his feet. "Everybody is happy. Hot dogs for supper?"

Everybody was happy with that announcement, too, and Windflower went to the kitchen to get supper organized.

Eddie Tizzard was not happy. Nor was Rob Skinner, who was standing in front of him with his fingers getting very close to Tizzard's chest and his voice rising even louder the more he got agitated. And he was very agitated at the moment.

"Stay away from his wife," he screamed at Tizzard, who was doing his best to remain calm and right on the edge of losing that battle.

"We're just trying to find out who might have wanted to harm your brother," he said again. "Who may have killed him. Don't you want to know?"

"Yes, I want to know," yelled Rob Skinner. "But I don't have any faith that you and your Keystone Kops are going to find that out. All you're doing is making a bad situation worse. Stay away from Mildred, you hear me? She's over there bawling her eyes out again."

"Okay," said Tizzard. "Maybe you can help me then."

That seemed to slow the other man down a little. "We think that your brother was doing some investing online. Did he ever approach you on that?"

"Sid always had some great idea about making money," said Rob Skinner. "Nothing ever came out of any of it. He asked me a long time ago about giving him some money to invest. I didn't have any, but I told him that I wouldn't even if I did. He stopped asking me."

"We found a lot of money in a secret account in his computer," said Tizzard. "Not paper money, but some kind of cryptocurrency."

"What's that?" asked Skinner.

"I'm no expert, but I think it's a kind of money that you can transfer around on the Internet, and eventually you can cash it in," said Tizzard. "Your brother had a lot."

This got Rob Skinner's attention. "You know, he did talk about a new investment scheme a little while ago. Said I should get in on it. Like an RRSP account, he said." Skinner was quiet for a moment. Then he spoke again. "If Sid had all that crypto money on his computer, can Mildred get that now?"

"I don't know," said Tizzard. "If he got it by legal means, I guess so. But people who are making money legally tend not to hide it away on their computer."

Skinner nodded. He had little more to say and had grown considerably quieter with the mention and possibility of money. Tizzard didn't care about his motivation. He was just happy to see the back of him as he left the detachment. Money was indeed the root of all evil, he thought as he finally had the office to himself. But then again, maybe Mark Twain was right. The root of all evil might in fact be the lack of money.

Chapter Twenty-three

Tizzard was on the late shift tonight, and that was okay with him. He needed some peace and quiet to work through everything that was happening. Carrie was looking after Hughie, and he would drop over to see him before bedtime and get some supper. But for now, he sat in his chair and looked out the window. He could see the same moon that Windflower had been watching a few minutes ago. He didn't know much about Grandmother Moon. He was more interested in reading Hughie *Goodnight Moon* right now. His son didn't appreciate it yet, but Tizzard did. At least, the act of reading.

But the full moon was always special to Tizzard, too. He remembered his dad calling the moon this time of year a Wolf Moon. There were no longer any wolves in Newfoundland, but at one time in the past there certainly were. They were believed to have died out completely about a hundred years ago when the caribou migrated north to Labrador. His father said that on very cold January nights, if you were very quiet you could hear them howling in the distance. Tizzard didn't hear any howls this evening, but he did hear Smithson come in with his last report of the day.

"I've got good news and bad news," said Smithson. "Which would you like first?"

"I have two fists," said Tizzard. "Which one would you like up the side of your head? It's been a long day, Smithson."

"The good news is that Leo Broderick's computer has some of the same links that were on Sid Skinners," said Smithson. "The bad news is that there's no connection to Slaney. His wife says they don't even have a computer."

"That's too bad," said Tizzard. "But he could still be involved, right?"

"Absolutely," said Smithson. "But without computer evidence it's harder to prove or even show."

"So, Slaney could have let Skinner or someone else handle the details?" said Tizzard.

"Yeah," said Smithson. "Once Commercial Crime does their complete scan, they will be able to tell us."

"How does that work?" asked Tizzard.

"Well, I sent them the data I loaded onto the cloud, and I will ship the copy of the hard drive to the airport on the taxi tomorrow morning. They'll have it by express tomorrow night," said Smithson. "If anyone else is mentioned, they will find it."

"Perfect," said Tizzard. "Thanks for your work on this."

"Great. See you tomorrow," said Smithson.

Tizzard ran through his paperwork, and as he was leaving to go see Carrie and Hughie, he saw a note in his in-basket from Betsy. Attached was a contract for services made out to Windflower. Betsy noted that they needed Windflower to sign it and asked if Tizzard could look after that for her. No problem, thought Tizzard. Windflower and Sheila's house was right on his way home.

The Windflower crew had just finished supper, and Winston was cleaning up when he heard a knock on the door. Still with his apron on, he and Lady went to investigate.

"Eddie, how are you?" said Windflower. "Come on in."

When his kids heard who it was, they both came running. Amelia Louise started the chant, and Stella was happy to join in. "Unca, Unca, Unca."

"I'm not interrupting anything, am I?" asked Tizzard as he picked up both squealing girls and pointed to Windflower's apron.

Windflower laughed. "Domestic bliss," he replied.

Tizzard, with Amelia Louise and Stella under his arms, came into the living room and said hello to Sheila. Sheila released the girls and gave him a big hug. "I just talked to Carrie. You're invited for supper Friday night."

"That sounds great," said Tizzard. "I guess you heard all the big news."

"How are you feeling about it?" asked Sheila. "Carrie was remarkably calm."

"Carrie is solid," said Tizzard. "I'm okay, too. We just have to see how it all works out. If need be, I still have paternity leave I can take, and Smithson is happy to transfer out. But I worry about the community."

"I know," said Sheila. "Council has already started working on it."

"Sheila is helping them put together a plan," said Windflower, who had ditched his apron but came back with another cup for Tizzard and the cookie tray. He poured Tizzard a cup.

Tizzard took the tea and a lemon square. "That's good," he said. "You know who to talk to. I talked to Majesky today. He seems pretty determined to move forward on this. Or maybe his hands are tied on the money side."

"Well, we're going to look at all options, including trying to get them to change their mind," said Sheila.

"I brought you this paper to sign," said Tizzard. "From Betsy. To make you an official contractor."

Windflower took a quick look at the document and got a pen to sign it. He handed it back to Tizzard, who gave Sheila another hug and lifted both girls in turn high into the air. He kissed them all over until both ran away screaming.

Windflower walked over to the door with Tizzard, went outside and closed the door behind them.

"Are you okay?" asked Windflower.

"Yeah, I'm surprisingly good," said Tizzard. "Even though there's an awful lot of going on, I feel okay on the inside, if that makes any sense."

"I understand," said Windflower. "I do believe that happiness is an inside job. But you have a lot of things to be happy about."

"I know," said Tizzard. "I even gave the troops a pep talk today. Just like you. Well, not exactly like you."

"If you need me, I'm here," said Windflower as Tizzard walked away and got into his car.

Windflower went back inside. Sheila had gone upstairs with the girls to give them their baths, and he took Lady for one last spin around the neighbourhood. The moon was full and shining down on them as the pair strolled along the quiet streets of Grand Bank. Lady stopped to attend to her needs, and Windflower gazed up at the face of the moon.

He said another prayer to Grandmother Moon. This one for Eddie and Carrie. Not that they be given any special attention. Just that they receive the love they deserved as good people trying to do good things in a sometimes uncaring world. That had to be worth something, he thought. Lady finished her task, and Windflower followed her lead as she took him down by the water and then back home safely again.

"Thank you, Lady," said Windflower when he finished drying her off. He gave her a Milk Bone snack, which she happily and noisily crunched right in front of Molly. The cat was super not impressed but relaxed her steely-eyed gaze when Windflower filled her bowl and gave her a treat as well. Lady tried to approach to take a closer look, but a sharp hiss sent her back to her corner.

Sheila was busy working at her computer, and Windflower came and gave her a shoulder rub.

"That is so good," she said. "I'm almost finished the first draft of the campaign. One more review and I'll send it off."

"Excellent," said Windflower.

"I've got the draft letters to the politicians and the petition to go up on social media. Then we'll plan an intercommunity meeting," said Sheila. "If you start my bath, I'll be up soon."

Windflower gave her one more shoulder squeeze and walked upstairs. He turned on the water and put in a dollop of Sheila's favourite bubble bath. Then he went to check in on the girls. Both were sleeping, perfectly quiet, like angels, he thought. Well, they were gifts from Heaven. He rechecked the bath, and when it was half-full, he turned it off and went to his bedroom to read his book. He finished one chapter and was about to start another one when he started to feel drowsy. He didn't hear anything else until he woke in a dream.

Chapter Twenty-four

Tizzard had come in just as Carrie was laying Hughie in his crib. He was almost asleep but seemed to smile at Eddie as he peered over the side of the crib. Then he closed his eyes and was gone.

"He waited up for me, and he smiled, too," said Eddie.

"That might have been gas," said Carrie. Then, seeing her partner's sad face, she came to him and hugged him. "I was only kidding," she said. "Your dad brought over some moose stew. Do you want me to heat you up a bowl?"

"Yes, indeed," said Tizzard, his mood brightening considerably.

Carrie warmed up the stew, which came with a thick piece of pastry over the top. Tizzard pronounced it delicious and made quick work of his portion. He had a cup of tea and played a game of crib with Carrie before he headed back to work. It was quiet, eerily quiet, as he drove around Grand Bank to do his visual inspection. He saw only one person walking their dog and not another soul.

There were lights on at the pub but only two cars in the parking lot. That was good, too, thought Tizzard. Little possibility of trouble there tonight. Not that there was ever much trouble in this little town. Maybe they didn't need a big police presence here anyway was his next thought. But then again, maybe the reason it was so quiet was at least a little bit about having their own RCMP detachment. That was enough questions for Tizzard as he made the turn back into the RCMP parking lot and went inside.

He spent a couple of hours cleaning up files and initialling documents that Betsy had piled up in his in-basket and then made himself a fresh pot of coffee. When it was ready, he had a cup with one of the homemade apple flips Carrie had gotten from Beulah. It was smooth and tasty and decadent. He almost fell asleep after that snack, but then the caffeine kicked in. You gotta love coffee, he thought as he put his coat back on to go out and do his highway tour.

Part of the job of the overnight shift was to do two tours of the highway between Grand Bank and Creston, just outside Marystown. That was their territory. One he would do now and one closer to the end of his shift in the morning. The highway was quieter than town tonight. Not a single car all the way out and only one coming out of the Garnish exit. He was coming back into the rolling hills near Grand Bank when he saw it on the side of the road. Actually, he saw the red eyes in the darkness first. He slowed as he got closer, and the animal froze in the headlights.

First, he thought it was a large dog. But then he realized it was a coyote. When he stopped the car, the animal started to move away, and Tizzard was ready to watch it scamper into the woods. But the coyote could only hobble and appeared to drag one leg behind it. Even so, it managed to climb over the snow, and all Tizzard saw was the swish of its tail as it disappeared into the darkness.

The rest of the night shift was even quieter than the first, and after Tizzard finished as much of the paperwork he could manage, he went back to the storage area to take a look around. There on the wall was the inventory sheet that somebody, likely Smithson, had started but never completed. That also sounded like something Eddie would do before he had all this responsibility. He chuckled to himself, picked up a clipboard and spent a couple of hours finishing it off. He had another chuckle when he brought it out and laid it on Smithson's desk.

Feeling pretty satisfied with himself, he put his feet up on his own desk and laid back. That was a mistake. Within a minute he was dozing off. A couple of more minutes and he was soundly asleep. Then he woke. In a dream.

As Tizzard was drifting off, Windflower was just waking up. He tried to recall as much of his dream as he could. That was the best time to remember it, as soon as you woke up. Sheila was sleeping quietly next to him, so he got up and walked downstairs. His plan was to write his dream down. He grabbed a pen and some paper as a very groggy Lady came to check him out. He patted the Collie on the head and started writing as fast as he could.

Tonight's dream was actually somewhat familiar. All his animal allies had gathered together to meet him. Usually that meant they had something to tell him. There was a moose, a beaver and a deer. And in the middle of all of them, chattering away, sat a rabbit. The same one from his previous dreams.

"It's the greedy one," said the rabbit when it saw Windflower.

"I'm not greedy," said Windflower, feeling a little defensive. The other animals stayed silent. That wasn't a good sign.

"Come and have some stew," said the moose, breaking the silence.

Windflower went to the pot in the middle of their circle, excusing himself as he brushed against the rabbit. "Rude, too," said the rabbit.

Windflower would have liked nothing better than to sit on that troublesome rabbit to quiet him, but he tried to get that thought out of his head. Too late. "And violent," said the rabbit, jumping back in mock horror.

"I'm sorry, Rabbit," said Windflower. "That was clumsy of me. And thank you for the stew," he said to the moose.

"At least he's polite," said the beaver. Windflower smiled at the beaver. "If not very bright," added the beaver.

Windflower sat and ate his stew and looked around him. As he did, he realized, again, that his allies were actually all elements of him. And that overall, he had a lot of strengths to go along with his weaknesses that they had clearly pointed out to him.

"Thank you," he said as he finished his stew and laid his bowl on the ground. "For the stew and your wisdom and guidance. How can I be less greedy?" he asked the rabbit.

"Finally," said the rabbit. "I told you before. You have to give it away to keep it."

The moose spoke up next. "You are a kind man, Winston. But your community needs you now, and you are holding back. Give freely of what you have received, and you will reap the rewards."

Right after those words were spoken, Windflower felt himself being lifted up and then gently placed back into bed with Sheila. She didn't even stir. And neither did he until the alarm clock went off in the morning.

Eddie Tizzard woke in his dream to a large coyote sitting on the floor in front of his desk.

"What are you doing here?" asked Tizzard.

"What are you doing sleeping on the job?" asked the coyote.

Tizzard started to stammer a reply when the coyote interrupted him. "It was a joke," said the animal. Tizzard didn't find it that funny.

"Don't take yourself too seriously," said the coyote, reaching a leg up to scratch the back of his head.

"That's pretty cool," said Tizzard. "I guess I'm supposed to ask you why you're here."

"Well, we have one thing in common," said the coyote. "We'll both eat anything."

"That's not true," said Tizzard. "I don't eat vegetables unless I have to."

"Grow up," said the coyote. "I'm here because I am the wisest, smartest animal of all."

"Really?" asked Tizzard.

"Man, you are so gullible," said the coyote. "No. Don't you know I'm the original trickster? I'm here to remind you to look twice, to check things closer. Not to accept things at face value. To look underneath the rock. You never know what you'll find. But first you have to wake up." With that, the coyote gave one small yelp and Tizzard woke up in his chair so quickly that he almost toppled over.

Tizzard went to the washroom and splashed water on his face to really wake himself up. Then, checking the time, he realized it was time to do his last rounds. He put a pot of coffee on to brew and be ready for when he came back and left for his trip around town and then out to the highway. Even less stirred in town since his last tour, and the highway was likewise as empty as the barrens outside of Grand Bank.

As the sun came over the hills, he kept a sharp eye out for the coyote he'd seen the first time around, but no luck. He came back into the detachment as Smithson was just pulling in. Perfect timing.

"Morning, Rick," said Tizzard as they walked in together. "I put on some fresh coffee."

"Super," said Smithson. "I could use a cup this morning. I stayed up late looking up more stuff about the dark web and money laundering. It goes on and on."

"Anything really interesting?" asked Tizzard, pouring them each a cup of coffee.

"Lots," said Smithson. "Mostly how many connections there are with Canada and both the dark web and illegal money transfers. The money doesn't stay here, but a ton passes through here."

"Interesting," said Tizzard. "Keep up the good work. I'm going home. Be safe out there. Oh, and I saw a wounded coyote out on the highway."

"Yeah? I saw it, too, the other night, hobbling around," said Smithson. "I'm surprised it's still alive. Miles Cheeseman who has the chicken farm out near Molliers has been looking for it with his shotgun. Said he'd lost two chickens and wasn't gonna lose any more."

"Well, it was moving pretty good when I saw it," said Tizzard. "See ya."

Tizzard texted Carrie to let her know he was on his way home. No reply. That meant she was sleeping or having issues with Hughie. Tizzard's grumbling tummy directed him to the parking lot outside of the Mug-Up café, and the alluring aromas led him inside. He ordered breakfast at the counter and took a seat in the window to watch the comings and goings of a Grand Bank morning.

He was sipping his coffee and waiting for his bologna and eggs when he saw them come into the café: Rob Skinner and a woman he hadn't seen before. He didn't think it was his wife, though. She looked too well dressed for him. The couple didn't see him as they took a table at the back of the Mug-Up. Tizzard pretended not to notice them as he ate his scrambled eggs, fried bologna, home fries and homemade toast as quietly as he could, paid his bill and slipped out the door.

He raced back to the detachment to get to Smithson before he went out on his morning routine. He was just leaving when Tizzard arrived.

"I'm putting you back on snoop detail," said Tizzard. He told him who he saw at the café. "I want you to find the story on that relationship," he added. "And while you're at it, can you find out if Rob Skinner was friends with Leo Broderick or if they had any connection? You don't have to be discreet. We need info and we need it fast. There's something going on here, I'm sure of it."

"Okay," said Smithson. "I'm on it."

Tizzard left the detachment feeling much better after both his breakfast and his chat with Smithson. Maybe we are getting somewhere after all, he thought.

Chapter Twenty-five

The morning routine at the Windflower house bordered on frantic. Sheila had given him the task of getting Stella ready for school, and that was proving to be a challenge. Amelia Louise was being her usual self, and that was not helpful to Windflower or Stella. First, Stella and then Windflower yelled at her to go to her room. Now she was in a full-throated cry, and Sheila had to come rescue Stella while Windflower tried to bribe Amelia Louise with her favourite toy and the promise of a snack. The toy idea flopped, but the snack idea seemed to slow Amelia Louise down.

He carried her downstairs and gave her a fig bar, which she grudgingly nibbled on and waved at her sister as Stella came down for breakfast. Stella ignored her and sat at the kitchen table to eat her cereal with her mother. Windflower came in to get another cup of coffee.

"Well, we've got the combatants separated," he said to Sheila.

Sheila smiled wearily. "Linda is coming at nine. That should give us enough time to get ready and over to Fortune. I bought our ferry tickets online."

"And it looks like a nice day for our trip," said Windflower, checking his phone. "Some snow coming in overnight. I hope it doesn't start before we get back."

"We should be fine," said Sheila. "Can you get the other one dressed while I help Stella get ready for the bus?"

"Absolutely," said Windflower. He went to the living room and put Amelia Louise over his shoulder and carried her squealing upstairs. After much struggle and a few tears, both of them emerged again downstairs, dressed and ready for the day.

Sheila and Windflower sat with Amelia Louise while she played with her breakfast. Until his phone rang. He went out to the kitchen to take the call.

"Windflower," he said.

"It's Anderssen," said the caller. "Are you coming over here?"

"We're on the ferry this morning," said Windflower. "What's going on over there? Have you seen Grimsby?"

"Is that Hans, the German with the red beard?" asked Anderssen. "I'm not an imbed. But because I can speak French and German, they sent me over."

"Yeah, the red-beard guy. He's one of ours," said Windflower.

"I didn't see him last night in the bar at the hotel," said Anderssen. "But he may still be around. I'm staying at a B&B just down the road. Some of them were talking about leaving, but that got postponed for some reason. I think they're getting suspicious."

"Okay," said Windflower. "I'll call you when I'm on Saint-Pierre."

"Everything okay?" asked Sheila.

"Perfect," said Windflower.

There was a knock on the door, and Amelia Louise and Lady ran to see who it was.

"It's my friend, Linda," said Amelia Louise proudly.

Sheila got Linda sorted out with all of Amelia Louise's snacks and the plans for later when Herb or Moira would pick up both girls after Stella came home from school. They thought that Amelia Louise would kick up a fuss when they left, but she had already moved on to showing her friend Linda all of her new toys. Windflower and Sheila left as quietly as they could and drove to the ferry office in Fortune, where they parked their car for the day.

Windflower got them both a coffee from the café, and they walked down to the wharf and through the customs shed to the ferry. They went into the cabin to escape the chill in the air and sipped their coffee as the boat slipped away from Fortune. There were only a handful of other passengers. All of them were speaking French and were most likely locals who had been visiting Newfoundland for shopping or to check on their properties in the Grand Bank area.

Many people from Saint-Pierre had bought second properties or cabins up in L'Anse au Loup on the outskirts of town.

They both knew a lot about the history of the area. Sheila had heard the rum-running stories from her parents and grandparents, and Windflower knew more about the recent activities like the 1994 RCMP raid at Terrenceville, code-named "Operation Bacon," which resulted in contraband and assets being seized with a total value of over $300,000.

Saint-Pierre was more than just a smuggling capital; it was the last vestige of the vast North American empire, New France, and a site for a settlement by the French since the early seventeenth century. It was later abandoned under the Treaty of Utrecht and then returned to France in 1763 at the end of the Seven Years' War. It was also known as a place of refuge for Acadian deportees from Nova Scotia.

Today, the tiny island and its uninhabited sister, Miquelon, were almost completely dependent on the same sagging inshore fishery as their Canadian counterparts and heavy subsidies from their federal government back in Europe.

They also had a chance to talk about what was going on in Grand Bank, and Windflower shared his latest dream.

"Well, that's a message that's pretty hard to misinterpret," said Sheila. "But it's your dream."

"I know I want to help," said Windflower. "The question is how best to do that without sacrificing my mental health."

"Or your safety," said Sheila. "It's not easy. But you'll figure it out. Remember, 'Self-love, my liege, is not so vile a sin, as self-neglecting.'"

Windflower gave her a squeeze. "Let's go up on deck. We're almost there."

Despite a growing wind, they went out on deck with all the other passengers and crew to make their entry into the harbour of the French island. It was a beautiful little harbour with dozens of small fishing boats tied up in the marina and colourfully painted wooden buildings lining the shore. They docked and went through French immigration and customs speedily and were on the main shopping street of the small town in good time.

Windflower made his call to Anderssen, but there was no answer, so he left a message asking him to call.

Then Sheila made the most of her half an hour shopping before the stores closed for lunch, while Windflower surveyed the streetscape and hustle and bustle of the prenoon crowd. She found a lovely little dress for Stella that she could use on Sunday mornings going to church and a sweater for Amelia Louise, plus a couple of cute stuffed animals for each of them. She also managed to get a nice multicoloured scarf with a French designer name that she was swooning over when she came out of the latest shop. Behind her, the clerk was putting up the "Fermé" sign to indicate that the long lunch break was about to begin.

Luckily for Sheila and Windflower, the restaurants and cafés were still open. They found a great crêpe restaurant on a side street just down from the main shopping area. They ordered a hot apple cider, and Sheila decided quickly on the vegetarian galette, which had cheese, mushrooms and fresh cream. Windflower couldn't imagine ordering anything but a crêpe at a crêpe restaurant, so he selected the Neptune crêpe with lobster, shrimps and scallops. Both were very pleased with their choices.

Neither of them really wanted it, but their server twisted their arms to order dessert. Not that they really needed much twisting. They ordered the crêpe cheesecake with fresh fruit and vanilla custard with whipped cream on top between them and two cappuccinos. Fully stuffed, they staggered back out in the winter afternoon and wandered down near the wharf while Sheila waited for the shops to reopen and Windflower for his call back from Anderssen.

The shop opening came first, and Sheila happily went inside the ladies' dress shop. Windflower stood outside for a minute and started walking down the street when his phone started ringing. It was Anderssen.

Chapter Twenty-six

The American said, "Things are going down now. Müller and most of his guys are on this afternoon's flight to Paris. Your guy is not going with them. I overheard one of them saying that they're not taking the rat back with them. I'm going to be staying here, and I'll check out the hotel after they're gone. But the shipment is going with two of the Germans on the ferry back to Newfoundland tonight. Interpol knows that Müller is on his way to Paris. I gotta go."

Windflower had a hundred questions to ask but no one to answer them. Luckily, he could still get mobile reception in Saint-Pierre, so he called Ron Quigley in Ottawa. He was on the phone with Quigley when Sheila came out of the shop and handed him a bag. She waved at him and proceeded down the street to a shoe store.

"As far as I can tell, Müller is going back to Paris with some of his crew, and some others are coming to Newfoundland tonight with what our American friend called a shipment," said Windflower.

"And Grimsby?" asked Quigley.

"No word," said Windflower. "Although Anderssen said he would check it all out after things die down around here. Which sounds like tonight."

"Okay," said Quigley. "You're on the ferry with whomever is coming back, so keep an eye on them. We'll have people waiting at the other end."

Windflower hung up with Quigley and waited for Sheila outside the shoe store. She came out a few minutes later with more bags for him to carry.

"Runners for Stella and Amelia Louise and a new pair of spring shoes for me," said Sheila. "You need anything?"

"I don't think we'll have any money left," said Windflower as Sheila smiled and continued on down the street, where she spotted a jewellery store. That could be trouble, thought Windflower as he watched her disappear inside the shop. He walked down a little farther and then saw something that caught his eye: "M. Laurin et Fils. Vin et Liquers Fines."

Wine and fine liquors. That might be my kind of place, he said to himself and pushed the door open. "Puis-je vous aider?" asked the man behind the counter, who Windflower assumed to be the father and probable owner.

"Non, merci," said Windflower, exhausting ninety-five percent of his French vocabulary. He motioned that he was going to look around. The shopkeeper seemed happy to ignore him, so he wandered around the store. He stopped at the Scotch section. This was really interesting.

He found a couple of bottles and checked the price tags. They were in Euros, so he did a quick calculation. Still, about half the price he would pay for one of these great whiskies back home. He picked a twelve-year-old Aberfeldy and brought it to the counter. "Bon choix," said the owner. Windflower used his Visa, which would make the actual calculation, and carried his prize outside, where he saw Sheila waving to him.

She had another smaller bag this time, but Windflower expected that this latest purchase from the jewellery store might be the dearest of all today. He didn't mind, since he had a special treat from today's trip, and together the two of them made the short trip back to the wharf and proceeded through to the terminal to wait for the ferry.

Sheila showed him her jewellery purchase. It was a beautiful set of pearl earrings that he knew would go perfectly with one of her black dresses for their next big social engagement. He opened his bag to show her his Scotch, and while they were waiting, he looked up the whisky on his phone.

As he read, he explained to Sheila that Aberfeldy was part of the famous Dewar family of Scotch whiskies. Sheila wasn't that interested and pulled out her phone to check her messages. He kept reading that it was made on the southern bank of the upper Tay River and was a multiple award winner. That made it a perfect choice to offer his old friend Vijay Sanjay, who had quite a collection of the "Golden Dram" and often invited Windflower over to taste his latest offering.

"And I got it for half-price," he said, trying to get Sheila's attention again. Just then he noticed two of the German men from the B&B come into the terminal. They both had knapsacks, and one was carrying a large duffel bag. They saw him and Sheila, and while they looked a little nervous, they came over to say hello. Or the best they could in their broken English.

They nodded in approval at Sheila's earrings and even more vigorously at Windflower's Scotch. "Guter Scotch whisky," said one of them. They loaded onto the ferry, and once again all passengers and crews stayed up on deck to see the boat out of the harbour. It was much colder now, and the wind had really picked up since this morning, so Windflower and Sheila waved goodbye to the Germans and went inside.

Sheila kept checking the messages on her phone, and Windflower settled back to try and enjoy the ferry ride. After about fifteen minutes, he noticed that the Germans had not come back in. He snuck back up on deck to take a peek around. That was when he saw the one with the duffel bag quickly throw it over the side of the boat, and then both of them almost scurried back downstairs. Windflower ran downstairs and managed to get into a washroom just before the pair came by.

After he heard that they passed, he went back up and took a look over the side of the boat near where they had been standing. He saw the duffel bag floating on top of the water and then something else. It had a blinking light on top of it. As quickly as he could he took out his phone, zoomed in and took several pictures. He sent them by text to Ron Quigley. Then he waited.

While Windflower and Sheila were enjoying their day on Saint-Pierre, Tizzard had a much quieter one back in Grand Bank. He had gone home in the morning after seeing Rob Skinner and the woman at the Mug-Up to find both Carrie and little Hughie were asleep on his bed. He snuck into the spare room and didn't hear a sound until just now when the baby was shrieking at his mother for some reason. He saw why when he came out of the bedroom.

Carrie was holding a spoon with some kind of baby goop in it, and Hughie was desperately trying to grab it out of her hand. He wanted the goop, but he wanted that receptacle more. Finally, Carrie gave in and handed it over. Then, of course, the baby wanted to dip that spoon into the goop. Soon there was more goop on Carrie and on the floor than in his bowl.

Tizzard tried not to, but soon he was laughing hard, and Hughie joined in with his father.

"Okay," said Carrie. "Over to you. I'm going to get changed for work."

Tizzard tried without success to extract the spoon from Hughie, but his grip was as strong as the metal in the spoon. Tizzard gave up and allowed his son to play with the spoon and the goop until he tired of it. Once that happened, he grabbed the baby and the highchair top and cleaned them both. By the time Carrie came out the baby was naked but clean.

"I don't know who the biggest baby is," said Carrie. "Give him to me. You get ready and we'll take him for a walk together."

Chapter Twenty-seven

Tizzard cleaned himself up, and soon he and Carrie and Hughie in the stroller were out in the cool midafternoon air. They had a pleasant walk, even though the wind picked up and a few flakes started to fall. By the time they got home, there was a full-fledged snowfall underway. Carrie was starting to get ready to go to work when Tizzard stopped her.

"Why don't you stay home and I'll go in?"

"But it's your day off," she protested.

"I'll take another day," said Tizzard. "I have to go see Doc Sanjay about the autopsy. If the snow keeps up, we might all have to be in later."

"Yeah, the forecast is now calling for at least twenty centimetres and wind gusts up to ninety kilometres an hour," said Carrie.

"Even better that you stay then," said Tizzard.

"Okay. I'll make you a sandwich and pack you a lunch," said Carrie.

"You are the best," said Tizzard as he hugged her and then took Hughie into the bedroom to change him and have a few moments play time before he headed back into work. He ate his sandwich while Carrie fed Hughie, and he got to give him one more kiss before he drifted off to sleep. He didn't go directly to the office; he wanted to see if Doc Sanjay had made any progress on the remains of the late Sid Skinner.

Tizzard parked outside the emergency entrance and walked in through the clinic, pausing to say good morning to all the patients and family members in the waiting area. Luckily, no one accosted him today about the poor job the Mounties were doing. Probably because they heard the news that the RCMP might be closing. There was something infinitely better about poor service than none at all.

In any case, Tizzard had made up his mind not to worry about it. He liked the Mark Twain quote about the subject:

"Worrying is like paying a debt you don't owe." He smiled to himself as he walked down the hallway to Doctor Sanjay's office at the back of the clinic. But the good doctor wasn't there. A helpful male nurse pointed him towards the operating area, and another nurse near that section told him that Sanjay was in Operating Theatre 1.

He found that door and was about to come in when a fully gowned and masked Sanjay met him on his way out.

"Good morning, young Tizzard," said Sanjay. "I am finished the first part of my postmortem examination of the late Cedric Skinner. Time for a break. Would you like some tea?"

Tizzard followed the doctor back to his office, where Sanjay got a pot out of the cupboard, put in some water, a helping of sugar and some spices and set the mixture to boil. When it started to boil, he added some milk and tea from a container on the counter.

"What are you making?" asked Tizzard.

"It's called doodh cha," said Sanjay. "It's a special Bengali chai tea."

When it was ready, the doctor poured them each a cup of the mixture. He opened a small tin and offered Tizzard one of the treats inside. They were small, round white cookies, or they looked like cookies to Tizzard. With a slice of pistachio on top.

Tizzard sipped the creamy white tea and bit into the cookie. "What is this? It's delicious. And so is the tea."

"We call them sandesh, but some people call them sandosh," said Sanjay. "They go perfectly with the doodh cha. Yes?"

"Yes indeed," said Tizzard, taking another cookie from the doctor.

"Good," said the doctor. "I'm glad you are enjoying the tea. They say back home, 'To have doodh cha not when you need it, but when you feel like you've deserved it.'"

"I deserve it," said Tizzard.

"I'm sure you do," said Sanjay. "What's going on with your old boss?"

"He's back on some kind of contract. Working with Quigley," said Tizzard, taking one more cookie when offered, although starting to feel the sickly effect of the sweet tea and the treats.

"Interesting," said Sanjay. "If you see him, tell him I was asking about him. I'd like to have him over for a game of chess and some Scotch tasting."

"I'll pass that along," said Tizzard. "So, anything to report so far?"

"It's still early for the late Mister Skinner," said the doctor. "But I can confirm that he, too, had a small hole in the side of his skull."

"Like Leo Broderick?" asked Tizzard.

"Very similar," said Sanjay. "And I also received this from my friend in the lab," he added, going to his desk to pick up an envelope. It was marked Federal Bureau of Investigation. "He sent me a message. But here is the proof. Our late friend Leo Broderick died almost instantly from batrachotoxin poisoning."

"The Venezuelan tree frog poison. In Grand Bank?" asked Tizzard.

"That would be correct," said the doctor.

"Who is going to believe that?" asked Tizzard.

"Well, my young friend, "'The facts are many, but the truth is one.'"

"That may be true," said Tizzard. "'But compliments win friends and honesty loses them.' And the same for public opinion."

"You've been studying the great poet, Tagore," said Sanjay. "Or listening to the wisdom of your elders. In any case, that's the truth, whether people accept it or not."

"Thank you, Doc," said Tizzard. "Especially for the treats. Let me know if you find anything else."

Chapter Twenty-eight

Windflower waited none too patiently for Ron Quigley's return call. When it came, it sounded very loud inside the small passenger cabin. He walked back up on deck to take it but was pushed back by spray from the ocean and a swirl of snowflakes that made it hard to stand up, let alone hear anything. He went back inside and stood in the small vestibule outside the cabin. He was pretty sure no one could hear him, and given the weather, it almost guaranteed that nobody, especially his German friends, would interrupt him.

"What's in the picture?" asked Quigley.

"It was a large duffel bag that one of the Germans threw overboard," said Windflower.

"Are you still on the ferry?" asked Quigley. "Do you know where the bag was dropped?"

"We're still on the ferry, probably thirty minutes from Fortune," said Windflower. "I can't be sure, but I would say that he dropped the bag about halfway. It had a light on it. I'm not sure you can see it in the pictures I sent."

"We did see that when we blew it up," said Quigley. "It might be a locator for a GPS."

"What's next?" asked Windflower.

"You keep an eye on the guys on the ferry. We'll have somebody tail them once they get to the other side. And we'll get our patrol boat out on the water," said Quigley. "To track the bag."

"You might have a bit of a problem on that end," said Windflower.

"Weather?" asked Quigley.

"It's really blowing, and the snow's coming down pretty fast," said Windflower.

"Well, that will make it hard for the bad guys to pick it up, too," said Quigley. "Any word on Grimsby when you were on Saint-Pierre?"

"It didn't sound good," said Windflower. "But Anderssen was going to check the hotel after everyone left and let me know if he found anything."

Quigley started to ask something else, but Windflower heard the cabin door creak open. "I gotta go," he said and hung up the phone, expecting to see one or both of the Germans come through the door. But it was only Sheila.

"I was worried about you," said Sheila. "It's getting pretty rough out there."

"I'm fine," said Windflower. "Luckily, we're not too far from Fortune. Let's go back inside."

The ferry ride got rougher for a few more minutes and then seemed to calm. That usually meant they were getting close to shore. That proved to be correct, and a short while later the passengers came up on deck to pass through customs and immigration in Fortune. Windflower claimed his bottle of Scotch and the girls' shoes as part of his claim while Sheila provided receipts for the rest. They were waved through just as the two Germans came through immigration.

Windflower noticed two of his old RCMP comrades in plain clothes waiting just outside the terminal. He gave them a brief nod of acknowledgement, but they had already spotted their targets and were following the Germans in the now raging snowstorm to the parking lot.

The Germans stopped and walked back to Windflower and Sheila.

"Wir brauchen eine Unterkunft," said one of them. Windflower looked puzzled. The other pointed to the sky. "Gasthaus," he said.

"I think they want a room at the B&B," said Sheila.

"Ja," said the first German. "B&B."

"Let me make a phone call first," said Windflower. The Germans looked happy while Sheila looked surprised. She followed him over to the side of the terminal, in out of the snow, while he made his call. "Who are you calling?" she asked. "Levi?"

He held up one finger and dialled Quigley. He walked back inside the terminal and made his call.

"They want to stay at the B&B," he said when Quigley answered.

"The Germans?" he asked. "Why not? You can keep an eye on them inside while our guys watch for any escape."

"They're not escaping anywhere tonight," said Windflower. "It's a full-fledged storm now. We'll be lucky to get back to Grand Bank."

"Great. I'll message the other guys. Did you see them?" asked Quigley.

"Two guys from Marystown. But I would keep them out of sight. It's pretty obvious that they're just cops out of uniforms," said Windflower.

"I'll pass that along, too," said Quigley. "Keep me posted on any developments."

Windflower hung up with Quigley and went out to find Sheila, who was now standing in the doorway with the two Germans.

"Okay, we're set for the B&B," he said.

The two Germans looked happy and both shook his hand.

"We'll see you over there in a little while," he said. When they looked confused, he pointed at his watch. "Ja, ja. Danke," they both said.

Windflower grabbed Sheila's arm and pulled her close to him as they made their way up the little hill to the parking lot to retrieve their car.

"Ron Quigley?" said Sheila when they had gotten out of the snow and into their vehicle.

"Yeah," said Windflower. "I'll explain later, but we'll need to get Beulah to help set them up again at the B&B. I'll have to stay there overnight."

"Okay," said Sheila. "I'll call Beulah. The girls should be ready. Let's swing by the Stoodleys' to pick them up, and then you can head over."

Windflower waited in the parking lot for the Germans to leave, and he followed a close distance behind. He could see another vehicle right behind him and guessed correctly that was Quigley's crew. The usually short drive took almost half an hour as the car in front took their time in the limited visibility. Windflower watched as the van finally reached the B&B, parked, and the two men inside almost immediately went across the street to the Mug-Up.

"Good," he said to Sheila, pointing to their soon-to-be guests. "I won't have to worry about cooking supper."

They drove back across town and picked up the girls from Moira and Herb, who looked a little relieved to see them go.

"They're a handful together," said Herb as Windflower carried out Amelia Louise and held Stella by the hand.

"Absolutely," said Windflower.

"But great fun, too," said Moira as she came to say goodbye and wave to Sheila through the snow.

"Gonna get a dump tonight," said Herb.

"Yeah, sure looks like it," said Windflower as he disappeared into the swirling snow. "Thanks again."

Chapter Twenty-nine

Windflower dropped Sheila and the girls off and went to pick up Beulah. By the time they got to the B&B, their two guests were sitting in their van in front, sipping on a coffee. Windflower opened the door of the B&B and waved them in. He checked them in and made a mental note of their names. Hendrik Schüller and Ulrich Riis.

While Beulah was making their beds, they opened a bottle of cognac that they'd brought back from Saint-Pierre and poured a shot into their coffee. They offered one to Windflower, but he had a bit of work to do. That included calling Ron Quigley to let him know that his people of interest were safe for the night. As he went to the kitchen to make his call, he looked out the window. He saw a lot of snow still coming down and near the side of the inn, a car with two men inside. His backup. He hoped he wouldn't need them.

Someone who did need backup was Eddie Tizzard. He'd gotten his dad to look after Hughie for a few hours and called Smithson back in for an extra shift. He put Betsy on notice, but unless the power went out, he would leave her alone for the evening. The Highways people had already closed the highway into Grand Bank from Marystown, and he'd sent Smithson out to do the last run. Just to make sure there was no one else out there on such a bad night. He could only hope that they wouldn't have a repeat of the last storm and find another vanload of stragglers.

Smithson returned with the good news that there didn't appear to be anyone stranded or in distress on the highway. That left them with the good citizens of Grand Bank to look after. As long as the power stayed on, people seemed quite content to weather the storm in the safety of their homes. Carrie was looking after the phones, and while it was steady, there was no panic. That changed just before midnight, when the temperature started to rise and the snow turned to more of a wintry mix.

Tizzard could tell when the changeover happened. Rather, he could hear it. The tell-tale tap, tap, tap on the windows of the detachment. Within five minutes of the first tap, the phone lines lit up, and soon all three of the RCMP officers were fielding calls and reassuring people that things would be okay. Even as they waited to see if, in fact, that would be the case. Luckily, most people were in bed and hopefully asleep when the lights went out.

Carrie had gone home by now to look after Hughie and to get a break from the phone. Tizzard hated to call Betsy, but he would need her now. She was already up and expecting the call. He sent Smithson to get her. His next was to Tom Hollett, the town manager, who was in his office as well.

"We'll get the gym set up again," said Hollett. "It's supposed to ease up later this morning, but people will be cold. Can we do anything about breakfast?"

"Why don't you call the manager at Sobey's?" asked Tizzard. "Some fruit and baked goods would do it. We can make big urns of tea and hot water for instant coffee. I'll get Betsy to organize it if you get the materials."

"Will do," said Hollett.

"Great," said Tizzard. Having the food looked after made all the difference. Carrie came back with more good news. First of all, she had Hughie, all wrapped up in a snuggly. She handed that bundle to Tizzard. "I had to bring him with me," she said. "Your dad was exhausted and needed a break."

"No worries," said Tizzard. "What else have you got there?"

Carrie passed over the bag, and Tizzard peeked inside. "Soup and leftover chili. I love you, Carrie."

She took the baby back. "You love to eat, Eddie Tizzard, more than anything. I know that. You go have your food, and I'll feed him in your office and then let him have a snooze in there. Okay?"

Tizzard didn't argue with that offer, and feeling particularly generous, he split his late supper with Smithson, who'd come back with Betsy.

"Hey, I found out who the woman was with Rob Skinner," said Smithson. "Marie at the Mug-Up told me. It's Marguerite Slaney."

"Paddy Slaney's wife?" asked Tizzard. "Now isn't that interesting. I wonder what they were talking about. We'll have to check that out. But not right now. See if you can help Betsy."

Betsy was very busy organizing the women for the continental breakfast and putting out the word to people that the gym at the high school was open as a warming centre. That, along with the fact that people were waking up in cold houses, kept the phones ringing off the hook and the RCMP officers busy ferrying people back and forth. She sent Smithson out to pick up the first load.

Windflower had heard the freezing rain start overnight but didn't know the power was out until he felt the chill in the early morning. That got him out of bed at the B&B to make sure everything was okay and that the emergency generator had kicked in. It would keep the lights on and allow him to start the stove, which was propane-powered but not enough to power the old oil furnace in the basement.

They kept the heat on a minimum over the winter. They'd learned their lessons with burst pipes and thousands of dollars damage in a previous winter. And he'd turned it up when they came in last night. But it wouldn't take long for the big old inn to cool down. Not enough to freeze the pipes in the short term, but chilly enough to wake you up. Although he couldn't hear much from the guest rooms. Maybe the cognac was still keeping them warm and asleep.

He made a cup of coffee and checked the weather outside. There was a beautiful glaze on top of the snow and on every surface the freezing rain had touched. Deathly beautiful, he'd once heard it described. While he was watching, he saw Herb Stoodley's van come into view and slide into a parking place in front of the Mug-Up. He opened the door and called out hello.

Herb waved back and motioned for him to come over. He grabbed his coat and boots and went outside. He started out quickly, but after a few slips and slides, he gingerly made his way across the street and into the dimly lit café.

"Morning, Herb," he called out.

"Morning, Winston," said Herb. "I'm just getting these space heaters set up. We can run our stoves and the emergency lights and a couple of these, but that's about it with the back-up running."

"Enough to do breakfast?" asked Windflower.

"Absolutely," said Herb. "What can I get you?"

"I'm okay for now," said Windflower. "But I've got a couple of guests who will be hungry when they wake up."

"Oh, those young fellers. Marie said they were here last night," said Herb. "They seemed nice to me when I met them. Very polite. Although I was just assuming they were polite. I don't understand much German."

Windflower decided to say little about his German friends. No point in getting Herb upset or letting the Germans know that he and the RCMP were on to them.

"If you can serve them, I'll send them over when they're ready," said Windflower. "Thanks, Herb." And Windflower was out of there before Herb could ask anything else.

Chapter Thirty

He walked carefully back to the other side and almost made it without incident. But just before he reached the B&B steps, his front foot found a very slippery patch, and soon his whole body flew out from underneath him. He didn't think he was injured at first, but as he tried to get up, he noticed that his wrist was scraped red and clearly bruised. And it hurt, a lot.

He managed to get to his feet, and that was when he noticed his two RCMP friends, still sitting in the same spot near the B&B. They weren't very good at this, he thought, and maybe he should go and point that out. But his wrist hurt too much. He grabbed the railing with his good hand and pulled himself up and inside the B&B.

He had another cup of coffee and was rubbing his wrist, which by now had swollen and was starting to turn a darker shade of blue with some violet mixed in. Beulah, who had stayed upstairs overnight, came into the kitchen. He tried to pretend that nothing had happened, but Beulah's mothering instincts kicked in, and she did her visual and then a very painful physical examination.

"I'd say it's broke, b'y," she said after she'd completed her inspection.

"No, it's just a sprain," said Windflower.

"You should get it checked out at the clinic," said Beulah, making herself some tea.

"It's fine," said Windflower, trying to hide the offending wrist behind his back.

"Suit yourself," said Beulah. "Do you want me to make breakfast this morning?"

"No thanks," said Windflower. "I'm going to suggest the Mug-Up. Herb Stoodley has the place opened up already. Have you heard anything from them this morning?"

"No, b'y," said Beulah. "But last night they went on and on, talking and yelling at each other. I think they were drinking. And maybe smoking some stuff on the balcony, too. My room was right above them."

"What were they fighting about?" asked Windflower, hoping that Beulah's German could give him some more information.

"It was hard to tell, exactly," said Beulah. "But one of them was really upset about a man called Ewe. Said they didn't have to hurt him. The other guy kept saying they didn't have a choice. I'm not sure they settled anything before I finally drifted off. If you don't need me, I'm going to go back to my room and say my prayers."

"Sure, sure," said Windflower, happy that she was leaving so that he could call Quigley with an update.

Eddie Tizzard was happy, too. They finally got the breakfast line going at the high school, and the people who made it there and those that the RCMP had picked up were working their way through it. The other good news was that the freezing rain had stopped, and the sun was starting to peek out from behind the clouds. The power was still out, though, and it might take some time to get back on. Smithson had reported that several wires were down across Grand Bank and that while crews were on their way, they were not the only community with problems today.

All of that meant that the council would have to keep the warming centre open for the rest of the day and that the Mounties would be on taxi service as required. That was okay with Tizzard. His dad was there with little Hughie on his knee, and many of the people there had come up to him to tell him how sad they were about the detachment closing. He realized that despite the complaints about service, especially about the men they had lost and were missing, that there was great support in this community for him and the work they were doing. No matter how it turned out, he felt pretty good right now.

He got himself a couple of croissants and a banana and went to sit with his dad. Carrie came by a few minutes later and took Hughie so Richard could have his breakfast, too.

"Even though it's kind of difficult circumstances, I love when the whole community can get together like this," said Richard.

Tizzard nodded. "Sometimes trouble brings good things, too."

"'Clouds come floating into my life, no longer to carry rain or usher storm, but to add color to my sunset sky,'" said his dad.

"That's beautiful," said Carrie. "Is that Tagore?"

"Yes, indeed," said Richard. "Here's another one. I got them from that book Doctor Sanjay loaned me. 'Let me not pray to be sheltered from dangers, but to be fearless in facing them.'"

"Okay," said Eddie. "Let's get Smithson and be fearless in going around town and marking off the places where the power lines are down."

Chapter Thirty-one

The three Mounties spent most of the morning doing exactly that, travelling around each street in Grand Bank and placing police tape around the electric wires that had fallen with the weight of the ice. And two areas where the poles had crumpled, too. Tizzard reported these locations to the Power people, who said that they'd put them on the list. All three returned to the high school at lunchtime. Betsy's cooking crew was now dishing out soup from three large tureens. They recruited the Mounties to deliver a few plastic containers to a handful of shut-ins who'd called Betsy and the RCMP for help. They had just returned from that pleasant job when the big lights in the gym came back on again. Sure enough, the power was back. Everybody in the gym was happy about that, none more than Tizzard.

This meant they could start winding down the emergency operations and get a break. But that still wouldn't be for a while. They had to monitor the areas where the lines were down, paying special attention to the places where the poles were down as well. But at least there was light at the end of the tunnel. "Okay," said Tizzard as he gathered his team together. "Let's have some soup, and then we'll get everyone back home again. Then we can get a break."

Someone who couldn't get a break, at least not yet, was Winston Windflower. His guests had gotten up before he had a chance to phone Quigley. With Betsy's help, he directed them across the street to the Mug-Up for their breakfast. They seemed pleased with that option. Windflower smiled and waved them off, but it was more of a grimace as the pain in his wrist increased any time he even gently moved it. It had also swollen more than Windflower could hide.

Ignoring that, he went into the back area and called Ron Quigley.

144

"The men are still here. Gone for breakfast," said Windflower. "And your undercover guys are sitting right out in the open."

"They're just beat cops," said Quigley. "But all we have right now. I'll get a message to them to try to be a bit more discreet. Anything else?"

"Yes," said Windflower. "Beulah heard them talking last night about a guy that got killed. Ewe somebody."

"Ewe Meeir?" asked Quigley.

"I don't know if Beulah got his last name," said Windflower. "Something about how they didn't have a choice but to kill him. You know of this guy, Ewe?"

"They found his body out on the highway after the last storm," said Quigley.

"Oh yeah, I think I might have heard something about that. He was German, too? Right?" asked Windflower.

"Ewe Meeir is a known associate of Gerhard Müller. With lots of connections to drug operations across Europe. His death was what sparked everybody's interest," said Quigley. "We might have to stop the two that are there for questioning. Can you hold them for another day?"

"Well, the weather won't help," said Windflower, looking out the window again. "But the slippery roads might. Along with our friendly RCMP detachment. Did you know they were thinking about shutting it down?"

"I did not," said Quigley. "But every couple of years somebody comes up with a crack-pot scheme to save money, so I'm not surprised. It's not Marystown's idea?"

"Nope," said Windflower. "It's Majesky, I hear."

"It must be part of a bigger plan then," said Quigley. "And if he's on board, it'll be harder to overturn."

"Well, Sheila's on that now," said Windflower. "I'll call Tizzard and see if he can help."

Eddie Tizzard was more than happy to help his old boss. "Sure, what would you like us to do? Arrest them?"

"No, not yet anyway," said Windflower. "We just need to delay them for a day or so. We can tell people that the highway isn't safe. Maybe have a roadblock put up outside of town?"

"That's not much of a stretch," said Tizzard. "It can't be good. I'll have Betsy put out a note saying that the RCMP recommends everyone stay off the highway for the next twenty-four hours. And if they still try to leave, we can set the roadblock up. How does that sound?"

"Perfect," said Windflower. "I'll let you know how it goes over here."

Windflower texted Quigley that he thought he bought another day with his German visitors. Quigley sent back a smiley face. That made Windflower smile again, but when he laid his phone down, his wrist was killing him.

"That's broken," said Beulah as Windflower came back into the kitchen. "Or a bad sprain, that's for sure. Look how swollen it is."

Windflower tried to tuck it behind his back again, but that hurt too much. He admitted defeat. "I just have to get our guests organized, and then I'll go over to the clinic."

His promise was still hanging in the air when the two Germans came happily strolling back into the B&B. With Beulah as his interpreter, he explained the roads situation. They didn't seem very pleased at the prospect of staying another night in Grand Bank but at the end shrugged and accepted their fate. Windflower booked them in for another night at the B&B and left them for Beulah to take care of while he went to the clinic. He called Sheila along the way.

"Oh my God, are you okay?" asked Sheila.

"I'm fine," said Windflower. "It's probably just a slight sprain."

It was not just a slight sprain, according to Doctor Danette White. "You're lucky. It's not broken. But there appears to be some ligament tearing."

"That's not good," said Windflower. "Is it?"

"No, that's not good," said Doctor White. "I'm going to wrap it to bring down the swelling, and you have to avoid using that wrist for the next couple of days. Apply ice for about twenty minutes at a time, three times a day. Come back and see me on Monday morning, unless the pain gets worse. Then come back right away."

"What about the pain?" asked Windflower.

"I'm going to give you some anti-inflammatory painkillers," said the doctor. "Hopefully, I won't see you again until Monday." She handed Windflower a small, sample bottle of painkillers and a prescription for more. "Only if you need them," she added.

Windflower nodded, thanked the doctor, and left. He was walking down the hallway to his car when he heard a familiar voice calling to him. "Winston, Winston."

He turned around and saw it was Doctor Sanjay.

"Vijay, how are you?" said Windflower.

"I am wonderful grand," said the doctor. "But what happened to you?" he asked, pointing to Windflower's bandaged arm.

"Oh, it's nothing, just a sprain," said Windflower. "A casualty of the freezing rain."

"That's too bad," said Sanjay. "I thought about staying at home, but I had a piece of business to finish off. The late Mister Skinner."

"What did you find out?" asked Windflower. "Tizzard told me you were doing the autopsy. He said you thought it might be some kind of exotic poison."

"Yes," said Sanjay. "We have been able to confirm that both he and the Broderick man had this poison present. I know our young friend is skeptical, but that's what the science says. And we have to follow the science."

"Indeed," said Windflower. "But how could Venezuelan tree frog poison get here in Grand Bank?"

"Obviously someone brought it," said Sanjay. "Who? That's a job for the RCMP. Tizzard told me you were helping out a bit."

"I am giving some advice," said Windflower. "I'm actually working on a special project with Ron Quigley."

"Very nice," said the doctor.

"Yes, and one of the benefits of this temporary assignment is that I got to go to Saint-Pierre," said Windflower.

"That's even nicer," said Sanjay. "You know there's a speciality wine and liquor store over there."

"M. Laurin et fils," said Windflower. "I stumbled upon the place while Sheila was shopping for shoes. I found a bottle that you might be interested in. A twelve-year-old Aberfeldy."

"Oh, my goodness," said Sanjay. "I just saw a note on that whisky in my Scotch tasting magazine. If I remember the write-up, they talked about aromas of dried flowers, honey, spice, and a hint of smokiness. It sounds divine."

"I thought about you as soon as I saw it," said Windflower. "And since you have treated me so many times, I would like to share it with you."

"You are too kind," said Sanjay. "And, of course, I accept."

"Great," said Windflower. "Maybe you and Repa could come over on the weekend. Have supper with us on Sunday. It's a little hectic, but Sheila and the girls would love to see you."

"I will check with Repa and confirm," said Sanjay. "But I am very excited. About the visit and the Scotch. Would it be a great imposition if I brought my chessboard?"

"No, that would be perfect," said Windflower. "We'll see you on Sunday, I hope."

Sanjay waved goodbye and went back to his office.

Chapter Thirty-two

Windflower went to his car and called Sheila with his good hand.

"It's a sprain," he said. "Doctor White gave me a bandage and some painkillers."

"And probably told you not to use it," said Sheila.

"Probably," admitted Windflower. "I saw Doc Sanjay at the clinic. I invited him and Repa to supper on Sunday. Hope that's okay?"

"That's perfect," said Sheila. "We haven't seen them in forever. Are Eddie and Carrie still coming over tonight?"

"I don't know, but I'll check in when I get back to the B&B. Our guests are staying overnight," he said.

"The roads?" asked Sheila.

"Yeah, I guess it's pretty treacherous," said Windflower. It wasn't a lie, he rationalized. Just not all of the information.

"Can you pop by here sometime along the way?" asked Sheila. "I desperately need a break."

"Why don't I take them over to the B&B with me for a few hours?" said Windflower. "Beulah is there, too."

"They would love that," said Sheila. "I'll get them ready."

Windflower had to take a circuitous route to get to his house. There were at least three streets along the way that had wires down or large branches across the road. He ended up circling around and passing the high school, where he saw several cars and RCMP cruisers and the truck from the Grand Bank Volunteer Fire Department. He spotted Eddie Tizzard's Jeep coming out of the parking lot and waved him down.

"Hey Sarge, how she's going b'y?" said Tizzard.

"It's good," said Windflower. "Just on my way to pick up the girls to bring them over to the B&B with me. You got lots of excitement going on over here."

"Yeah, but we're almost done now," said Tizzard. "There's only a couple of dozen people left without power, and most of them have generators. That leaves a handful who need help overnight, and our friends from the fire department are taking over from here."

"That'll be good," said Windflower. "You can get a break. Are you and Carrie still coming over for supper?"

"Absolutely," said Tizzard. "Carrie's taking a break right now, and I'm on my way to join her. Smithson can hold the fort until after supper, and I'll take over."

"Okay, see you then," said Windflower. A few minutes later, he was putting Stella and Amelia Louise in the car. He walked back to check in with Sheila one more time. "Everything okay for tonight?" he asked.

"I'm good," said Sheila. "I've got some casseroles in the freezer I can thaw, and I think I've got another loaf of that garlic bread you like so much."

"Mmmm," said Windflower. "I'm looking forward to that. We'll be back in a few hours."

Amelia Louise and Stella were even happier when they got to the B&B and saw that Beulah was there. She doted on them, and they totally loved her. Pretty soon she had them in the kitchen baking cookies. Windflower left them alone to their task, and since the two Germans were safely in their rooms above, he walked across the road to check in on Herb Stoodley.

The café was busy, but Herb still had time to sit and chat for a minute with Windflower. Herb talked about how much he and Moira had enjoyed having the girls over. "We never had the blessing of children of our own," he said. "But I think being a grandparent might be the best deal of all. One of my favourite authors, Gore Vidal, once said to 'never have children, only grandchildren.'"

"That's a good one," said Windflower. "Although I love being a dad, especially here in Grand Bank."

Herb nodded his agreement. "Why don't you stay then?"

"What do you mean?" asked Windflower.

"Well, if all fails, there will be a one-person detachment here in Grand Bank. You'd be perfect for it," said Herb.

"I'm retired, in case you forgot," said Windflower. "Besides, maybe one of the crew here wants to stay."

"I dunno," said Herb. "Smithson won't want to be here on his own. And Tizzard and Evanchuk are a team, so how's that going to work out? You should think about it, anyway."

"Thanks, Herb," said Windflower. "I've got lots to think about already. See you soon."

Back at the B&B, the girls could not wait to show him the results of their labour. Mostly Beulah's labour, thought Windflower, but he congratulated Amelia Louise and Stella while thanking Beulah. When he tasted the oatmeal raisin cookies, he pronounced them delicious, much to the delight of the girls, who had another cookie to celebrate. The sugar in the cookies kept them going and active until it was time to go home for supper.

Windflower got Beulah to check with their guests to see if they would like take-out chicken for supper. They were quite happy with that choice, and Windflower picked it up from the take-out and left them with Beulah so that he could go home for supper. When they arrived, Eddie and Carrie and Richard and Hughie were all in the living room while Sheila was busy in the kitchen getting their meal ready.

He said a quick hello to the Tizzards, who were quickly enveloped by his daughters, and went to help Sheila.

"Whatever it is, it smells delicious," said Windflower. "What is it, and what can I do to help?"

"Can you chop up some broccoli and put it in the steamer? Then we're almost ready to go," said Sheila. "It's just a chicken casserole. I like it because you can put whatever you have in the fridge in it."

Sheila took the garlic bread in tinfoil out of the oven. Windflower finished the broccoli and helped Sheila separate the steaming bread into two baskets.

"The girls made cookies with Beulah. They're pretty good," he said.

"Great," said Sheila. "We can have them with some ice cream for dessert. Call the troops. We're ready."

Eddie and Richard Tizzard gushed about the casserole while Carrie fed Hughie in the living room. Once she was finished, Eddie took the baby on his lap while she had her supper, too.

"So, I hear you're leading the charge on keeping the cop shop open," said Eddie to Sheila.

"I'm just making up some of the plan," said Sheila. "I think it will be up to the community and the RCMP, of course, to figure out where this is going. How about you guys? Do you have a plan B?"

"I'm not sure we have a good plan A," said Carrie. "It's hard enough to manage everything with just Hughie and the two of us. Plus, all the help we get from Richard and Eddie's sisters. It would be hard to leave all that support."

"But we might have to, if worse comes to worst," said Eddie. "We can postpone the outcome a little, but I would think that if the detachment closes or goes down to one person, we're likely going to have to move."

Windflower listened carefully to the conversation but said little. Richard Tizzard was the next one to speak up. He'd taken Hughie and was bouncing him on his knee. The baby seemed to be really enjoying the ride.

"You know you both could get a job at the RCMP in Marystown," he said. "At least you'd be close enough to come visit whenever you wanted. I think it'd be pretty hard to say goodbye to this little guy."

Eddie looked at Carrie, and she stared back. "We'd always come visit or you could come see us," he said. "But you know, if we do have to move, we could consider something on the island. I could talk to Bill Ford."

"Why not?" asked Carrie. "That would buy us at least two more years around here and maybe more. We could even keep our house here."

That was the end of the adult conversation as Stella and Amelia Louise had "captured" Eddie and were taking him "prissner," according to Amelia Louise. Sheila managed to get the security forces back to the table for cookies and ice cream, but by now Hughie had enough and was screaming so much that Carrie had to leave early and take him home. Richard and Eddie Tizzard left shortly afterward.

Chapter Thirty-three

Eddie helped his dad get into the Jeep and then came back to thank Sheila and kiss the girls goodnight. Sheila took them upstairs for bath time while Windflower got his coat and Lady's leash and went out with Eddie.

"Sanjay says hello, by the way," said Eddie. "He's hoping to get together with you soon."

"I saw him at the clinic," said Windflower. "He and Repa are coming over on Sunday."

"That'll be nice," said Eddie. He paused for a moment and then spoke again. "You know, you should consider the Grand Bank job if that's how it unfolds. Smithson's getting out of here, and I think that Marystown or somewhere else on the island might be a better fit for us."

"You're the second person to suggest that today," said Windflower. "But I don't know. I might think about it if it came up, but it wouldn't look very good to have me trying to get a job while Sheila's trying to save the detachment, would it?"

"I guess not," said Tizzard. "But you should still think about it. And if they offer it to you, which I think they might, remember the bard. '"Who seeks, and will not take, when once 'tis offer'd, shall never find it more.'"

"Good one, Eddie," said Windflower. "You may be right. 'We must take the current when it serves or lose our ventures.'"

"Goodnight, Sarge," said Eddie.

"Goodnight, Eddie," said Windflower. He waved goodnight to the Tizzards and started his evening stroll with Lady. He was just coming on the wharf apron when his cell phone rang. It was Beulah.

"You better come back, b'y," said Beulah. "I heard them German boys talking, and I think they're going to take off."

"What did they say?" asked Windflower, almost immediately regretting that question, since his German was negligible.

"Heute nacht verlassen," said Beulah. "And die polizei."

"The police," said Windflower, recognizing that word. "Thanks, Beulah. I'll be there soon." He ran back to his house and dropped off Lady, not even stopping to tell Sheila what was going on. He would call her later. He jumped in his car and raced to the B&B. The van was still in the parking lot. He circled around the block and found the RCMP undercover vehicle in a laneway on the street behind the B&B.

He parked, walked up to the other vehicle, and tapped on the back window. They unlocked the door and let him in the back seat.

"We're not supposed to have any contact," said one of them, whom Windflower recognized as Elliston. The other man he didn't know spoke up. "We can't talk to you," he said.

"Listen, I don't have time for chit-chat," said Windflower. "We think the Germans are going to try to leave tonight. If they do, you'll be the lead. Be ready." Windflower left that car and went back to his own. His next call was to Ron Quigley, but no answer. He left a message and started to go around the block to the B&B. As he turned the corner, he could see the van starting to move. He turned off his lights and ran to the RCMP car behind him.

"They're going," he said. The two men started their car, and Windflower watched as they crept out into the night. He saw the flash of their lights a few minutes later as they braked to go around a corner. He jumped back in his car, and without any lights on he followed behind them.

When he got to the edge of the highway, Elliston and his buddy were standing by the barricade that had been moved aside. And there was no sign of the Germans and their van. "What do we do now?" asked the other RCMP officer.

"Follow them. But stay far enough behind so they don't see you," said Windflower. "I've got a message into Quigley. Give me your cell phone number. I'll call you."

Windflower punched the number into his phone. "Go, go," he said.

The other car sped off in the darkness without its lights, and Windflower hoped they'd be okay and that they could somehow stay out of the Germans' sight. He had limited faith in either of these things happening.

He phoned the RCMP in Marystown and talked to the duty sergeant. He agreed that they would put a spotter on the highway outside of Marystown to keep an eye out for the van. "Thanks," said Windflower. "I'll try to get you more direction. But for now, we're just observing. None of us has orders to intervene."

"I'll pass that along," said the duty sergeant. "I'll call Inspector Ford, too."

"Perfect," said Windflower as he hung up. Now, like ninety-five percent of all police work, we wait, he thought. While he was waiting, he called Sheila.

Eddie Tizzard was back at the detachment when Smithson came in from his tour around town. "Almost all cleared up," he said. "The Power guys and the council did a good job of cleaning things up. We should be fully operational by tomorrow."

"That's good news," said Tizzard.

"I have some other news, too," said Smithson.

"Do you enjoy torturing me?" asked Tizzard. "I can make your life miserable, you know."

"I did a check on Rob Skinner, and nothing showed up," said Smithson.

"That's your big news?" said Tizzard.

"Nothing on Rob Skinner Senior. But Rob Skinner Junior, that's another matter," said Smithson.

"His son?" asked Tizzard.

"Arrested in Fort Lauderdale, coming back from Bogotá, Colombia," said Smithson. "Currently serving fourteen years in Florida State Prison. And when he's finished there, our guys want to talk to him about something."

"Money-laundering," said Tizzard.

"Maybe," said Smithson. "How do you want to handle this?"

"You phone Bill Ford and let him know what you found out," said Tizzard. "Ask him to pass it up the food chain and see what, if anything, they would like us to do down here."

"Okay, I'll phone him now," said Smithson.

Chapter Thirty-four

Tizzard took a couple of minutes to think about the news that Smithson had shared. Some of the pieces of the jigsaw puzzle were starting to fit into place. Maybe, just maybe, they were getting somewhere. He hadn't had much more time to ponder things when Smithson came back in.

"Inspector Ford is going to make a few calls and get back to you," he said. "But he's working on the Germans right now. I guess the two at the B&B made a run for it. They're waiting for them in Marystown."

"Why didn't we hear about it?" asked Tizzard.

"I dunno," said Smithson. "I put up the barrier, like you told me. They must have moved it and took off. There's two undercovers following them, and Windflower knows about it."

"I'll call Windflower," said Tizzard. "Why don't you go home and get a rest?"

"Okay," said Smithson. "But I had one more idea. What kind of a search have we done for Paddy Slaney?"

"The usual," said Tizzard. "Local, regional, national. Looking for him in hospitals, jails, homeless shelters."

"What about international?" asked Smithson.

"I don't know," said Tizzard. "Why don't you do that tomorrow after you get a break?"

"Okay," said Smithson. "Goodnight."

Tizzard said goodnight to Smithson and called Windflower.

"Why didn't we get the call?" he asked when Windflower answered.

"No time," said Windflower. "They were out of here so fast, I only had a chance to get Elliston and his partner on the chase. Then I called Marystown to head them off at the pass."

"Any word on them yet?"

"No, but you better keep your eyes out," said Windflower. "They might decide to turn back, especially if they get wind they're being followed or see the trap in Marystown. I have little faith that our undercover guys could stay that way for long. And to be fair, it's hard to hide when you are one of only two vehicles on the road."

"Okay," said Tizzard. "I'm on overnight, and I'll keep my eyes peeled when I head out on the highway later."

"Good luck with that," said Windflower. "I'm going home to bed, at least until something else happens. It can be totally quiet around here, and then everything breaks loose."

"I'd settle for some of that quiet you're talking about right now," said Tizzard. "Goodnight, Sarge."

Windflower hung up, turned off the lights in the downstairs of his house, and went up to bed with Sheila. Somewhere in the middle of the night, his cell phone rang. He opened it, brought it into the bathroom and closed the door.

"Sorry for getting you up," said Quigley. "But I thought you'd want to know. We've got the Germans. They ran the barricades in Marystown when they spotted our guys but crashed into a pole shortly afterward."

"We told them the roads were bad," said Windflower. "How are they?"

"It's hard to believe, but they're both fine. Beat up a little and tons of scrapes and scratches, but according to reports from the scene, they're going to be okay," said Quigley.

"That's good," said Windflower. "Anything back on tracking that package that went overboard?"

"Not yet, but our patrol boat will be out again tomorrow," said Quigley. "The weather has been so bad that nobody has been able to get out there. And how did my undercover apprentices do?"

"They had a poor start but picked it up," said Windflower. "There might be some salvation there."

"Good," said Quigley. "I'm going to keep them on the team for now. I thought that they could split up and cover the land along the coast. What do you think?"

"Maybe," said Windflower. "But that's a lot of coastline to cover. If you have two vehicles, I would suggest one from Point May to Allen's Island and the other between Lord's Cove and Lawn. That's where we've been picking up smugglers over the last few years."

"I remember that now," said Quigley. "Good advice. I also need your help with another part of the case."

"What's that?" asked Windflower.

"I want you to interview our two German guests. In Marystown," said Quigley. "With someone."

"But I don't speak German," said Windflower. "Not Beulah?"

Quigley laughed. "No, not Beulah. Smithson. Did you know he spoke German?"

"I don't think I did," said Windflower. "But somehow I'm not surprised. He is an interesting young man. I guess I can do it with his assistance."

"Great," said Quigley. "I'll let Bill Ford know that you will be interviewing Riis and Schüller as soon as they're in fit condition. Probably tomorrow, is that okay?"

"Sure," said Windflower. "Get Bill to give me a call. You might also want to let Tizzard know. He's feeling a little left out right now."

"I thought he had enough on his hands," said Quigley. "The corporal 'doth protest too much, methinks.'"

"'Our wills and fates do so contrary run, that our devices still are overthrown; our thoughts are ours, their ends none of our own,'" replied Windflower.

"Nice," said Quigley. "A little Hamlet to say goodnight. Thank you, Winston."

"Talk soon," said Windflower. "Now, if you'll excuse me, I have a pillow with my name on it." He hung up and as quietly as he could slipped back in bed beside Sheila. He was soon out cold.

Chapter Thirty-five

Eddie Tizzard still had the night ahead of him, but he didn't really mind that. Despite the fact that he was tired, he loved the peace of the RCMP detachment at night. He went out soon after and pushed the barricades at the entrance of town farther to the side. That danger had certainly passed. He ran his Jeep slowly out over the hills and bends near Grand Bank until he came to the barrens.

Out here, there was nothing but him and nature. Tonight, the moon was hidden behind thick clouds, so the only light was from his vehicle. He turned that off and sat in the almost perfect darkness. It was strange, but he didn't feel alone. He could feel all of the other creatures, large and small, that lived out here. He could still feel the warmth of the spirits of the humans he had interacted with most recently.

He could also sense the presence of something else. Something different. Maybe it was the wind or the darkness itself. Or maybe it was just a feeling. But he certainly felt it, and its company stayed with him as he started his car and drove towards Garnish. He was not a religious man, but it really did feel like he had been touched by a power greater than himself. He didn't feel afraid of this power. In fact, he felt comforted somehow. He also knew, without knowing how he knew, that he didn't have to understand this power. All he had to do was accept it. Once he did, he felt even better.

On his drive back from the end of his highway tour, he paused around the same spot and said a silent prayer of thanks. It seemed like the right thing to do. He wasn't quite sure who or what he was praying to or about. But after doing it, he felt great. And he had more energy to complete his shift. He wasn't sure what had happened to him, but he was going to run with it. Maybe he could talk to his dad about this experience.

Richard wasn't religious either. He'd left the religion of his youth a long time ago and wasn't going back any time soon. But he'd been studying Eastern religions and traditions for a while now, and part of that journey had been to read and try to interpret some of Tagore's writing. He'd often quote the Bengali poet to his son. One about faith came to Eddie Tizzard's mind right now: "Faith is the bird that feels the light and sings when the dawn is still dark."

He would definitely talk to his dad about this later, he thought as he came back into Grand Bank and parked in front of the detachment. But before anything else, he needed a snack.

When Windflower woke again, it was to a much more pleasant sound than the harsh ringing of his cell phone. He could hear Stella and Amelia Louise singing a song they'd made up, or at least it sounded made up, in one of the other bedrooms. Sheila was still sleeping peacefully beside him.

Saturday morning was one of his favourite times of the week. Usually, he got to sleep in, but seeing how serene Sheila looked, he decided to get up with the girls. He would have to leave for part of the day to go to Marystown anyway. He checked his phone, but there were no messages, so he padded over to the other side to check out the activity. He peeked into Amelia Louise's room, but nobody was there. He could hear them next door.

He soon figured out that they were playing *American Idol*, with Stella and Amelia Louise being the judges. They had arrayed all their dolls against one wall of the bedroom, and one by one they picked one out and then each pretended to sing a song for them. Stella had quite a versatile choice of songs, but Amelia Louise only really had two, "Twinkle, Twinkle, Little Star" and "Let It Go" from the *Frozen* movie.

After the singing, the other got to be the judge and make comments. Once again, Stella had a variety of comments, which wasn't surprising, since her younger sister usually fell asleep before the show was over. Stella would say things like "I love your voice or "Come back next year," or even "You're going to the Top Ten." From Amelia Louise, her comment was always "You are amaaaaaazing." The third time Windflower heard that one, he couldn't help but laugh a little out loud. The girls grabbed him and pulled him into their game.

He agreed to play, but only if they did it downstairs and he was allowed to make some coffee. The girls conferred and agreed to his conditions. They took as many dolls as they could carry and brought them downstairs to the living room to get set up. Windflower closed his bedroom door to try to give Sheila a break and went to the kitchen to put the coffee on. He let Lady out into the backyard and checked the weather.

Cool and damp this morning, with a light frost on the windows. But the possibilities of a nice weather day. But it was early, and around here that could and did change quickly. He brought Lady in, took the first early drips of coffee and went to join the girls. Of course, he was now a judge in their game, too. "But don't be mean like Simon," said Stella. Windflower promised he wouldn't, and while he sipped his coffee and then got another cup, he passed a splendid hour of fun and entertainment with two of his favourite people in the world.

He finally begged off and walked upstairs to see Sheila and bring her a cup of coffee.

"I thought I heard you up," he said.

"Thank you," said Sheila as she took the cup of coffee. "And thank you for the break. I needed it. But this is your morning to sleep in."

"I have to go to Marystown," he said.

"That's too bad," said Sheila. "Did they catch the bad guys you were talking about last night?"

"Yeah, they're in Marystown," said Windflower. "Ron Quigley wants me to interview them."

"What time do you have to go?" she asked.

"As soon as I get the word," said Windflower. "But not before I make waffles."

"I love a man who can cook," said Sheila. "Do you want me to get up to look after the girls? You might struggle a bit with only one good hand."

"Nah," said Windflower. "I'll be fine. I'll get them to help me."

"Good luck with that," said Sheila as Windflower went back downstairs.

Sheila turned out to be right. The girls helping degenerated into a screaming, pouting, foot-stamping event that got both girls sent to their rooms until Windflower finished breakfast. When he got the first batch ready, he called them out, and they came back down as if nothing had happened, ready to start over completely fresh. We could learn from that, thought Windflower as he called Sheila to share the next waffle.

Eddie Tizzard was sitting outside the Mug-Up waiting for Herb Stoodley to open up. He was starving and nearly cried when he saw Herb's van pull up in front of the café.

"How long have you been here?" asked Stoodley.

"Not long, just waiting for breakfast," said Tizzard.

"Well, you're right on time," said Stoodley. "Come in and I'll put the coffee on. You can keep me company while I make your breakfast. I assume you want the usual."

"Yes," said Tizzard. "Two eggs, bologna, home fries and beans if you have them."

"Whole wheat toast?" asked Stoodley.

"I'll have an extra order of toast, too, please," said Tizzard.

"You're a hungry boy," said Herb. "Busy last night?"

"Not overnight, thank goodness," said Tizzard. "But after two emergencies in one week, I don't think we could take much more."

"Do you know if our German visitors are coming over for breakfast this morning?" asked Stoodley.

"They're gone, b'y," said Tizzard. "Took off in the middle of the night."

Stoodley gave Tizzard a cup of coffee and took one for himself while he was waiting for the home fries to warm up. "Too bad," said Stoodley. "They were good tippers. Are they in trouble or something?"

"Don't ask me," said Tizzard. "I'm just the local copper. But I hear they were involved in an accident near Marystown."

"Well, I hope they're okay," said Stoodley. "Your breakfast is about ready. Go take a seat and I'll bring it over."

Chapter Thirty-six

A few minutes later, he delivered as promised and Tizzard dug in. Stoodley got the coffee pot and refilled their cups and then came back to sit with his breakfast customer.

"You know we really appreciate everything you do around here," said Stoodley. "We know we're lucky to have people of your quality looking after us."

"Thank you, Herb, that's very nice of you to say," said Tizzard, pausing momentarily from his breakfast. "I know that. Maybe I'm just getting a bit tired and worn down these days."

Stoodley left him to finish his breakfast and went to help the next customers who came in, an older couple who smiled at Tizzard as they sat at a table across from him. He smiled back and went to the cash to pay his bill.

"On the house," said Herb Stoodley. "Thank you for your service to the community, Corporal."

"Thank you, Herb," said Tizzard. "You are very kind."

"'I can no answer make, but, thanks, and thanks,'" said Stoodley.

Tizzard nodded to Stoodley, and as he was leaving the older couple waved to him. "Gratitude, gratitude," he said to himself as he left the café and walked to his car. He was on his way back to the detachment when his phone rang. He pulled over and answered his cell phone. It was Bill Ford.

"They'd like to have Smithson go to Marystown today," said Ford. "They need him to translate for Windflower."

"The Germans?" asked Tizzard.

"We've got them both here," said Ford. "Can he do it?"

"I'll give him a call," said Tizzard. "It's his day off, but I'm sure he'd jump at an adventure."

"You used to be like that, too," said Ford.

"I'm an old hand now," said Tizzard. "'Life is as tedious as a twice-told tale.'"

"Oh my God," said Ford. "Now you're quoting Shakespeare too. Let me know about Smithson. I'm assuming he's a yes. I'm calling Windflower now."

Tizzard hung up and drove to the detachment. Carrie's car was out front.

"Morning," said Tizzard, giving her a peck on the cheek.

"Good morning, my love," said Evanchuk. "Everything okay on the night shift?"

"Cool," said Tizzard. "Is Hughie at Margaret's?"

"Yeah, I just dropped him off," said Evanchuk. "I said you'd be over to get him whenever you get up later."

"Perfect," said Tizzard. "Oh yeah, I guess the Germans took off last night but crashed their van. They're okay, and Windflower is going over to Marystown to interview them. I have to call Smithson to tag along as interpreter."

"He'll like that," said Evanchuk.

"I bet he will," said Tizzard.

Windflower knew what the call was about before he answered it. Luckily, they'd finished breakfast and had moved on to a group game of Jenga. Amelia Louise had just crashed the tower, again, as he went to the kitchen to take the call.

"Morning, Winston," said Bill Ford. "We're ready when you are to interview our friends."

"What kind of shape are they in?" asked Windflower.

"I looked in on them a little while ago, and they were both sleeping like babies," said Ford. "They both had painkillers last night, so I expect they'll be stiff and sore when they wake up."

"And grumpy," said Windflower. "Is Smithson on?"

"I just talked to Tizzard," said Ford. "He'll be happy to go, I'm sure."

"Okay," said Windflower. "We'll be over right after lunch."

His next call was from Smithson. "When do you want to go?" he asked Windflower.

"Let's go around noon," said Windflower. "You're up early on your day off."

165

"I just got the call and wanted to let you I'm ready when you are," said Smithson. "It'll be a bit of an adventure."

"Yeah," said Windflower. "Pick me up at noon."

"We've got a couple of hours," he said to Sheila. "Smithson is picking me up. He's very excited about going to Marystown."

"He's young," said Sheila. "Going to Marystown is a break, something different. Plus, he gets to go with you."

"That's nice," said Windflower as he was surrounded by his daughters.

"Pleeze, Daddy," said Amelia Louise.

"We need you for our game," said Stella. The girls each grabbed one of Windflower's arms and pulled him into the living room.

"Great," said Sheila. "You play that game, and I'll go get groceries."

Windflower looked at her pleadingly, but Sheila grabbed her purse and car keys and was out the door in a flash.

"Okay, prisoner," said Stella.

"Yeah, prissner," said Amelia Louise.

"I was afraid of this," said Windflower.

Eddie Tizzard wasn't afraid at all. But maybe he should be. He was clearly in a dream. That much was for sure. But he was also flying. Without a plane. And he wasn't afraid at all. Somehow this was the most exciting and yet calming experience he'd ever had. He was high above the clouds, floating through the world. He decided to see if he could dip down below the clouds to see what was underneath all that white stuff.

He dipped his arms and started drifting downward, and the clouds kind of parted before him. Like he was slicing through smoke or vapours. Soon, he could see something far below him. The farther he dipped, the more he could see. He could make out some shapes on the ground. He was flying over Grand Bank. He looked for familiar landmarks. There was the lighthouse and the wharf with the fish plant on the other side.

He flew a little farther and saw the town hall and the high school and then the supermarket and the clinic. But no people. Not a single person in all of Grand Bank on a clear Saturday morning. Where were all the people? He flew over the Cape, the large outcropping of cliff that towered over Grand Bank and looked out to the islands of Saint-Pierre and Miquelon across the way. He managed to land on top of the Cape and stood on the highest point to get his bearings.

He was standing there with the wind blowing in his hair when a large seagull plopped down beside him. He looked at the gull, and the gull stared back at him.

Finally, the gull spoke. "I like the view up here on a nice day. You can see across the water and down into town as well. My family used to fish over there, on Brunette Island."

Tizzard thought he recognized the voice.

"Yeah, it's me, Sid Skinner," said the gull. "Amazing, eh, this ability to fly? People make fun of seagulls all the time, but I like this life, er, death, whatever it is. I can be a seal or a fish or a bird. Pretty neat, isn't it?"

Tizzard had to admit it was pretty neat.

The seagull, Sid Skinner, was in a talkative mood. "There were three hundred people over on the island at one time. That's before our family got resettled in the 1950s. My grandfather would still climb up here in his eighties to look over and talk about the old days."

"That's pretty sad," said Tizzard. "Our family had to move off Ramea when the cod fishery collapsed."

"I know," said the gull. "Thanks for talking with my wife. I appreciate that. In return, I will grant you one favour."

"Are you allowed to do that over there?" asked Tizzard. Then he thought about it some more and started making a long list of things he wanted in his head.

"Be careful what you wish for," said the gull.

Tizzard thought again. Somehow, all those thoughts of money and a new house and trips to exotic places just vanished, and he came back to his senses. "Is Paddy Slaney alive?" he asked.

"Yes," squawked the seagull, and he flew off. Tizzard tried calling out, but soon all he could see was a flash of white, and the bird was gone. Before he could do anything else he found himself being pushed by the wind closer and closer to the edge of the cliff until he suddenly fell over and was falling, falling, falling. Until he hit his bed and woke with a start.

Chapter Thirty-seven

He jumped involuntarily and went to the bathroom to splash some water on his face. He looked in the mirror and could see that he was still alive. And that he looked very tired. He went back to bed and tried to go back to sleep. But that idea had passed. What didn't was the idea that the seagull or Sid Skinner or whatever that was had planted in his brain. Paddy Slaney was alive. He wanted to go and run and tell somebody. But maybe that wasn't the best approach, at least until he had some actual proof of this theory told to him by a talking sea gull.

It was something, though, and even if it was just hope, Tizzard clung to it and held it close. He lay awake in bed, thinking about what seemed impossible a few hours ago. Paddy Slaney isn't dead. His next thought was, if he wasn't dead, then where on earth was Paddy Slaney?

Smithson came by to pick up Windflower right at noon. He managed to get away from the grasp of his daughters, kissed Sheila, and ran out to the car before he could be taken "prissner" again.

Smithson drove slowly through town and out to the highway. The two men had exchanged niceties, but neither seemed in a big mood to talk. Windflower reached into his bag and pulled out the CD that Herb Stoodley have given him.

"You mind?"

"Not at all," said Smithson.

They listened to the music together as they travelled out through Grand Bank proper and then into the countryside. The piano concerto was the perfect accompaniment to the vast emptiness of the landscape, and it carried them along past the Garnish turnoff and then into the outskirts of Marystown.

"That was quite nice," said Smithson. "I always liked Rachmaninoff. He is such a polished composer."

"He should be," sad Windflower. "He started piano lessons when he was four."

"Apparently, he also had the largest hands in classical music history," said Smithson. "They said his hands could span an octave and a half on the piano."

"No wonder he was so good," said Windflower. "Did you play the piano?"

"Not my instrument. Too much practice," said Smithson. "But I always admired piano players. Even the modern ones like Jerry Lee Lewis. He once said his fingers had brains in them. 'You don't tell them what to do—they do it.'"

"That's funny," said Windflower as they came into Marystown. "Let's stop at Tim Hortons. I wouldn't mind getting a bagel and a coffee. You hungry?"

"I could eat," said Smithson.

"Great," said Windflower as Smithson turned into the parking lot and they walked into the café. "I'll call Inspector Ford once we order."

"What do you want?" asked Smithson. "I'll order while you make the call."

"Thanks," said Windflower. "I'll take an everything bagel, toasted with butter and two slices of cheddar cheese and a large black coffee." He got them a table and called Bill Ford.

"We're at Tim Hortons," said Windflower. "We can be over there in twenty minutes."

"Perfect," said Ford. "Do you have a preference for who goes first? Riis or Schüller?"

"Nope," said Windflower. "Surprise me."

Smithson was back soon after with the bagels and coffee. Windflower offered him five bucks, but he turned it down.

"My treat," he said.

"Thanks," said Windflower.

Both men enjoyed their meal and coffee and sitting at a table by the window, watching the steady parade of cars and pickup trucks move through the never-ending drive-through.

"It's always busy here," said Smithson. "No matter when you come."

"People love their coffee," said Windflower. "In St. John's they've had to pass a by-law restricting drive-throughs because they're interfering with traffic. Lots of cops I know would love to retire and operate one themselves."

"Not me," said Smithson. "I want to explore. See the world. Or at least as much of it as I can."

"You're young," said Windflower. "Your priorities change when you get older."

"I think I'll always want adventure," said Smithson.

"Try having two kids," said Windflower. "That's an adventure and a half. Let's go do our work."

They drove the short distance to the RCMP building in Marystown and parked out front. Windflower knew the way to Bill Ford's office, and Smithson tagged along behind. They said hello to Ford's admin person and waited for Ford to come out of his office.

"Sorry," he said. "Dealing with HQ," he said. "I'll fill you in along the way." They walked to the basement, where Ford gave the duty officer directions to bring Riis up to Interview Room C.

Inside the interview room, Ford gave them an update on what he heard from the higher-ups. "They've got Gerhard Müller in Europe," he said. "But they need something from our guys here to tie him to the package that we believe is floating in the water somewhere between Newfoundland and Saint-Pierre. They'd also like to know about Grimsby, although they fear the worst. Finally, they would like to see if these two know anything about Ewe Meeir."

"No pressure," said Windflower. "Did they give us anything to offer in return for them spilling the beans on their boss and incriminating themselves?"

"Surprisingly, yes," said Ford. "I have been told that you have the authority to offer them full immunity and witness protection for evidence that will lead us to the recovery of the drugs and can directly link Gerhard Müller to the package."

"Wow," said Windflower. "They must be desperate to get that Müller guy."

"They're getting tons of pressure from the Americans. You know what they're like. And as soon we squeeze them as hard as we can, we have to turn them over to the Europeans. The French, Dutch, Germans and Interpol all want them."

"Popular people," said Windflower as there was a knock on the door. "That must be our friend Riis."

Chapter Thirty-eight

An RCMP constable ushered the prisoner into the room. Ford led the man to a seat opposite Windflower and Smithson and left with the other officer. He would watch the interview on the other side of the one-way mirror.

Ulrich Riis looked to be somewhere is his late twenties. He was of slim build, with a stubbly beard and what Windflower thought were beady eyes. Then he saw the crack in his John Lennon-style glasses and realized the man was squinting. He had a bandage on his hand, and as Windflower looked closer, he could see bruising on the side of Riis's head from the accident.

"Good morning. I'm Winston Windflower and this is Constable Smithson. We have some questions for you," said Windflower. He nodded to Smithson who repeated his words to Riis. There was no response from the prisoner.

"I was on the ferry, if you remember," said Windflower. He paused to let Smithson translate. "I saw you and your friend throw the package overboard." Smithson translated, but still nothing from Riis. In fact, he was now rubbing his arm and staring at the floor.

"Okay," said Windflower. "I have a limited time offer. I can get you completely off with everything and get you access to the RCMP witness protection program. But you have one hour to decide. I'm going to make the same offer to your friend. Maybe he'll be more eager to play the get-out-of-jail-free card."

Smithson had waited until Windflower finished and then tried to translate what he heard into German. He struggled a little with the "get-out-of-jail-free" concept, but Windflower heard the word "freiheit" and assumed that his amateur translator had got the message across. Riis stayed mum, although Windflower noticed that he did pay a little more attention to the last couple of words from Smithson.

"Okay, we're done for now," said Windflower. He walked to the door and opened it. "You can take this man back to his cell, Constable. And we'll have Schüller now. Thank you."

Bill Ford came back into the room. "Not much there," he said.

"Early days," said Windflower. "Let's see if we can play one off against the other. They're being kept separate, right?"

"On separate floors with a guard outside their door," said Ford as there was another knock on the door. Hendrik Schüller was led in and limped towards the table, where the constable helped him into his seat.

After Ford and the other officer left, Windflower sat for a moment to size up the new prisoner. Schüller was tall and lanky, with long, stringy hair. He glanced at Windflower and then quickly averted his eyes. His face was covered in cuts, some small and some fairly big gouges. He was lucky, thought Windflower. At least a piece of the windshield had caught him on impact. He had the tell-tale bruises as well of a fully operationalized air bag.

Despite the physical damage, Schüller seemed rather nonchalant about sitting in a jail in what for him was the absolute middle of nowhere. He had a half-smile that spoke a little about entitlement or privilege, or maybe a combination of both, thought Windflower.

"So, your friend has told us a lot about your operations," said Windflower, turning to Smithson for translation. Smithson had just started when Schüller put up a hand to stop him. "We don't need that," he said in English with just a hint of a German accent. "His German hurts my ears."

Smithson started to say something, but Windflower slowed him down. "That's great. We can move much faster. As I was saying—" Schüller interrupted again.

"I want a lawyer. I know my rights," said Schüller.

"I don't believe you understand the predicament you are in right now," said Windflower. "You are a German citizen in a Canadian jail, with some very serious charges pending against you. You have no rights. If you want, I will advise the German embassy in Ottawa that you are being held in custody. Or you can hang around for the Americans or the Dutch. They all want you. Or you

174

and I can have a friendly chat, and if you can corroborate what your friend Riis had to say, then maybe you can get a similar deal to the one that he has."

"What kind of deal?" asked Schüller.

Those were the magic words to Windflower. He knew that once he had someone asking him questions about a deal, they were halfway there.

"I'll give you the same offer as I gave Riis," said Windflower. "Immunity and witness protection, but we want everything about Gerhard Müller and your involvement, and we want that last package you threw overboard."

"We lost contact with the package," said Schüller, slipping further into Windflower's tentacles. "That's gone. Can I still get the deal?"

"That depends on what you have to say," said Windflower. "What was the plan for the package?"

"It had a tracker on it, and Müller hired a local fisherman to get it and bring it into Canadian waters," said Schüller. "He was then supposed to leave it in a cove, and me and Riis were supposed to pick it up and drive it back to the mainland. Somebody else was taking it over the border to Chicago."

"But you two panicked and took off?" asked Windflower.

"We could feel the heat," said Schüller. "We knew you were a cop right from the first time we saw you. And those two goofs in the car outside the B&B were a joke."

"Where were you supposed to meet the fisherman?" asked Windflower.

"Some place that begins with an L," said Schüller. "But I don't remember it. It was on a piece of paper in the van."

"My colleague here will take your initial statement," said Windflower. "If things check out, I will forward the info to my superiors along with your request." He left Schüller with Smithson and went to talk with Bill Ford.

"We're moving," he said when he saw Ford. "Did you get all that?"

"Yeah," said Ford. "Good work. What's next?"

"Where's their van?" asked Windflower.

"It's in the impound."

"Get somebody over there and get them to search everything," said Windflower. "We're looking for a piece of paper with a location that begins with L. Maybe it'll have somebody's name on it as well. That would be even better."

"I'm on it," said Ford.

"Okay," said Windflower. "I'll call Quigley."

Ron Quigley was pretty excited about Windflower's news. "That's super. But we have to move quickly now. The word is that the Americans want our two guests for a case they're making down there, and we know when they want something, they usually get it."

"If we can find out where the package is being brought to, we may still be able to retrieve it," said Windflower. "Bill's trying to find that now."

"Great," said Quigley. "Listen, maybe if you get the place and the name, we could get Schüller to arrange a meet."

"Sure," said Windflower. "We'd have a better chance of getting the stuff back that way. Should I still try to get Riis? We may not need him anymore."

"You might as well," said Quigley. "You never know what these guys will say, especially about each other. Did you get anything about Grimsby?"

"I didn't even ask," said Windflower. "I'll go back to both of them on this."

"Ask them about the German that was found on the highway as well," said Quigley. "Ewe Meeir."

"Will do."

He walked back into the interview room. Schüller was back talking in German, and Smithson was feverishly trying to write it all down in English. They both looked up at Windflower, as if he had interrupted a secret mission or something.

"We will need some more info," said Windflower. "What happened to Grimsby?"

"I don't know anybody by that name," said Schüller.

"Your friend with the red beard."

"You mean Weber?" asked Schüller. "I honestly didn't know his other name. He got found out by Müller and was disposed of."

"What do you mean by disposed of?" asked Windflower, a little shocked at the callousness of the response. And once again woken to the fact that despite their innocuous looks, Schüller and his associates were cold-blooded criminals running a massive international drug smuggling ring. He paused for a moment to collect himself.

"We'll need to know everything you know about this," said Windflower. "Who did the disposing, by the way?"

"Müller," said Schüller. "He insisted on taking care of internal matters personally."

"Write that down," said Windflower to Smithson. "Tell Smithson everything you know about Grimsby and what happened." Then he paused again. "And if you know where we can find his remains."

Schüller nodded. Smithson just sat there with his mouth wide open.

Chapter Thirty-nine

Windflower gulped and continued. "What about Ewe Meeir?"

"Same thing," said Schüller. "It was Müller. Him and Meeir were close, really close. But he thought that Meeir was getting too far into sampling the product. He said it was bad for business."

"I want you to document that, too," said Windflower. This time Smithson nodded. "I'll be back."

Windflower needed a break. He walked upstairs and out through the front door. He started walking and didn't stop until he was almost out of town. He stopped by the park near the entrance to what could be called downtown Marystown and watched as a parade of ducks came swimming towards him. They were hoping for some lunch, but he had nothing to offer them. They squawked loudly and swam back across the pond, where a couple was coming back from a walk through the woods.

That cheered him a little, and he needed it. Once again, he was reminded of the harsh nature of police work and how little he had missed that part. But just being by the water helped to refresh and almost rejuvenate him. He took one more big breath of the brisk afternoon air and went back to the detachment.

When he got back to the interview room, Bill Ford was waiting for him. "We took Schüller back to his cell. Young Smithson needed a break, too."

"Can't say as I blame him," said Windflower. "It's tough, especially hearing about another officer."

"Yeah," said Ford. "But you know that we're the only ones standing in between them and total chaos."

"I know," said Windflower. "But it's still hard. Let's get the other guy back in here." While Ford went to call up Riis, Windflower walked outside to find Smithson. He was coming around the side of the building.

"I was getting some air," said Smithson.

"I had to get out for a few minutes, too," said Windflower. "Are you okay?"

"Not really," said Smithson. "But I will be. I have been learning about vicarious trauma and how to deal with it. I have an online counsellor now, and I try to talk to her about it whenever it comes up."

"That's really good," said Windflower. "I find physical activity works for me, too. Having a dog helps."

Smithson smiled. "I think I'm going to get a dog in my next posting. For now, it'll have to be yoga and breathing exercises."

"Are you going to apply for a specific posting?" asked Windflower. "Back closer to Ontario?"

"I hope so," said Smithson. "My dad has passed, but my mom is still alive. I would like to be closer if I could. Maybe Manitoba."

"Good luck with that," said Windflower. "Let's go finish this off." He and Smithson walked downstairs and into the interview room, where Riis was sitting with the RCMP escort. Windflower nodded his thanks to the officer and sat in front of Riis.

"Ich habe dir nichts zu sagen," said Riis. Then he sat back in his chair and folded his arms.

"Constable, can you read a little bit of what his friend Schüller had to say?" said Windflower to Smithson.

Smithson started to read from his notes, and Riis sat up a little straighter in his chair. Windflower let him go on for a little while and then asked him to stop.

"Your friend was quite helpful in describing the operation and in particular your role in it," said Windflower. "And yes, he got a deal. Unfortunately, that option is no longer open to you, and I will be advising the Americans that they can come pick you up at their convenience. Goodbye, Herr Riis."

"Wait, wait," said Riis.

"Oh, now you can speak English. Thank you," said Windflower.

"I can tell you who killed the cop," said Riis.

"Start talking," said Windflower.

"I want a deal," said Riis.

"Tell me and take your chances," said Windflower.

"It was Schüller," said Riis. "He was Müller's hit man. He did Meeir, too."

"Tell me about Weber," said Windflower. "Smithson will write it down. Go."

* * *

Tizzard shook himself awake and jumped in the shower to try to shake off the drowsiness he still felt, despite his sleep. He made himself a sandwich and then drove to his sister Margaret's to pick up Hughie. She was giving Hughie a bottle but handed him over when Eddie came by. At first, the baby screamed when he temporarily lost his bottle, but almost smiled when he saw his dad. At least that was Tizzard's interpretation.

After the feeding, he thanked his sister for her help and drove over to visit his dad. Richard Tizzard was happy to see both his son and grandson and put on the kettle to make some tea and enjoy their company.

"Do you ever have dreams?" asked Tizzard.

"Sometimes," said Richard.

"Do you remember them? Are they like kind of real?" asked Tizzard.

"Most of my dreams these days are about the past," said his father. "Your mom often comes to me in my dreams now. But when I was younger I used to have more of them. It seems to me looking back that whenever there was a big change happening in my life, they would happen more often. Those dreams were very real. But I have to say that I almost never understood them until what I dreamt about came true."

"That's interesting," said Eddie as he rocked little Hughie in his car seat chair. "My dreams seem to be about other people these days. Even cases I'm working on."

"That doesn't mean they're not about you," said Richard. "It's your dreamworld. It has to be at least a part about you, even as it might seem to be all about somebody or something else."

"Hmmm," said Tizzard as he looked down to see Hughie dozing off. "I better get this little guy home," he said. "Thanks, Dad."

"I don't know what you're thanking me for, but you're welcome," said Richard. "Enjoy the rest of the day. Unless you have other plans."

Eddie laughed at his dad's corny joke and left for home with Hughie. He laid his son in his crib and called in to Betsy to see what was happening at work. Not too much, according to Betsy. That was fine with Tizzard.

"Is Smithson back yet?" he asked.

"No, he's still in Marystown," said Betsy. "I can message him if you'd like to find out when he will be coming back."

"Thanks, Betsy," said Tizzard. "Ask him to call me."

Chapter Forty

Tizzard hung up, and for the first time in a long time, he had a few hours off and nothing that he had to do. He made himself some more tea and found a package of cookies in the freezer. He found the latest issue of the local rag, the *Southern Gazette*, and started reading. A big ad from the Grand Bank Council was in the middle of the paper, with a link to an online petition. "Save Our RCMP" was the headline in large block letters. We could use a bit of saving, thought Tizzard as he opened the cookies and enjoyed a brief respite from his normally hectic schedule.

Back in Marystown, Smithson's phone pinged with the message from Betsy, but he was still actively engaged in taking the statement from Ulrich Riis. Windflower had stepped out again to confer with Bill Ford and to give Quigley another update. He came back into the interview room as Smithson and Riis were finishing up. Before Riis went back to his cell, Windflower asked him about the fisherman they were supposed to meet.

"Do you remember his name or where you were going to meet him?" asked Windflower.

Riis shook his head. "I don't remember the guy's name, but the place was Lama something."

"Lamaline?" asked Windflower.

"Yeah, that's it," said Riis.

As Riis was led away, Bill Ford came rushing in to talk to Windflower. "We've got a name," he shouted. "Kevin Edwards in Lamaline."

"Riis just confirmed it's Lamaline," said Windflower. "Call Quigley again and let him know. Plus, your guys are over in the area. Smithson and I are going to head back. He'll leave his notes, and if you need to talk to us, you know how to get us."

"I suspect the bigwigs will want to take over now," said Ford. "That's fine with me."

Windflower and Smithson started to leave when Windflower's phone rang. It was Ron Quigley. Windflower put him on speakerphone and gave him the latest info from the interviews. Ford told him what he had just found out.

"Do you have a phone number for that Edwards guy?" asked Quigley.

"Yeah. Do you want it?" asked Ford.

"I was thinking that we could get Riis to set up a meeting and arrange to pick up the package," said Quigley. "Can you arrange all that, Winston?"

"We probably could," said Windflower. "Can we take Riis back with us and let him stay in Grand Bank tonight?"

"Bill, can you let Elliston and Williams stay with him tonight?" asked Quigley.

"Sure," said Ford. "I'll send an escort over with him, and you let them know to meet Windflower in Grand Bank."

Smithson and Windflower drove around to the back of the building, where Riis was put in their car. They waited until another RCMP cruiser came out of the parking lot and flashed the lights at them.

"Can you drive?" asked Smithson once he made sure that their prisoner was secure in the back seat. "With your hand and all. I have to call Tizzard."

"Sure," said Windflower. "I'm not an invalid." He pulled out of the lot and started towards the highway with their escort car trailing closely behind. Near the Shoppers Drug Mart, Windflower saw a familiar sight. He pulled off the road and parked next to a red truck, where a man was handing over a plastic bag to another person.

"The fish man," said Windflower. He walked over and asked what the freshest fish was today.

"It's all fresh, b'y," said the man in the truck. "But I would recommend the halibut. Came in on the truck last night. It looks gorgeous."

"I'll take two large steaks, if you got them," said Windflower.

The man went to a large white freezer and pulled out a large chunk of halibut. He took a knife and quickly sliced off two nice-sized chunks of fish. "How are dese, b'y?" he asked Windflower, holding them up, one in each hand.

"Perfect, my friend," said Windflower. "Wrap 'em up."

While the fishmonger was wrapping his fish, Windflower called Sheila. "I've got some halibut."

"That's great," said Sheila. "Get enough for us and the Sanjays tomorrow night. I thought we'd get pizza tonight." Windflower could hear his girls yelling "pizza, pizza" in the background.

"Better give me another big piece," he said to the man who was handing him his original order.

"No problem, b'y," said the man and quickly wrapped the other piece of halibut. Windflower paid while chatting with Sheila and promised to be home soon. "That would be good," she said. "I'll need a little break."

"No worries," said Windflower. "See you in a couple of hours."

Back in the car, Smithson was talking with Tizzard, and it didn't seem to be going that well. Smithson put his phone on speaker so Windflower could hear as well. "What do you mean you're bringing a prisoner back with you?"

"Eddie, it's me, Winston," interrupted Windflower. "Sorry for not letting you know before. This is all happening at short notice. We're bringing back one of the Germans, just for one night. Bill Ford has assigned Elliston and Williams to look after him tonight, so you don't have to do anything."

"Why am I the last to know about stuff that's happening in my own shop?" asked Tizzard, sounding a little aggrieved.

"Things move fast, sometimes, Eddie, you know that," said Windflower. "It's not about you, or me for that matter. We're just pawns in this big game." Tizzard was quiet, and Windflower took the opportunity to try to smooth the waters. "Listen, we've got a big sting operation moving with Riis and a guy in Lamaline. Why don't you come along with me? It'll be like old times."

Tizzard liked that idea, a lot, despite his annoyance and perceived injustices. "When will it happen?"

"Probably tomorrow morning," said Windflower. "Smithson can cover off the detachment and you come with me. Okay?"

"Okay," said Tizzard.

"See you soon," said Windflower.

"That was cool," said Smithson. "You brought him right around. He's under a lot of pressure these days. We all are, really. But Eddie, I mean Corporal Tizzard, takes it so hard."

"We all need some support," said Windflower. "And to know that what we do is appreciated. Most people take what you do every day for granted. Until they really need you. Now, enough work talk. Let's listen to that CD again. It's in my bag."

Smithson fished the Rachmaninoff CD out and popped it into the player. The two men enjoyed the music and the scenery and didn't talk again until Windflower came closer to Grand Bank.

"You want me to drop you off home to get changed or anything?" Windflower asked.

"No, I'll just keep on going right now," said Smithson. "I'll get a break later. Besides, I've still got to do some more research."

"What are you working on?" asked Windflower.

"We're looking for Paddy Slaney," said Smithson.

"I know that," said Windflower as he took the first exit into Grand Bank and drove towards the detachment.

"I mean we're expanding our search," said Smithson. "There might be an international connection."

"Really?" said Windflower.

"Yeah," said Smithson. "Sid Skinner's nephew is in jail down south for drug smuggling, so we're looking to see if Slaney shows up on the international radar."

"Good luck with that," said Windflower as he parked the car. "Let's get our guy inside."

Chapter Forty-one

With the other two RCMP officers as sentries, they brought Riis into the detachment and put him in a cell. Windflower and Smithson went back outside and shook hands with their colleagues who were heading back to Marystown. Eddie Tizzard was coming down the hallway when they came back in.

"He doesn't look like much," said Tizzard.

"He may be the key to a massive drug bust," said Windflower. "Let's get some coffee and go talk to him."

Smithson went off to do his Internet searching while Tizzard and Windflower approached Ulrich Riis's cell. "We'd like you to set up a meeting with the fisherman to retrieve the package," said Windflower.

"What's in it for me?" asked Riis. "So far, all I have is your promises. I want a guarantee now. No prosecution and a new identity, like you said. And a hundred thousand dollars, American."

"I can't do that," said Windflower. "Not the money, that's for sure."

"Well, find someone who can," said Riis. "And I want my agreement in writing."

Windflower walked away from Riis and into Tizzard's office.

"What are you going to do?" asked Tizzard.

"Make it somebody else's problem," said Windflower. He called Ron Quigley.

"Let me ask about the money," said Quigley. "But we're not putting it in writing. That will come later when we move him into a safer location."

"Okay, see what you can do," said Windflower. "I'm moving ahead anyway. You have a problem with that?"

"Be my guest," said Quigley.

Tizzard followed Windflower back to see Riis. "Okay. I've got the money," he said.

"Where's the paperwork?" asked Riis.

"That's coming later," said Windflower. "Will you make the call?"

"Not until I get it in writing," said Riis.

"Get Smithson," Windflower said to Tizzard, who gave him a puzzled stare but did as he was told and came back a minute later with Smithson.

Windflower handed the phone to Smithson. "Dial this number," he said, and he read the number out to Smithson. Smithson started dialling in the numbers. Before he pressed "send," Windflower stopped him.

"Last chance," said Windflower, and he asked Smithson to hand him the phone. "You may still get immunity and relocation based on your testimony, but if he makes the call, you lose the money. Your call?"

When Riis didn't move, Windflower gave the phone back to Smithson. "Wait," shouted Riis. "Give me the phone. Your little plan wouldn't have worked anyway," he said smugly. "You don't know the code word."

"But you do," said Windflower, passing over the phone.

Riis pressed "send," and it rang for a few minutes. When it was answered, Riis put it on speaker.

"Hello," said a voice at the end of the line.

"Is this Kevin Edwards?" asked Riis.

"Yes, b'y. Who's dis?" asked Edwards.

"It's Ulrich Riis. I'm calling you to collect our package. Have you got it?"

"Yes, b'y, I got it," said Edwards. "But what's da code word?"

"Adam," said Riis.

"Where you been?" asked Edwards. "I was spectin' ya yesterday. And deres two of dem Mounties hanging around the area. So we's got da be careful."

"We had a minor problem, an accident," said Riis. "How do I find you?"

187

"Meet me at da café in Lord's Cove, and we'll go from dere," said Edwards. "If the weather holds, we can go out and get it in the morning. Have ya got da rest of me money?"

"I thought you were already paid," said Riis.

"No, b'y, only half," said Edwards. "Ya owes me anudder tousand. This is dangerous work, b'y."

"Okay, I'll bring it. Nine o'clock?" asked Riis.

"Yes, b'y," said Edwards.

"Now we have to get a thousand dollars," said Windflower. "How much you got in petty cash?"

"A couple of hundred, maybe," said Tizzard.

"Well, break out the RCMP debit card," said Windflower. "We're going big-time, Eddie."

"What about me?" called Riis. "Can I get something to eat?"

Elliston and Williams were just coming in as Windflower and Tizzard were trying to figure out what to do with that request.

"Welcome, gentlemen," said Tizzard. "Your guest is ready to receive you, and he's hungry, by the way."

The two other Mounties looked a little shell-shocked but walked down the hall to see Riis.

"I've made it somebody else's problem," said Tizzard. "Learning from the best."

Windflower laughed and pretended to be offended by the comment. "'He does me double wrong that wounds me with the flatteries of his tongue.'"

"See you later, Sarge," said Tizzard.

"See you in the morning, Eddie," said Windflower. Then he remembered he didn't have a car. No worries, he could use the walk. So, too, could Amelia Louise, Stella and Lady when he got home. Another quick walk around the block, and then it was time for supper. Sheila had ordered the pizza, a large meat lover's and a plain cheese. Somehow, Amelia Louise had developed a taste for plain pizza, and Sheila was happy to have her make at least one somewhat healthy choice.

She'd made a large salad and cut up carrots and a cucumber for veggies. Windflower deposited the pies in the middle of the kitchen table when he came back from the pizza shop and everybody dug in.

Tizzard was about to go home to see Carrie when Smithson rushed into his office. "I think I may have found a trace of Paddy Slaney."

"What do you mean a trace?" asked Tizzard.

"A man named Patrick Slaney was arrested in Bogotá and then released. That's the best I can figure out. My Spanish is not as good as my German," said Smithson.

"I guess you still need a Spanish girlfriend," said Tizzard. "So, where is he now?"

"I can't follow what happened. It says 'tranferido,' which I think means transferred, but I can't figure out where," said Smithson.

"Let me try Quigley," said Tizzard. "He's in with the big Drug guys now." He called Quigley's number. "I wonder if you can do us a favour. We're tracking a local guy and think he may be mixed up with drugs in South America. Smithson's got a lead but needs some help. Anything you can do?"

Quigley thought for a moment. "The Americans might be able to help. Here's my contact at the DEA. Tell Smithson to tell him that I said to call."

"Perfect," said Tizzard as he wrote down the name and number. "Hugo Rodrigues, DEA," he said as he handed him a paper with the number that Quigley had given him. "See what he says. I'm going home, and Carrie will be back soon. Can you hang on?"

"Absolutely," said Smithson. "I've going to phone this guy right now."

Chapter Forty-two

Eddie Tizzard drove home to see his wife and baby. They were both happy to see him. Carrie was especially happy since Eddie said she didn't have to stay overnight at the detachment.

"Elliston and Williams are both there," he told Carrie. "If you do the tour around town and then a spin up to the highway, we should be good. Forward the emergency line to your cell phone, and if we get a call one of us can go."

"That is so great," said Carrie. "We almost never get a night together anymore. I'll get Hughie fed and straightened away and go right over. There's stew in the fridge that you can microwave."

"Excellent," said Eddie. "I'm starved."

Winston Windflower, on the other hand, was stuffed. He'd had two large slices of pizza, meat lovers, of course, a small helping of salad and then a piece of lemon meringue pie that Sheila had picked up from Beulah.

"This is the best pie ever," he exclaimed as he ate the last of a very large slice.

"Until the next pie you come across," said Sheila with a laugh. The girls went to the living room and were playing with their dolls. That gave them a few moments of relatively quiet time together. "So, how did things go today?"

"It was good," said Windflower. "I actually liked being on an assignment versus a real job. It was, like Smithson said, an adventure. But I have to work tomorrow. At least in the morning."

"That sucks," said Sheila. Windflower could see her thinking.

"I'll try and be home as soon as I can," said Windflower.

"I know," said Sheila. "I'm just wondering if I'm brave enough to bring Amelia Louise to church with me and Stella. The last time, I thought we'd all get kicked out."

"She's not the church-going type," said Windflower. "I have an idea. Maybe Herb would take her for an hour while you're in church. Do you want me to call him?"

"Sure," said Sheila. "The café is not open early on Sundays. Moira goes to church, too, so he might enjoy the company."

Windflower called Herb, and he was more than happy to oblige.

"I'd love that," said Herb. "Me and Amelia Louise will have a grand old time. Why don't you get Sheila to drop her off along the way to church?"

"That's all set," said Windflower as the two girls came back into the kitchen and ended the adults-only time. "Let's watch a movie," he said.

The girls screamed "yes" and started calling out their favourites. They almost always wanted *Frozen* or the *Lion King*, again. But Sheila convinced them by bribing them with an offer of popcorn for the newest *Despicable Me* movie. At least that was a movie that she and Windflower hadn't seen before.

After the movie, the girls were still quite active, so Sheila allowed them to put their coats on over their pajamas and go with Windflower and Lady for her last walk of the night.

It was cool and clear, and the girls marvelled at how many stars appeared in the sky. Usually, they were in bed by this time. Windflower tried pointing out some of the major constellations, but they, especially Amelia Louise, were being too silly, so he let them have their fun and enjoyed the walk. When they got home, he took Amelia Louise for story time while Stella went with Sheila.

Windflower went to Stella's room first and pulled out a book from her shelf. He brought it over to Amelia Louise, who already had half a dozen books on her bed to choose from. He pushed them aside and laid on the bed with his book. It was called *The Sky Is Full of Stars,* and while it was a little older book, it had all the basics about the night sky in a way that young children could understand and enjoy.

Amelia Louise loved the book, and Windflower had to read it three times. By then, she could point to some of the constellations like Orion and Leo the Lion and call them by name. She was very pleased with herself going to sleep, and Windflower was pretty pleased just to be her dad. He was still smiling when he went downstairs to sit with Sheila.

"What's so funny?" she asked.

"Not funny, just happy," said Windflower, and he told her about Amelia Louise and the sky book.

"I have that feeling just about every day," said Sheila. "We're pretty lucky."

"We are indeed," said Windflower. "Do you want to watch another movie?"

"No, let's play crib."

Windflower tried to talk her out of it, but to no avail. Soon she was back with the cards and the cribbage board. "Cut for deal," she said.

Windflower loved Sheila, and he liked playing cards. But sometimes it was a little stressful when they played together. She was highly competitive and hated to lose. Tonight, he thought he would try a different strategy. He threw away his best cards and still got higher scores than her. He even led with a five, which is a big no-no in crib, and Sheila didn't have a ten card. Three times. Despite all his efforts, he won the first game and then the second, and when he won the third, she threw the cards on the floor and stomped upstairs.

Windflower picked up the cards and put everything away. When he got upstairs, he could hear the bath running, even with the door closed. He slipped into bed and was nearly asleep when he felt Sheila slip in beside him. "Sorry," she whispered in his ear. He just pulled her closer, and soon they were both gone to sleep.

Unfortunately for Windflower, he woke in the dreamworld a little bit later. He looked around to get his bearings. It was winter and nighttime. Maybe it wasn't a dream at all, he thought. Then he looked a bit farther away. It was certainly a dream. There was a hockey game going on, and it looked to be on Grand Bank harbour. He had never seen the water freeze in the harbour, or even heard of that happening. It was the Atlantic Ocean, after all.

But there it was, frozen. With hockey players all over it and people cheering alongside the makeshift rink. When he walked closer, he could see that one team had a familiar badge on the front of their uniforms, the RCMP badge with its distinctive bison head and the Maintiens le Droit saying. "Uphold the Right," said Windflower instinctively. Then he recognized some of the players. There was Eddie Tizzard and Ron Quigley and a speedy Carrie Evanchuk racing down the wing to score a goal. He walked up to the goalie and said hello. "Hello," said Bill Ford, pulling down his mask to show Windflower his identity.

"What's going on?" asked Windflower.

"We're playing hockey," said Ford, looking at Windflower like he was crazy, which he certainly felt at the time. He felt even worse when the ice started to shake and crackle, and the next thing you knew, someone had fallen through the ice. Windflower looked around to find out who it was. Eddie Tizzard was missing. Could it be Tizzard? Windflower didn't even think. He ran towards the crack just as Eddie was coming up, maybe for the last time. He reached out his hand and stretched as far as he could without falling in himself. Then he woke up.

Chapter Forty-three

This was a disturbing dream. Partly because his friend had fallen through the ice. But also, Windflower really didn't know how to interpret this dream. He couldn't go back to sleep and went downstairs to think about it. His Auntie Marie and Uncle Frank had both told him to write down his dream as soon as he could, so he grabbed a pen and some paper off Sheila's desk and started to write. Not just about the dream, but also what he felt. That was the really important part about dreams.

His first feeling was one of concern for Eddie. He sure didn't want anything to happen to him. Eddie Tizzard was like the younger brother he'd never had, and he recalled when Eddie had been shot and nearly died a few years ago. But this dream didn't feel as bad as that. Then he realized that as always, dreams were never about the other people in your dreams. They were always about you.

So, what was his subconscious telling him? As he wrote, some things became a little clearer. He'd heard one time that seeing someone falling through ice was a warning signal to pay more attention to your own issues and problems. But that wasn't it either. It felt like the ice was a metaphor for some part of him that had not yet come to the surface or been recognized. Even by himself. He thought about that a bit and then started writing again.

What came out next surprised him. The message that he was getting was to try to break free of old thinking and behaviours that no longer served him. That he needed to find a new direction in his life. Well, that last part wasn't as much of a surprise. But a good reminder that his old life was passing, and it was time, past time, to start planning a new one. How to do that was a longer-term issue. One that he wasn't going to resolve tonight. He put away the pen and put the paper into his jacket in the closet.

He said goodnight again to a curious and confused Lady and went back up to bed.

Eddie Tizzard wasn't having any dreams at all, and that was quite fine with him. He'd got Hughie to bed and was starting to doze off when his cell phone rang. He thought it was Carrie telling him she was on her way home, but it was Smithson.

"I found him," said Smithson.

"Paddy Slaney?" asked Tizzard. "Where is he?"

"New York City," said Smithson. "He's in protective custody as a witness against a drug cartel. The DEA have him in a secure facility there. But we can't talk to him. No one can. Not even his family, according to my contact. If they know where he is, the cartel will find him, too. Right now, it's better if everyone thinks he's missing. Or dead."

"Wow, that's amazing," said Tizzard. "Good work. But what do we do next?"

"I've got a call into Quigley to see if we can't get more info about Slaney. But I think we should also follow up on Rob Skinner and that whole connection," said Smithson.

"Good idea," said Tizzard. "But aren't you tired? Don't you ever sleep?"

"Nah, I'm good," said Smithson. "It's not like I got big plans for tonight in downtown Grand Bank."

"How are our guests?" asked Tizzard.

"Riis is out cold, and Elliston is snoring in the cell across from him," said Smithson. "I think the other guy is having a nap in your office. Apart from that, everything is quiet over here. Evanchuk's gone out for the highway run, and I think she said she's going home afterward."

"Good night, Smithson," said Tizzard, and he hung up and went into the bedroom to read his book. That didn't last long, and he was half asleep when Carrie came home. She snuggled in, and he didn't hear anything until the baby monitor went off early in the morning. Carrie was still sleeping as he took Hughie downstairs and got him changed.

The next time Windflower woke up, it was morning. Still dark, but morning. He looked at the radio clock alarm and saw that it was just before seven. Everyone else was sleeping as he went downstairs and put on the coffee. He let Lady out back and grabbed his coat, and this morning, his pipe.

He sat on the steps of the deck and unwrapped the pipe from the blanket. He put a small amount of his sacred tobacco in the stone bowl and lit it. He took a couple of puffs to get it going, breathing out the smoke quickly so that it mixed with the cool air and rose above his head. Then he waited. This morning it was like the smoke from the pipe created a bubble that completely encircled him. Then the bubble lifted off the ground, and soon he was flying above his house and farther, up into the clouds.

Then, almost as quickly as he had risen, the bubble came to a rest in what looked like to be inside of a cloud. The bubble opened, and he walked out. Soon he could see people, lots of people, in twos and threes standing around, talking. For a change, he did not recognize any of the people in this dreamy cloud. No one seemed to know him either. He finally realized that they couldn't see him or hear him. At least, none of them would respond to his questions.

He saw a man with a long white beard and walked up to him. Maybe this guy could help. "Excuse me," said Windflower. "Where am I? Is this Heaven or something?"

The man with the beard laughed. "This is definitely not Heaven. It is a waystation."

"Like somewhere in between here and there?" asked Windflower.

"Something like that," said the man. "The people here are all talking to somebody from their past. They're trying to recover something they lost or something they were supposed to find but didn't."

"I don't understand," said Windflower. "Why am I here?"

"To find the person who can help you get to where you're supposed to go," said the man. "If not, you end up back here. Again."

"You mean I've been here before? I don't remember that," said Windflower.

"You're not supposed to," said the man. "But at least you found me this time. That's an improvement."

"So, can you help me?" asked Windflower.

"I'm not supposed to," said the man.

196

"It is my dream," said Windflower, surprising himself with his boldness.

"In that case, the thing you are looking for is not another person. Maybe that's why you have had so much trouble finding it," said the man. "You are trying to find your confidence or self-confidence. Do you remember losing it?"

Now Windflower had to think hard. And fast. But not fast enough, because he could feel his bubble come back over him, and he was soon floating away again. He tried to ask more questions, but it was too late. Before he knew it, he was back sitting on his deck with Lady staring directly into his eyes. "I'm okay, girl, let's go in," he said.

He thought he saw faces in the window looking out at him, but by the time he got back inside, the faces had disappeared into the living room. He overheard Stella telling Amelia Louise not to worry. "Daddy says he's doing something like cerrymonny, but really he's just smoking. We can tell Mommy when she gets up."

Chapter Forty-four

He asked the girls, "How is everybody out here this morning?"

"We're fine, Daddy," said Stella. Amelia Louise, who'd been sworn to secrecy, said nothing.

"Do you guys want pancakes for breakfast?" he asked.

"Yes, please," said Stella.

"Me, too, pleeze," said Amelia Louise. "Wif chocolate chips."

"Coming right up," said Windflower.

Windflower had just gotten the first batch of pancakes on the frying pan when he heard Sheila coming downstairs.

"This is a nice treat," she said. "You are a one-armed magician."

"I try," said Windflower. "And I do have to go to work soon."

"Don't forget we have the Sanjays for supper," said Sheila.

"No worries," said Windflower. "I'm hoping it will only be this morning. I think I'll marinate the halibut before I go." He dished up the pancakes and called the girls.

Sheila got a cup of coffee and noticed that they were both unusually quiet. "What's going on with you two this morning?"

"Nothing," said Stella.

"Nuttin," said Amelia Louise.

"I don't think so," said Sheila. "Something is up."

"Daddy was smoking again," blurted out Amelia Louise.

"Shush," said Stella. "It was a secret."

"Why is it a secret?" asked Sheila.

"Cuz we didn't want to get Daddy in twubble," said Amelia Louise.

Sheila looked at Windflower. He just smiled back. "It was my pipe," he said. "Here's your pancakes. Unless I'm in trouble…"

"No trouble here," said Sheila. "Pass the maple syrup."

Eddie Tizzard was cooking breakfast too. Little Hughie was having a little snooze in his chair when Carrie came downstairs. "Bacon, I love that smell in the morning," she said.

"There's coffee, too," said Eddie. "I have to leave after breakfast, though. I'm going with Windflower and the German to see if we can get his package back."

"Okay," said Carrie. "As long as you feed me first."

"No worries, ma'am," said Eddie, and he split the eggs and bacon between them, grabbed a piece of toast and sat to have his breakfast. Hughie woke up about halfway through, but Carrie looked after that, and Eddie got to enjoy his little family before it was time to go.

"I'm going to take your car, if that's okay," he said. "We'll need to be incognito for this morning. I'll leave my Jeep in case you need to go anywhere."

"Be my guest," said Carrie. "I'm not planning on going anywhere."

Eddie texted Windflower that he was on his way and drove to pick him up.

Windflower's phone pinged right after he'd finished whipping up the marinade for the halibut. He'd whisked together some white wine, lemon juice, oil and rosemary and tossed the halibut and put it in the fridge.

"Can you turn this a couple of times during the day?" he asked Sheila. "Then it'll be perfect for the barbeque when I get home."

"Sure," said Sheila. He heard a car outside and ran with both girls to the window to see Tizzard arrive.

Amelia Louise and Stella were jumping up and down with their usual "unca" chant, and when Tizzard saw them, he came to the door to greet them. After visiting for a few minutes, Windflower and Sheila managed to get the girls off Tizzard, and the two men made their escape.

"You're lucky," said Windflower. "You could have been kept 'prissner' all day."

Tizzard laughed. "That would be fine with me."

When they got to the detachment, they saw Smithson's cruiser out front next to the white sedan belonging to Elliston and Williams. "What's he doing here?" said Tizzard.

"I thought you might want some help with the operation," said Smithson. "I've got a recording device already set up if you want to use it."

"That's great," said Windflower. "How's it work?"

"It's just a basic wire with a remote microphone and receiver," said Smithson. "One end could be clipped on Riis and the other on you. I can record from back here."

"That is super," said Tizzard. "Good job, Smithson."

"Set it up," said Windflower. "Thanks."

Smithson put the wire on Riis and then hooked Windflower up. "I can monitor from here and respond if anything happens," said Smithson.

"Okay," said Windflower, gathering Tizzard, Elliston and Williams together. "Here's the plan. Tizzard and I will head past the café and find a spot to park out of sight. We'll control the road to St. Lawrence. Elliston, you drive Riis right to the door and let him out to talk to Edwards. Williams, after we all leave, you take Smithson's cruiser and stop off the road somewhere outside of Fortune. You have the road back towards here. Everybody got it?"

All of the Mounties nodded their agreement, and Elliston went to get Riis.

"No screwing around today," said Windflower. "You take delivery of the package and we come back here."

"Make sure you get my money," said Riis with a snarl.

"We're gone first," said Windflower. "Elliston, you wait until we give you the all-clear and then follow with Riis and park in front of the café. Then, Williams, you follow. Let's go."

Tizzard and Windflower drove out of Grand Bank and quite soon after passed through Fortune. Once they were out of Fortune, they were almost completely in wilderness as they travelled along the rugged coastline. They passed by Point May and through Lamaline before passing the café in Lord's Cove. The café had once been a bustling summer restaurant and take-out but was now closed permanently after the pandemic. No sign of anybody or any vehicles, so Windflower called back with the okay to move. Tizzard found a woods road just before Lawn, drove down a ways and then turned around to face the road while still being almost completely out of sight.

Chapter Forty-five

Windflower heard Elliston talking to Riis as they got into the car, and then silence. Elliston texted him when they arrived at the café. He didn't have to wait long. "There's a car," said Elliston. Windflower could hear the car door open and then Riis talking. Another voice came on. "Have ya got my money?" asked the other man. Windflower couldn't hear anything, but it must be okay because the man then said, "Okay, b'y. Come with me."

"Follow him," texted Windflower to Elliston.

He heard the other man saying, "Just you."

"No man," he heard Riis say. "He follows. Just in case."

Windflower heard a car door open, and he was guessing Riis was going somewhere with Edwards. He texted Elliston again. "Open your phone and put it on speaker, and then you can tell us what's going on."

Elliston called back. "We're heading back towards Lamaline," he said. "Now he's turning down the Point au Gaul road. He's heading to a shed near the water."

Windflower could hear Edwards and Riis talking, and a few minutes later he heard nothing.

"What's going on?" asked Windflower. He could now hear Riis talking, not in the speaker but on Elliston's cell phone.

"Get out of the car," said Riis.

Windflower could hear doors opening and closing, and then nothing.

"Let's go," he yelled to Tizzard.

Tizzard swung his car back onto the highway and raced back in the direction of Elliston's car. He sped down the narrow road towards Point au Gaul and saw Elliston waving his arms.

"Both of them are gone," said Elliston. "Riis had the bag, and Edwards took off behind him. They were heading towards Lamaline."

"Jump in," said Tizzard. Windflower called Williams to get him to come towards them, and Tizzard got back up to the main road as fast as he could. They spotted Elliston's car on the beach in Lamaline, and they could see a small boat motoring off into the distance.

"Now what?" asked Tizzard.

"That's a very good question," said Windflower. "I'll call Quigley."

"We've got a problem," said Windflower. "Riis and the package and the local guy are gone. On a boat heading somewhere, but we have no way to know where."

"Hang on," said Tizzard. "I called Smithson. He just texted me back. He said that in addition to the microphone, he also slipped a GPS tracker into Riis's inside jacket pocket. It's small enough that he won't know it's there."

"Did you get that?" he asked Quigley.

"Riis is gone, but you can track him?" asked Quigley.

"Correct," said Windflower.

"Okay. Keep a presence on the scene there," said Quigley. "I'll alert our patrol boat and see about getting us a chopper."

"Got it," said Windflower and hung up. "Elliston, see if the keys are still in your car."

Elliston went to the vehicle and gave Windflower the thumbs-up sign. "You stay here. Me and Tizzard are going back to the detachment." They drove along the highway back to where they found Williams near the side of the road in Smithson's cruiser.

"You stay here," said Windflower. "Call Elliston, and he can give you an update. Stop anybody coming through here and turn them back towards Fortune. Tell them there's an incident on the highway up ahead. And keep your eyes open for anything coming the other way."

They left Elliston and went back to the detachment to wait for the next developments. They'd just finished a cup of coffee when they heard the familiar noise of a helicopter flying overhead. The noise only got louder as the chopper went in for a landing in the parking lot of the clinic. Tizzard and Windflower drove over to check it out.

The rotors of the engine were slowing down by the time they got there, and a familiar face jumped out of the helicopter. It was Corporal Ted Reid, the long-time RCMP chopper pilot in this region.

"I heard you were retired," said Reid when the noise died down a little. "Nice to see you, Eddie."

Both of the other officers stepped closer to shake hands with Reid.

"I'm only back short-term," said Windflower. "On a contract. Tizzard's in charge now."

"He's running this operation," said Tizzard. "But nice to see you again."

"I hear I'm looking for a boat," said Reid. "Any more descriptive than that?"

"Just a small fishing boat with at least two people on board," said Windflower. "But we think there's a GPS. We planted one. Hopefully, it's still in place."

"Smithson set it up," said Tizzard.

"The tech whiz," said Reid. "Is he at the detachment? I'll radio him and get any coordinates he has. I'll get back up. One of you want to come with me as a spotter?"

"I've been before," said Windflower. "Why don't you go with Ted? I'll call Smithson and bring your car back."

Tizzard looked wide-eyed at Windflower. He'd never been in a helicopter before. "Sure," he said. "I can do that if you'd like."

"Let's go," said Reid as he and Tizzard climbed back into the chopper.

Windflower stood back from the helicopter as it roared to life and slowly rose above him. He looked around. Almost every window at the clinic was filled with spectators taking in the show. It was certainly the most excitement that many of them had seen in Grand Bank for a long time. As the helicopter flew out of sight, he waved goodbye to the people at the clinic and drove back to the detachment.

Up above Grand Bank, Tizzard could see everything, but with the noise, heard little. He could see Reid's lips move under his helmet and assumed he was talking with Smithson. "I've got a read on the GPS," Reid shouted to Tizzard, who nodded back. Soon the helicopter was zooming over the waterway between Grand Bank and the islands across the way. Reid swooped the helicopter down closer to the shoreline of Brunette Island, and Tizzard started looking closely for activity below.

"There," he shouted, and Reid went towards where he was pointing. Below them was a fishing boat floating on the water. But they couldn't see any people. Reid flew the helicopter over the small island but still couldn't see much sign of life. There were a few ramshackle and dilapidated structures that used to be houses. But not much remained of those. He turned to Reid and shook his head. "Can't see anything. But they could still be down there."

Reid nodded. He started talking again on his headset. Tizzard couldn't hear, but he thought he saw Reid mouth the word "Windflower." He was right.

"There's a pretty good bet that's the boat," said Windflower. "There'd be no reason for anybody to be over there right now in the middle of winter. I'll call the location in to the patrol boat, which is supposed to be in the area. Can you hang around up there for a little while?"

"Yes," said Reid. "I've got plenty of fuel. We'll keep circling around until the patrol boat gets here." He hung up with Windflower and made a circling motion that Tizzard figured out quickly. "We're waiting for patrol," he shouted back.

Windflower called Bill Ford. "Can you let the patrol boat know we found our people on Brunette Island?"

"That's good," said Ford. "I heard it didn't go well this morning."

"Stuff happens," said Windflower. "Can you get the captain to come pick us up at the wharf in Grand Bank? We'll need reinforcements."

"Sure thing," said Ford. "Good luck."

He got Smithson to contact Elliston and Williams to get them to come back and meet them at the wharf. His next call was to Ron Quigley.

"Make sure you get the package," said Quigley.

"We'll try," said Windflower. "That will be the hard part. But we'll do our best."

"You have the authority to do whatever you need to make that happen," said Quigley.

"Okay," said Windflower. He and Smithson got some long guns out of the armoury and put on their vests. They brought more weapons and protective gear for the other two officers. "Better to be safe," said Windflower as they drove to the wharf. Along the way, they passed the United Church parking lot, which was full of cars. It wasn't lost on either of the RCMP officers that while the good people of Grand Bank were inside enjoying their pleasant Sunday morning service, they were heading to a potentially dangerous and possibly even deadly situation.

Chapter Forty-six

They had a few quiet moments at the wharf until Elliston, Williams and the RCMP patrol boat had all arrived.

High in the air over Brunette Island, Tizzard and Reid kept a watchful eye for activity below. Tizzard thought he saw something and pointed it out to Reid. As they neared, they could see a thin line of smoke coming from one of the old, abandoned buildings. Reid called Windflower, who had just gotten on board the RCMP boat.

"We think we might have a location," said Reid. "It is on the near side of the island, almost directly across from Grand Bank. You can't miss the boat on the water once you get close. There looks to be a pathway up from the water."

"Great," said Windflower. "I'll call you when we get over. We're just leaving Grand Bank."

Reid circled back over the open water and picked up the RCMP patrol board with Windflower and his fellow officers on board. They watched as the boat slid across the water, found Kevin Edward's boat and pulled up alongside. Windflower and Smithson went aboard carefully with their weapons drawn. They went into the cabin and came out moments later giving the all-clear sign, which was visible to Tizzard and Reid as they hovered above.

Windflower and Smithson went on shore and waited for the other two officers. When everyone was ready, Windflower led the way down the pathway. They disappeared briefly from Tizzard's sight and then reappeared near the rickety structure where he had seen the smoke. He couldn't hear anything but the chopper roaring in his ears.

Windflower approached the door to the building, which at one time was likely a fisherman's summertime dwelling. Even for years after the island was abandoned, men came and stayed on the island for the short summer fishing season. He called out to whomever might be inside to come out with their hands up. At first, there was no response. But then Windflower saw some movement. He tensed, and the men behind him tightened up as well.

He saw Ulrich Riis come out first with his hands up. "Don't shoot," he cried.

"Hold your fire," shouted Windflower. He didn't want anxiety or adrenaline to get anybody killed. He indicated to Smithson to arrest Riis. Smithson grabbed him, put him in cuffs and took him a few yards away from the scene, where he got him to sit on the ground.

Then Kevin Edwards, the local fisherman, came out in the same manner. Windflower grabbed Edwards and put him in cuffs. He sat him on the ground, too. Elliston and Williams were left to guard him while Windflower went to Smithson and Riis.

"That wasn't very bright," said Windflower.

Riis simply stared sullenly back at him.

"Your deal's off," said Windflower.

"You know what?" said Riis. "You got nothing on me but a bunch of made-up conspiracy theories. I'll take my chances."

Windflower left Riis and walked back to Edwards.

"You're in a lot of trouble," said Windflower.

"I'm always in trouble, b'y," said Edwards. "Youse guys always got it in fer fellers like me. I'm only tryin ta make a livin'."

"Well, this time you hit the jackpot," said Windflower. "Importation of narcotics, to start with. That's probably good for ten in a federal pen. Plus whatever else we find when we start poking around your house and your boat and your shed."

"Hang on a minute," said Edwards. "I ain't involved in no dope. I may have muggled a bit of booze. But not da dope."

"That's a bit hard to square with getting paid two thousand dollars," said Windflower.

"I taut it was cigarettes," said Edwards.

"Take him back to the boat," said Windflower. "Keep him away from Riis."

Windflower called Quigley as the men were being escorted back to the patrol boat.

"We got Riis and the fisherman, but no drugs," he said. "We're going to take a look around the building we found them in, but unless Edwards is really dumb, and I don't think he is, it won't be easy to find. We're not even sure it's over here. He may have dumped it already."

"Make Edwards an offer he can't refuse," said Quigley. "Offer him the reward."

"But he's the smuggler," said Windflower.

"We need the drugs to make our case all the way up the line," said Quigley. "I told you. Do whatever you need to do."

"Okay," said Windflower. He walked back to the patrol boat and got Smithson to come back with Edwards. The three of them went a bit away from the boat, and Windflower found a tree stump to sit on. He motioned to Smithson to bring Edwards to stand in front of him.

"You don't seem too worried about going to jail," said Windflower.

"No, b'y," said Edwards. "Dere's worse places to be. I been dere before. Hoccupational azard we calls it."

"Good. You'll be happy then," said Windflower. "But I'm assuming you got a wife and a family."

"Jus me and the missus now," said Edwards. "But I sees my grandchildren every day."

"Well, you won't be seeing them for a while," said Windflower. "Unless."

"Unless what?" asked Edwards.

That was a good sign for Windflower. An opening. He walked through. "Unless you want to make a deal. One that could make you a rich man."

"So, why didn't you say dat in da first place?" said Edwards. "I'm jus a biznessman, ya know."

"I can offer you immunity if you tell us everything you know. And there is a reward for the return of the package you were holding for our German friend," said Windflower.

"How much of a reward?" asked Edwards.

"If you tell us everything, agree to testify in court and we recover the package intact, we can give you five thousand dollars," said Windflower.

"That's more dan double whut dose udder fellers were payin'," said Edwards. "Yes, b'y, I can do dat."

"Okay," said Windflower. "Show us where the package is."

"Take dese tings off and I'll show ya," said Edwards.

Windflower indicated that Smithson should take off the man's cuffs. Edwards rubbed his hands and walked back towards the old structure where they'd been hiding out. He walked past that building and came to a small shed that was barely standing. He opened the creaking door and went inside. He emerged a few moments later with the large canvas knapsack that Windflower recognized from the ferry.

He let Smithson bring Edwards back to the patrol boat and laid the knapsack on the ground. He unzipped the still soaking-wet canvas and looked inside. There was plastic wrap sealed tightly around the contents. But he could see what looked like thousands of small pink and green pills. Maybe tens of thousands.

Chapter Forty-seven

Windflower called Quigley. "We've got the package," he said.

"That's great," said Quigley. "Did you check inside?"

"Yes," said Windflower. "Thousands of pills, wrapped up tight in plastic. Edwards will testify, and it only costs you five grand."

"Excellent work, Winston," said Quigley. "There might be a bonus for you, too."

"I'm just happy nobody got hurt," said Windflower. "We're going back to Grand Bank, but I'm going to suggest that all of this and Riis get transferred back to Halifax with Reid, if that's okay."

"That sounds good," said Quigley. "I'm assuming that the local guy is not going anywhere."

"Not till he gets his money," said Windflower. "We'll get his statement and release him. He's staying put."

"Great job," said Quigley.

Windflower thought so too as he walked back towards the patrol boat. Riis was inside in the cabin, and Edwards was sitting on the deck.

"Can I bring me boat back over?" asked Edwards. "If not, it'll be stranded over ere, and ya never knows bout da weather round ere."

"Smithson, you go with Edwards," said Windflower. "Come to the wharf in Grand Bank right behind us."

Smithson got in Edwards's boat and got ready to follow the RCMP patrol boat back across the water. Just then, the helicopter made a dip and came closer to them. Windflower raised both hands with a thumbs-up gesture. He told the captain of the RCMP boat that it was okay to go back to Grand Bank. He called Reid in the chopper.

"We've got the prisoners and the package," he said. "And you've got a couple of passengers to deliver to Halifax along with the package. I'll get Elliston to go as the escort."

"Perfect," said Reid.

Minutes later, the RCMP helicopter landed at the clinic and was met by Windflower and his crew. "We have time for coffee?" asked Reid once the rotors had slowed down.

"Let's all go to the detachment," said Windflower. "I'm sure Eddie can find us a snack."

Back at the detachment, Eddie Tizzard did indeed find them a box of cookies to go along with a fresh pot of coffee. After their break and a thank-you from Windflower, the officers split up to finish off their duties for the day. Elliston and Williams had checked in with Bill Ford and got the okay for Elliston to accompany Riis to Halifax. Smithson drove them, along with Reid, back to the helicopter while Williams headed back to Marystown.

Windflower went to see Kevin Edwards to get his statement.

"Can I call my missus?" asked Edwards. "She worries bout me when I'm away longer than spected."

Windflower took Edward's cell phone out of his plastic bag of belongings and handed it to him. He went back to get him a cup of coffee while he made the call.

When he came back, he handed Edwards the coffee.

"I don't spose I could ave a smoke?" asked Edwards.

"You're still in pretty big trouble here," said Windflower. "Until we get your statement down and can confirm it."

"I still gets me money, right?" asked Edwards.

"Yes, if it all works out," said Windflower. "You know you'll have to give up smuggling as part of this deal, too."

"I'm tired of the muggling game," said Edwards. "Like the fellers on TV says. Too much risk and not enough reward. If you gives me dat money, I won't need to. I'll retire."

"Good plan," said Windflower, turning on the tape recorder. "Now let's hear your story."

An hour later, Windflower reassured Edwards that his money would be on the way soon, once he transferred this tape and got it sent to RCMP HQ. Feeling pretty pleased with himself that he wasn't going to jail and had money on the way, Kevin Edwards got a ride from Smithson back to pick up his car at the café in Lord's Cove.

The office was empty for the first time that day, since Tizzard had gone home. Windflower sat back in his old chair for a minute to think about his day and what Edwards had just told him. The drug story was an old one, with hardcore criminals always wanting to increase their share of a lucrative market. The more experienced interrogators at RCMP in Halifax or Ottawa would get Riis and Schüller to spill their stories. He was actually more interested in how that whole crew ended up in Grand Bank and how they roped Edwards into their scheme.

According to Edwards, he was approached last year by a friend who asked him if he would be interested in a small job. Edwards wouldn't say who this friend was. He said that "ya can't rat in yer own ouse, b'y." Windflower understood that. He'd seen it before with the local smugglers and rumrunners who plied their trade between here and Saint-Pierre. But when it came to the Germans, Edwards had no such compunctions.

He'd been contacted first by a man he called Weber. That was the RCMP guy, Grimsby, Windflower remembered. That must be how he gained the trust of Gerhard Müller. Weber made all the arrangements and arranged for the first thousand dollars to get to Edwards. Weber had then called a couple of days ago to tell him to turn on a GPS tracking device that had already come in the mail.

"I turned it on, but nuttin appened," said Edwards. "Then the udder day it jus went crazy, blinking and everything. As soon as da weather cleared, I went and picked it up out of da water and put it in da old shed on da island. I didn't even look inside."

That was probably true, thought Windflower. This was a straight-up smuggling job for Edwards. He might have guessed what it was. He just didn't want to know. Either way, they had the package, and all the real bad guys were going into the justice system. He couldn't say they were going to get punished. That wasn't his part of this work. His part was done.

He went to Betsy's office, uploaded the recording on her computer and emailed it to Ron Quigley. One more chat with him and his day was done.

"Well done, Winston," said Quigley. "We couldn't have done this without you."

"Thanks, Ron," said Windflower. "I know we've done good work here. But what about all the guys who are going to get deals out of this? I'm not worried about Kevin Edwards. He was ready to get of the game anyway. But Riis and Schüller..."

"We do our best," said Quigley. "You know that. You also know that sometimes 'to do a great right, do a little wrong.'"

"I get it," said Windflower. "I just don't like it. But I guess 'what's done cannot be undone.'"

"Very good," said Quigley. "We'll talk soon. You never know when I might have another project."

"Bye, Ron," said Windflower, too tired to think of any wittier quotes to parry with. He packed up his bag and left to walk the short distance home. That walk did him good. By the time he got home, he was ready to give Sheila a break from the girls, and they all headed down to the brook with Lady in tow to see the neighbourhood ducks.

Chapter Forty-eight

Eddie Tizzard was enjoying a few well-deserved hours off work. Although he had to admit that flying in the helicopter with Reid today was an excellent adventure. He had time to play with Hughie and give Carrie her own break, which she took by having a long bath and reading her book.

Eddie got Hughie down for a nap just as she was coming into the living room.

"I feel alive again," she said.

"I feel good, too," said Eddie. "Even though I have to go in tonight."

"Too bad," said Carrie. "But at least we get a few hours together. We should make the most of it."

"I agree," said Eddie.

Back at the brook, Windflower had given up all the bread he had to the girls, who, along with the ducks, were still demanding more. "Sorry, girls," he said. "We've got to go home. The Sanjays are coming for dinner."

That led Amelia Louise, soon joined by Stella, to start up a "doc, doc, doc" chant that didn't stop until they were nearly home. Doctor Sanjay's familiar black car was parked in their driveway.

The girls ran in to envelop the doctor in hugs, which he gladly reciprocated. Sheila and Repa Sanjay were sitting on the couch in the living room. Windflower went to say hello to Repa and then managed to get Vijay away from the girls. Sheila and Repa finished the rescue mission and took the girls to the kitchen. They were soon busy chopping vegetables and getting the salad ready.

Windflower pulled out the tray with the new bottle of Scotch and two tasting glasses. He went to the kitchen and came back with a water jug and two more glasses. He let Sanjay have the honour of opening the whiskey. Before he poured them their taste, he sniffed the aroma of the Aberfeldy. "Smells like dried flowers, with just a hint of smokiness," said Sanjay.

He poured about an ounce into both glasses. Windflower sniffed it first and then took a sip. "I can taste the peat, but maybe apples and something else," said Windflower.

Sanjay followed. "Yes, I can taste that too, and maybe oranges or something more exotic like tangerines. Even a bit of vanilla. It is gorgeous. Great choice, Winston." They finished their drink, and Windflower poured them both a glass of water.

"Do we have time?" asked Sanjay, pointing to the chess set he had brought with him.

"It won't take you long to beat me," said Windflower.

That turned out to be true. But with a promise of another game after supper, Windflower went to get the grill ready for the halibut. He went outside, lit the barbeque and went back in to get the fish, which Sheila had arranged on a platter for him.

"Thank you, Sheila," he said. "Anything else for the grill?"

"Yes," said Sheila, passing him a large tinfoil packet. "Mixed vegetables with butter and garlic."

Windflower took the veggies out first and came back in to socialize a little with the Sanjays before cooking the fish. They were both excited about the pending visit of their eldest son and his wife and two grandchildren.

"We haven't seen them for two years," said Repa. "So we can't wait to get our hands on those little kiddies."

"That will be so nice," said Sheila. "It will be like come home year all over the province this year. Everyone will want to visit their families."

"It looks like young Tizzard and his wife will have to leave if the situation doesn't change," said Doctor Sanjay. "That will be a big loss to the community."

"Not to mention the loss of policing services," said Windflower.

"Well, we will do our best to overturn the decision," said Sheila. "But I have to admit that early indications don't look good."

"I always think that some good can come out of all situations," said the doctor. "Maybe we have to think about it a little differently. Tagore says that 'everything comes to us that belongs to us if we create the capacity to receive it.'"

"Interesting," said Windflower. "Excuse me, I have to grill the fish."

He took his platter of fish and went out to the grill. He had heated the grill to medium. He placed the halibut on the grill and closed the lid, leaving it to seal its juices on one side. After a couple of minutes, he opened the grill and gently turned the fish, again closing the lid. A few more minutes, and then he opened the grill and poured the remaining marinade over the fish. He turned it and let it sit for a few more minutes.

He checked it, and when the pieces started to flake, he knew it was done. He plated the fish and brought it in along with the steaming hot vegetables. Sheila had placed the salad in the middle of the table and had a bowl of baked potatoes ready for serving. Windflower handed over his food and sat at the head of the table with the girls on either side and the Sanjays beside them. Sheila dished up food for everyone and passed around the plates.

"This fish is wonderful," announced Doctor Sanjay, a sentiment echoed by his wife. Everyone, even the girls, seemed to enjoy their supper, and for dessert Sheila had a surprise. She brought out what looked like a fruitcake, but when she sliced it, Repa's eyes grew wide. Sheila gave everyone a slice, along with a scoop of ice cream.

"Oh, my goodness," said Repa. "Is that what I think it is?"

"It's a petha cake," said Sheila.

"Oh, my goodness," said Repa. "It's perfect."

"What does petha mean?" asked Windflower.

"It's candied ash gourd," said Vijay. "Where did you get it?"

"I ordered it online," said Sheila.

"Thank you so much," said Repa. "It's an old family tradition to have petha cake as a great celebration. We are very honoured."

"Some call it the Indian Christmas cake," said Vijay. "Thank you so much, Sheila. And Windflower for the delicious fish."

Sheila beamed, and Windflower was pretty happy, too. The Sanjays stayed a little longer and then left for home. Before they left, Sanjay invited Windflower to come at his convenience so that they could finish their chess match. He also had a new Scotch to try out. "It's a Glen Dronach. I can't wait to try it. I hear it has hints of raisins, chocolate and orange peel," said Sanjay.

"It sounds delightful. I'll be over soon, I promise," said Windflower as he said goodbye to his friend.

"Don't forget," said Sanjay. "'You can't cross the sea merely by standing and staring at the water.'" Windflower laughed and waved goodnight to the Sanjays.

Sheila took the girls upstairs for their bath while Windflower went with Lady for her last walk of the evening. The night was cool, but not as cold as usual. That usually meant one thing: more snow was on the way. He wasn't particularly worried. His job with Quigley was nearly done, and now he could get back to focusing on the hardwood floors at the B&B.

With that pleasant thought in mind, he walked Lady around town and then headed back to his nice warm and snug house, feeling grateful for his lot in life.

Chapter Forty-nine

Eddie Tizzard was heading back into work feeling pretty blessed as well. He'd had time with his son and special time with Carrie finished off with a large slice of chicken pot pie courtesy of Beulah's kitchen. He parked in front and went in to see Smithson.

Smithson was excited to see him. He'd managed to get through the system and talked to somebody on the inside who was responsible for the Paddy Slaney case.

"They're trying to get Slaney to roll over on the younger Skinner guy," said Smithson. "So they're very interested in talking to us, especially when they heard about all the goings-on up here."

"Great," said Tizzard. "What else did you find out?"

"My contact said that Slaney was given one call. And he called his wife," said Smithson.

"Marguerite Slaney knows that he's alive," said Tizzard. "Interesting. Do you know when this call was made?"

"My guy said it was in the last couple of days," said Smithson. "Maybe that's why she was meeting with Rob Skinner."

"Maybe," said Tizzard. "I know you're supposed to be off tomorrow, but can you come in early and pick up Marguerite Slaney? I'm going to go over to see Rob Skinner first thing."

"Sure," said Smithson. "But I can go home now, right?"

"Absolutely," said Tizzard. "See you in the morning."

Smithson left, and Tizzard got himself organized for the evening. He and Carrie had agreed to split the overnight shift, and he would go back to get her sometime after midnight. For now, he made himself a fresh pot of coffee and got cracking on the new stack of paperwork that Betsy had dropped off in his basket.

Windflower came back and looked after the pets before heading up to see Sheila and the girls. She had done a joint reading session with them tonight, so all he had to do was put Amelia Louise to bed. She still managed to get him to read *Goodnight Moon*, but he was quite happy to do that and tuck her in tight.

Sheila was sitting in front of the fire when he came back down.

"That was a nice visit," said Sheila.

"That was very kind of you to make that cake," said Windflower.

"They have done so many nice things for us, I just wanted to do something special," said Sheila.

"Well, you succeeded there," said Windflower. "Both of them were very pleased. What are you working on?" he asked as Sheila was typing on her laptop.

"Trying to come up with some more ideas for council to kick around about saving our detachment," said Sheila. "The word from Halifax is that this is a done deal."

"I'm not surprised," said Windflower. "Once I heard that Majesky was behind this, I had my doubts."

"One person here hardly makes a lot of sense," said Sheila. "How would they do the patrolling, never mind all of the other functions?"

"Maybe you should think about policing differently," said Windflower. "There's lots of other models out there now where there are less uniformed police and more public and community involvement. You will still need some police as a deterrent to the really bad guys, but most laws are followed because people agree with them. Like a speed limit, for example. Yes, there are some speeders, but most people stay within a safe range based on the driving conditions."

"That's good," said Sheila. "I think I'll do some more research on that."

"Glad to help," said Windflower. "But if my services are no longer required, I'm going up to read my book."

"I'll be up in a while," said Sheila. "You can warm up the bed for me."

Windflower did exactly that, but he made it so nice and comfortable that his book soon gave way to his pillow, and he promptly fell asleep. He felt Sheila move in alongside him some time later, but he didn't wake as she snuggled in and didn't stir again until the alarm went off in the morning.

Tizzard had a quiet evening at work and was tired too when it came time to go pick up Carrie. She was sitting watching TV when he came in. They had a cup of tea together before Carrie said goodbye and headed to work. Tizzard peeked in on Hughie, who was sleeping peacefully. Soon Tizzard was doing the same.

Windflower heard Sheila get up and followed her soon after. He took a quick look out the window. Snow, and lots of it, on the ground already. But it was that perfect-looking winter snow, nice and clean and fresh. Like the world was getting a beautiful whitewash. He checked the app on his phone and was happy to see that it would likely continue this morning and then taper off to flurries later. That was perfect, he thought as he put on his robe and padded downstairs.

For a change, it was only him and Sheila. She was working on her laptop at the kitchen table.

"Good morning, beautiful," said Windflower.

"It's a PD day today," she said. "So, no school. I let the girls sleep in."

"Good plan," said Windflower.

He kissed her on the forehead and put on the coffee. Then he grabbed his smudging gear and went outside while he waited for it to brew. With Lady at his heels, he pushed the door open and walked out onto the snowy deck. He managed to get his bowl lit and smoking and took a few moments to let the sacred medicines waft around him. He loved that combination of smells early in the morning as the sage and sweetgrass and cedar mixed in with the tobacco.

He allowed the smoke to penetrate his pores, and it was almost as if it went inside his spirit as well. Then he laid his bowl on the table and said his prayers. This morning it was almost all about gratitude, and he took the time to think about and pray for the happiness and well-being of the people he cared about. Sometimes he wondered where all these prayers went, but this morning that didn't seem to matter. It felt good to pray, especially for others. At the end, he prayed briefly for himself. Not that he should receive any special gifts or treatment, but that he have the courage and strength to deal with whatever came his way today.

He called Lady and went back inside. He poured himself a coffee and got one for Sheila.

Chapter Fifty

Sheila said, "I have some ideas I want to run by you."

"I can see that you've been busy," said Windflower. "How can I help?"

"I've been thinking about different models and approaches for policing," she said. "There's some great ideas out there."

"Like what?" asked Windflower, sipping his coffee.

"One idea is to have trained civilians instead of police patrol the roadways," said Sheila. "We don't need armed police officers to do routine traffic work."

"Well, I think the *Highways Act* requires an authorized force to do that work," said Windflower.

"Yes, but that's the highway," said Sheila. "What about if the RCMP continued to look after the highway, but the communities in the area took over the street patrol?"

"I guess so," said Windflower. "What about the drug dealers and the other bad guys? Who's going to look after them?"

"Who's looking after them now?" asked Sheila. "We all know who they are and where they live. Why aren't they under arrest?"

"They do get arrested when we catch them out in the open," said Windflower.

"That's good," said Sheila. "But how do they get to operate behind the scenes all the time?"

"Because people in the community don't say anything," said Windflower.

"That's why we need to have more community involvement with policing," said Sheila. "We have to start policing ourselves and call in experts when we need them. And we may not always need an armed police officer. What were most of your calls about?"

"Traffic accidents and domestic disputes of one sort or another," said Windflower.

"Exactly," said Sheila. "Lots of communities all over the world, from Europe to Australia, have devolved local traffic to by-law people and put together crisis intervention teams to deescalate difficult or violent situations."

"What about if somebody has a gun?" asked Windflower.

"Good question," said Sheila. "How many times have you showed up to a domestic dispute and been threatened with a gun?"

"It doesn't mean it can't happen," said Windflower.

"That is true," said Sheila. "But we don't have a gun culture here in Grand Bank. If people have guns, it's for hunting, not for shooting each other. Maybe it's time we started acting out of what is real and what is happening in our towns and not what we're afraid might happen."

Windflower didn't have an answer for that, and he didn't have time to think up one because he heard two little girls come running down the stairs.

"It's a holiday," said Stella.

"Mila get holiday, too," said Amelia Louise. "Don't I, Daddy?"

"Yes, indeed you do," said Windflower.

Amelia Louise smirked at her sister as if to say "I told you so."

"Let's have breakfast, and maybe we can go sliding," said Windflower. That's what they called tobogganing around Grand Bank. Whatever it was called, the girls were pretty happy.

Windflower got them their cereal and let them eat in the living room watching cartoons on TV to give Shelia a few more minutes to finish her work. Windflower made her and him a boiled egg and toast. After breakfast, he cleaned up while she got the girls ready to go outside.

The best and safest place for sliding in Grand Bank was on a steep hill up near the cemetery, and once everyone was bundled up, he put the girls on the toboggan and pulled them along to the hill. Lady, of course, was their escort, and she was pretty excited just to be outside. Windflower remembered looking back at his house as he was leaving to see Molly sitting in the window watching them. She had that cat look. The one that said, "You people and that dog are crazy. Why would you go out in that cold and miserable weather when you could stay warm and toasty inside?"

But neither the humans nor the dog minded being outside. Going down the hill five or six times on the toboggan with Lady running alongside was so much fun. Coming back up, not so much, at least for Windflower, who had to drag both the sled and the girls. He finally begged off and led his troops homeward.

Eddie Tizzard was pretty happy this morning, too. Hughie had slept through the night, and father and son had some great crack-of-dawn bonding time together. He'd changed, fed, and then changed Hughie again, and now he was having a bottle before another naptime. What a life, thought Tizzard as Hughie dozed off. He burped him one more time and then laid him in his crib. And still had enough time to cook scrambled eggs and bacon for his lovely wife, who was just coming home from work.

"I might just keep you," said Carrie as she came in smelling the bacon.

"Who knew that bacon was the secret to a girl's heart, too?" said Eddie. "Anything happen overnight?" he asked as he served them both breakfast.

"Quiet as Grand Bank itself," said Carrie. "A car slid off the road just outside of town, and I gave the driver a ride home. The tow truck will get the vehicle later."

"Looks pretty out there," said Eddie.

"It's nice," said Carrie. "Even better, it's supposed to stop by noon."

"That is good news," said Eddie. "I'm going over to see Rob Skinner this morning. Smithson found his son in jail in the States, and Paddy Slaney is alive, too."

"Wow," said Carrie. "Is Rob Skinner involved in all this?"

"That's what I hope to find out as soon as I clean up."

"I'll do that. You cooked," said Carrie.

"Thank you, my love," said Eddie. He gave her a tight squeeze and left for work. Rather than go into the detachment, he went directly to Rob Skinner's house. Skinner lived in a modest bungalow down near the brook. The house wasn't remarkable in any way, but the driveway featured several vehicles that looked brand-new, a pair of sparkling Ski-Doos, and behind them a large motorhome. Tizzard couldn't remember where Rob Skinner worked, but wherever it was, it clearly paid well.

He walked up to the front door and knocked. A woman appeared, likely Rob Skinner's wife, and she directed him to the doorway on the side of the driveway. Tizzard should have known. Few people used their front doors in Grand Bank. They were reserved for special guests like the clergy who might visit once a year. All others used the side or back doors. Tizzard followed her directions and was met at the side by Rob Skinner.

Chapter Fifty-one

Rob Skinner asked, "Can I help you?"

"I'd like to talk to you," said Tizzard. "Do you have a few minutes?"

"A few," said Skinner as he opened the door wider to let Tizzard in. "But I have to take my missus to Walmart in Marystown."

Tizzard followed Skinner into the kitchen and sat on an offered chair at the table. He noticed that the kitchen had been recently remodelled and had all new appliances. "Nice job on the kitchen," said Tizzard.

"Thanks," said Skinner. "The missus likes it. That's what's important. How can I help you?"

Tizzard paused for a moment to think about how he wanted to handle this. He decided to go straight to the heart of the matter. "When was the last time you spoke to your son?"

Skinner's face started to turn red, but surprisingly he kept his cool. "Robbie has always had trouble with drugs," he said. "That's no secret. I haven't talked to him in a while. It's not easy to get access. But you probably knew that already."

Tizzard nodded. "I saw you with Marguerite Slaney the other morning. What were you talking about?" While he waited for a reply, he could hear Skinner's wife moving around inside the living room. Either that or the question sparked Skinner, and he jumped up in a rage.

"That's none of your business," said Skinner. "What right do you have to come into my house and talk about my son and that poor woman? Why don't you do your job and stop harassing innocent citizens? Get out of my house," he yelled.

Tizzard could hear him still yelling as he walked down the driveway and back to his car. "That went well," he said sarcastically to himself. He drove to the detachment. Smithson's cruiser was parked out front. He said good morning to Betsy.

"She's in your office," said Betsy.

Smithson came out of the back with a cup of coffee.

"Did she ask any questions when you said we wanted to talk to her?" asked Tizzard.

"No," said Smithson. "It was like she was expecting us. Do you want me to sit in?"

"Sure," said Tizzard as he walked to his office.

"Good morning," he said to Marguerite Slaney. "Can I offer you some coffee or tea?"

"No, thank you," said the woman. "I guess you want to talk to me about Paddy."

"Yes," said Tizzard. "But first, what do you want to tell us?"

"I wasn't sure if I was allowed to say," said Marguerite Slaney. "Paddy said to be very careful because he could still be in danger. And if they thought I knew where he was, they'd come after me."

"When did you find out he was still alive?" asked Tizzard.

"It was just the other night that he called," said the woman. "He wouldn't even tell me where he was. Do you know?"

Tizzard ignored that question. "I saw you with Rob Skinner the other day at the café. What were you talking about?"

Now Marguerite looked flushed. "We were just having a chat. He lost his brother, and Paddy was missing..."

"I think there's more to it than that," said Tizzard. "What did Rob Skinner tell you? Is he involved in some way?"

The woman moved from flustered to afraid. She clutched her purse tightly and her lips even tighter. She said nothing.

"You need to talk to me," said Tizzard. "Somebody around here is going to be in big trouble."

"Do I need a lawyer?" she finally asked.

"If you've done nothing wrong, why would you need a lawyer?" asked Tizzard.

"Am I under arrest?"

"No," said Tizzard.

"Then I'll like to leave. Will you drive me back home?" she asked Smithson.

Smithson looked at Tizzard. "Just give us a moment, ma'am," said Tizzard. He got up and motioned for Smithson to follow him.

Tizzard walked down to the lunch area and poured himself a cup of coffee. "What are you going to do?" asked Smithson.

"I don't know yet," said Tizzard. "But Marguerite Slaney knows something. Maybe she knows a lot. I have to figure out how to get her to talk."

"I agree," said Smithson. "But you can't hold her for not talking."

"I know," said Tizzard. "I'm just letting her sweat a little right now." He took his time and sipped on his coffee. After a few more minutes, he started walking back to his office with Smithson right behind him.

"Are you sure there's nothing you want to tell us?" he asked Marguerite.

The woman stayed silent in almost the same pose as when they left her.

"Okay," said Tizzard. "Constable Smithson will drive you home. But don't leave town, ma'am. We will want to talk to you again. Also, we would ask you not to be in contact with Rob Skinner, at least for the next few days. If that is agreeable to you, you are free to go."

The woman nodded and rose to follow Smithson out to his car.

Tizzard walked behind them. When he saw Marguerite get in Smithson's cruiser, he turned to Betsy. "Can you get me Judge Prowse on the phone, please, Betsy?"

Smithson came back as Tizzard was hanging up.

"The good judge has agreed to give us a warrant," said Tizzard.

"For what?" asked Smithson.

"For you to put a trace on Marguerite Slaney and Rob Skinner," said Tizzard. "Skinner said he was going to Marystown this morning, so you can get inside his house this morning."

"I can do something outside of the Slaney house, but it's hard to get inside unless she leaves," said Smithson.

"Do what you can on the outside and then wait for her to leave," said Tizzard. "She likely will have to go out for shopping or something. What about cell phones?"

"Unless we have the phones, we can't do much, but we can get cell phone records, and we can track movements easily enough. Do you have their cell phone numbers?" asked Smithson.

"It's in the file," said Tizzard. "Betsy will have them."

"I'll call the provider and set that up right away," said Smithson. "This is exciting. Like espionage."

"Yeah, just like that," said Tizzard, a little cynically. "I'm going to check the bank records of both of them, too,"

Both men went to see Betsy. Smithson may have been the office tech wizard, but Betsy knew how to get anything they needed. Anything.

Chapter Fifty-two

An hour later, Tizzard was going through the banking records of Marguerite Slaney and Rob Skinner.

Skinner's was the most interesting. Several large deposits from an account that he would have to get Smithson to check out and regular monthly deposits of a couple of thousand dollars at a time. It looked to Tizzard like a salary or maybe a commission of some sort. Then the money got transferred out again, but it wasn't clear where those monies went. More for Smithson to look into. What was it that Windflower used to say? "Always follow the money," Tizzard said out loud.

Windflower wasn't following much right now. He was on his way to the B&B to see how Levi and his dad, Jerimiah, were making out with the hardwood floors. When he got there, he was very impressed. They had just applied the final coat, a water-based polyurethane.

"It's actually called a topcoat," said Jerimiah Parsons. "We've put two coats on underneath, and all we have left is to roll it in."

"Great job," said Windflower. "The floors look even better than new."

"Glad you're pleased," said Jerimiah. "Levi here will finish up. I've got a few things to do at home."

"Send me your bill," said Windflower. "I really appreciate your help."

"No charge for me," said the father. "It was nice to be working with my son for a change."

"Well, thanks very much," said Windflower. "I might have to give Levi a bonus."

Both the older men laughed, and Levi looked like he would like to crawl under the newly finished hardwood floors. Windflower shook hands with Jerimiah Parsons, gave Levi a wave and started back home. He drove by the RCMP detachment, saw Tizzard's Jeep and decided to drop in to say hello.

"Morning, Sergeant," said Betsy. "Nice to see you." She started to come out from behind her desk to give him a hug, but Windflower was too fast for her. "Nice to see you, too," he said as he slipped by and went to Tizzard's office.

"Hey, Sarge," said Tizzard.

"You're in a good mood today," said Windflower.

"I think I'm starting to crack the great mystery," said Tizzard. "At least I've got some solid leads. Do you want to hear about it?"

"Sure," said Windflower. "Got time to go to the Mug-Up?"

"Always have time for a snack," said Tizzard.

Windflower drove to the café, followed by Tizzard in his Jeep. It was busy at the café, but that wasn't a surprise. They waited until someone left and took a table near the back of the tearoom. Marie came by soon after to take their order. The usual two coffees, but this time an order of homemade raisin toast.

"My treat today," said Windflower. "It's love your local police day."

Tizzard laughed. "We could use a little love. Although my sense is that the worst is over. At least for us. What happens with the town after they lose the detachment, that's another story."

"Sheila is working on a plan," said Windflower. "They survived before the RCMP. They'll survive afterwards."

"My dad told me that they never had a municipal police force here. Nor in much of Newfoundland outside of St. John's," said Tizzard. "They had an outfit called the Newfoundland Rangers."

Herb Stoodley came by with their tea biscuits. He also brought the coffee pot and filled their cups, pouring one for himself. "Mind if I join you? I heard you talking about the Rangers."

"What do you know about them?" asked Windflower.

"I actually did a bit of research on this," said Stoodley. "Back in 1935, the Commission of Government created the Newfoundland Ranger Force to provide government services in remote areas of Newfoundland. They became an important link between government and people in small and rural areas, especially in Labrador. They did just about everything, from inspecting logging

232

operations to collecting customs duties and even issued relief payments. And, of course, they were the only law in the land. When they finally disbanded it, many of the Rangers joined the RCMP."

"Wasn't there an incident involving the Rangers in Grand Bank?" asked Tizzard, who by now had finished his toast and was debating whether or not he should lick the crumbs off his plate.

"Yes, indeed, Corporal," said Herb. "Back in the forties, there was a big push to form a town in order to bring in water and sewage. The only way to finance that was to incorporate. But not everybody thought it was such a great idea. They didn't want to pay the taxes that they knew were coming. The arguments got so heated that the Rangers were brought in to keep the warring factions apart."

"Interesting," said Windflower. "Thanks for the history lesson, Herb."

"You're welcome," said Stoodley as he took their plates and went back to the kitchen.

"So, what's next in your investigation?" asked Windflower.

"Well, we've got two key people that we need information from," said Tizzard. "But neither seems that interested in talking to us."

"Maybe you have to make it worth their while," said Windflower. "Give them an incentive."

"What do you mean? Bribe them?"

Windflower laughed. "The RCMP doesn't bribe people, Eddie. We encourage them to do the right thing, either by punishment or reward. And the fact that you have two people involved is even better. Maybe you can play one off against the other."

"That's good," said Tizzard. "But how am I going to get them to speak out against one another?"

"Who are we talking about?" asked Windflower. "And what do you know so far?"

"Marguerite Slaney and Rob Skinner," said Tizzard. "We've got a warrant to tap their phones, and Smithson is working on that now. And I've seen them together. We know that Paddy Slaney is hooked up in some DEA investigation in New York, and Skinner's son is in jail down there, too."

"Drugs?" asked Windflower.

"Yeah," said Tizzard. "Maybe money laundering as well. Smithson found tons of bitcoin, some crazy Internet currency that's worth millions, on Sid Skinner's computer. I just had a look at Rob Skinner's bank account, and there's lots of money in there that didn't come from working odd jobs around town."

"Wasn't there something about Colombian tree frog poison as well?" asked Windflower.

"Doc Sanjay is convinced that's how Leo Broderick and Sid Skinner died," said Tizzard. "And young Skinner was involved in the drug market down in South America."

"Good," said Windflower. "You've got lots of angles to explore. Especially the money."

"I thought about you this morning," said Tizzard. "I remember you saying to always follow the money."

"Also good," said Windflower. "Greed is a dangerous motivation and one that is most often on display in criminal activities, especially murder. Back when Quigley and I were at the RCMP training academy, we had an instructor who loved Shakespeare. He described *The Merchant of Venice* as a deep warning against greed. He also used to show how powerful money and greed were as motivators. I never forgot that."

"That's interesting, but how do you think I should approach all of this?" asked Tizzard.

"I think I might go after Skinner first," said Windflower. "From what you've told me, he's got some suspicious financial transactions that you could ask him to explain. I don't think you've told me anything you have on the woman."

"Would you come with me while I interview Skinner?" asked Tizzard. "I could do it on my own, but I think I'd prefer to have you with me."

"Sure," said Windflower. "I could do that. Let me know when."

Chapter Fifty-three

They brought their cups to the front, and Windflower paid their bill. He headed home while Tizzard went back to the cop shop. Smithson came in not long after.

"I've got the Skinner's house phone tapped, and I ran a wire on the outside of Marguerite Slaney's as well," said Smithson. "And I've got a phone log from Rob Skinner's cell phone."

"Anything interesting?" asked Tizzard.

"Calls to Marguerite Slaney starting two days ago. And numerous calls from international numbers. I checked the area codes. Florida and Cali, Colombia."

"Do we know who he called in Florida?" asked Tizzard.

"No big surprise," said Smithson. "Florida State Prison."

"His son," said Tizzard.

"Exactly," said Smithson. "There's no way of figuring out who called him from Colombia. Might have been his son. Or anybody."

"Can you get phone logs from Skinner's and Marguerite Slaney's home lines as well?" asked Tizzard.

"Yes, I can do that," said Smithson. "It will be interesting to see if there's any of the same numbers showing up."

"Exactly," said Tizzard. "Very interesting.

Windflower had some soup with the girls and took them for another walk with Lady. When he got back, his cell phone rang. It was Ron Quigley.

"Hey, Ron, how she's going, b'y?" asked Windflower.

"She's going grand," said Quigley. "I wanted to give you an update on the happenings with your favourite Germans. Schüller and Riis are falling over each other now, each one blaming the other for everything. And we discovered Grimsby's body. Anderssen tells us that the local gendarmes found it in a dumpster out back of the hotel."

"Well, that's too bad," said Windflower. "That's pretty dangerous work."

Both men were silent, reflecting on that sombre thought. Finally, Quigley spoke again. "Despite that great loss, there are lots of wins here, though. Gerhard Müller's operations have been dealt a great blow, and the man himself has been handed over to the Germans, who insisted on prosecuting one of their own. We're still negotiating with the Americans about the fate of the others."

"I guess that's some version of justice," said Windflower. "Tizzard's got an interesting case going on down here."

"I heard a little bit about the DEA and South America," said Quigley. "Are you helping him out?"

"Just informally," said Windflower.

"Why don't you stay on contract with us and give me a full report of what's happening and what unfolds?" said Quigley.

"Can't you get that from Tizzard?" asked Windflower. "I don't want to step on his toes."

"I'll call him," said Quigley. "Tell him that you will be my liaison from the HQ Drug Squad. He'll like the help."

"Okay, as long as you check in first, I'm good," said Windflower.

"Hey, maybe you'll get lucky and we'll find something we can use," said Quigley.

"'Fortune brings in some boats that are not steered,'" said Windflower.

"Don't 'mock the good housewife Fortune from her wheel, that her gifts may henceforth be bestowed equally.'"

"That is very good, Ron. *As You Like It*," said Windflower. "Nice."

"Be even nicer if you get us some intelligence," said Quigley. "Keep me updated."

"Bye, Ron," said Windflower.

"Ron Quigley?" asked Sheila, who came in as he was finishing his call.

"Yeah, I got another contract. Or maybe it's an extension," said Windflower.

"Maybe you'll get a job out of this," said Sheila.

"I already have a job," said Windflower. "Assistant caregiver," he added as Amelia Louise and Stella came in and started tugging on his legs.

"C'mon, Daddy," said Stella. "We want to do crafts."

"Yeah, Daddy, cwafts," said Amelia Louise, who was trying to drag a large container of supplies behind her.

"There you go, big-shot consultant," said Sheila, laughing. "Cwaft time."

Windflower got out the craft supplies and started laying some of them on the kitchen floor. He figured it would be easier to clean up in here. He was right.

Tizzard, on the other hand, was still trying to figure out how he was going to clean up his case when he also got a call from Ron Quigley.

"Good day, Corporal," said Quigley. "How are things in beautiful Grand Bank?"

"Things were good right up until the phone rang," said Tizzard. "I hope that you are calling to make my day and not break it."

"'O ye of little faith,' Corporal," said Quigley. "But I understand completely. I remember the dread I felt when the call came from Ottawa. I, however, come bearing good news. So, 'give your thoughts no tongue.'"

"Now I'm really worried," said Tizzard.

"I have asked Windflower to assist you in your case as the liaison with the HQ Drug Squad," said Quigley.

"He's already helping me. Are you asking him to take over?" asked Tizzard.

"No, no, no," said Quigley. "You're in charge. He follows your lead. But he also sends me a report of whatever you and he find out. It sounds like you've got some sort of South American drug connection going on down there, and we need intelligence on it. If it's happening in Grand Bank, it's likely happening other places."

"Okay," said Tizzard. "I'm good. Anything else? Aren't you going to wish me good luck?"

"'Good luck is often with the man who doesn't include it in his plans,'" replied Quigley. "Let me know if there's any problems. Otherwise, I'll hear from Windflower in due course."

Chapter Fifty-four

Tizzard hung up and called Windflower. "I hear we're a formal team again," he said.

"Yeah, except you're the boss now," said Windflower. "Go easy on me."

Tizzard laughed. "I'm going to pick up Rob Skinner for a chat. Wanna come with me?"

"I'm ready," said Windflower. "I've had enough crafts for one day. Why don't you swing by and pick me up? The girls would love to see you."

"See you soon," said Tizzard. True to his word, he was in Windflower's driveway a short while afterward and not long after was rolling around the floor with Amelia Louise, Stella and Lady. Windflower pulled him out of the pile and they managed to get out the door with the "unca, unca, unca" chants lingering behind them.

"That was fun," said Tizzard.

"Try it every day, all day," said Windflower. "I don't know how they do it."

Tizzard smiled and drove directly to Skinner's house.

"Lots of toys around," said Windflower, pointing to the snow machines and the travel trailer.

"He has many sources of income, according to the bank," said Tizzard. "That's one of the things I want to talk to him about." He parked the Jeep, and he and Windflower walked to the back door.

"You again?" said Rob Skinner. "Haven't you bothered us enough lately? What do you want now?"

"We want to talk to you," said Tizzard. "We can do it here or down at the detachment. Your choice."

"I got nuttin to say," said Skinner, and he moved to close the door. Tizzard put out his arm and stopped him.

"It's not a request," said Tizzard. "More of a demand."

"Am I under arrest?" asked Skinner.

"You're the second person that's asked me that today," said Tizzard. "I could if you want me to, or you could come along with us."

"I thought you said I could do it here," said Skinner.

"That offer expired, and my last one is going fast," said Tizzard. "Either you come now, voluntarily, or we arrest you. Your choice."

"I gotta tell the missus I'm going out," said Skinner. He was back with his jacket on a minute later and followed Tizzard out to his vehicle. Tizzard opened the back door, and Skinner got in. Windflower got in the passenger side, and they went back to the detachment. Smithson had left for his break. He would come back in at midnight.

Tizzard brought Skinner into the interview room and pointed to a chair. "We'll be back," he said. Windflower followed him back to the break room, where Tizzard made a fresh pot of coffee.

"I don't know what we'd do without coffee," said Tizzard.

"We'd be pretty tired, that's for sure," said Windflower as they waited for the coffee to brew. "I assume you're letting him stew for a few minutes. Good idea."

"I think I learned that from you," said Tizzard. "He's probably tired, and I don't think he had his supper yet, so he may be hungry, too. Even better."

"How are you thinking about handling it?" asked Windflower as Tizzard poured him a cup of coffee and sat with one of his own.

"He didn't react well to the questions about him and Marguerite Slaney, so I thought I'd start with the money," said Tizzard.

"Good plan," said Windflower. "He seems to have a lot of disposable income, and you have the bank statements."

"Ready?" asked Tizzard. He went to his office and picked up his file with the printout of the bank statements.

"I am recording this interview," he said to Skinner, who sat in the chair across with his arms folded and a scowl etched on his face. Tizzard said the time and date out loud. "Present for this interview with Robert Skinner are Corporal Edward Tizzard and Winston Windflower, RCMP consultant."

"What's he doing here?" asked Skinner.

"He's assisting me," said Tizzard. "Now, let's get right to it. What are your sources of income?"

"Well, b'y, I got a disability pension from when I hurt my back, so that limits my physical labour," said Skinner. "But I still manages to get a few small hobbles here and there. Nothing big."

"Where did the money come from to buy the machines in your yard?" asked Tizzard.

"My wife had a bit of money that her father left her when he died, and we don't have many expenses now that it's just the two of us," said Skinner.

"What about all this money?" asked Tizzard, pushing across the copies of the bank statements.

"I think I wants a lawyer," said Skinner.

"We haven't charged you with anything. Yet," said Tizzard, letting the last word hang in the air. "We're just asking questions. Although if you don't answer, then we can only assume that you're hiding something."

Skinner just sat there. If anything, he gripped his arms tighter.

"Tell us about your son," said Tizzard. "Have you talked to him lately?"

"No," said Skinner.

"Well, according to your phone records there are several calls from a Florida number that we have identified as coming from Florida State Prison," said Tizzard.

"Okay, Robbie called me," said Skinner.

"That's better," said Tizzard. "Although I must admit that your lying does have me somewhat concerned. Let's get on the same page here, okay? Tell me about your son."

"You know he's in prison, and you know what for," said Skinner. "What he does has nothing to do with me."

"Unless you have been receiving money from him," said Tizzard. "Then it could be proceeds from an illegal operation."

"I don't have any of that money," said Skinner, realizing that he had better start swimming before he drowned.

"So where did it go?" asked Tizzard.

Skinner had no response.

"It looks like money laundering to me," Tizzard said to Windflower. "What do you think?"

"I'd say so," said Windflower. "Even if you were just the vehicle to pass the money through, you might be liable for ten years in Canada. More if it's prosecuted in the United States."

Skinner was mulling this all over now. "I still wants a lawyer."

"Okay," said Tizzard. "I'm not going to charge you right now. But don't leave town. We will want to talk to you some more."

Skinner looked a bit shocked that they were letting him go but got up to leave. "Don't suppose you'll drive me home?"

Tizzard ignored that last request, and through the window he and Windflower watched Rob Skinner turn his collar up against the wind and start walking home.

Chapter Fifty-five

Tizzard said, "We didn't get much, but I think we might have shook him up a little, let's see what he does next."

"He's not innocent, that's for sure," said Windflower. "But it's hard to imagine him as the brains of this operation either. Did you get a file on the son?"

"I'm not sure. Let me check with Smithson," said Tizzard. He texted Smithson and soon after got a ping back. "He's going to email Florida and will get back to us."

"I guess the next person on your list is Marguerite Slaney," said Windflower. "Do you want to talk to her today or leave it until tomorrow?"

"I think we'll wait," said Tizzard. "We've laid out enough rope. Let's see if one of them hangs themself. Or the other. I'll give you a ride home if you'd like."

Windflower got home at his favourite time of day, suppertime. Sheila had made a vegetarian lasagna, and Windflower nearly went weak in the knees when he opened the door.

"Come sit down," said Sheila. "I didn't hear from you, so me and the girls made lasagna."

Both girls beamed at him as he sat and took his plate from Sheila, along with a scoopful of steamed broccoli. They stared at him as he took his first bite. "This is delicious," he said. "Who made this great supper?" Stella and Amelia Louise raised their hands.

"Thank you so much," said Windflower as he dug into his cheesy pasta. "It's very good," he said to Sheila. "Where did you get time to make it?"

"It's not that hard with the precooked noodles that we already had," said Sheila. "And it only takes about thirty-five or forty minutes in the oven. I made another one and froze it."

"Wow, you are amazing," said Windflower as he passed his plate over for another helping.

Eddie Tizzard was having a nice supper, too. It was Carrie's day off, so she surprised him with one of his favourite dishes, baked rabbit. He knew what it was as soon as he opened the door. "Oh my god," he said. "Where did you get the rabbit?"

"Your dad dropped it off," said Carrie. "He said Jarge had a few snares and got a couple, so he brought your dad a brace. He's having one at Margaret's tonight and dropped the other one off for us."

"That is great," said Tizzard. "What a grand way to come home. You, a rabbit supper, and Hughie. Where is he?"

"He's down right now but will probably wake up soon," said Carrie. "Why don't you check on him?"

Tizzard kissed Carrie and went to the bedroom to peek in on the baby. Hughie was sleeping but stirring around a little. But not quite yet. That would give Tizzard a chance to get cleaned up, and just as soon he was coming out of the bathroom, he heard the baby.

"I got him," he called out. He picked up a still groggy Hughie and laid him on the change table. He cleaned his bum and put on a clean diaper with the baby watching his every move. When he was done, Tizzard raised him high above his head and held him there as the baby squealed with delight.

"You guys having fun?" asked Carrie as she laid Tizzard's supper on the table and took the baby. She could feed him while her husband had his supper.

"I love rabbit," said Tizzard. "Baked rabbit, boiled rabbit, rabbit stew, bottled rabbit. I loves it all, b'y."

"You know it's actually a hare? A snowshoe hare," said Carrie.

"I just know it taste's sum good, b'y," said Tizzard as he picked out a tender morsel of the brown meat. "You made the pastry, too. It's perfect. And so is the gravy."

"I'm glad you enjoy it," said Carrie.

"Aren't you having any?" asked Tizzard.

"Very funny," said Carrie. She'd had rabbits as pets when she was a youngster and couldn't imagine eating one. "I had a nice salad and a piece of broiled fish. Very healthy."

"So was this rabbit, by the taste of him," said Tizzard.

"You're so bad, Eddie," said Carrie, handing him back the baby. "Do you have to go back in?"

"Only for a little while to talk to Smithson," said Tizzard. "We've got some stuff on Rob Skinner. Money issues."

"Maybe it's connected to all that bitcoin that was on his brother's computer," said Carrie.

"If it is, Smithson will find it. He's a genius with this stuff," said Tizzard.

When he went back to the detachment a little while later, Smithson proved him right.

"I can't connect all of it," said Smithson. "But I did manage to track Rob Skinner's bank transfers. They all go to a series of accounts in Europe. Switzerland, mostly. You remember we had some money laundering stuff a while back?"

"Yeah," said Tizzard. "Aren't there some banks that are on Interpol's list of suspected money launderers?"

"The Swiss authorities have been dealing with this for years. They recently passed a law to make it harder for banks in their jurisdiction to engage in money laundering activities," said Smithson.

"But they haven't stopped it?" asked Tizzard.

"No," said Smithson. "They're trying. Their big problem is that many banks are private. Right now, they are investigating four managers at one called Julius Baer."

"And that is important why?"

"Because that's where most of Rob Skinner's transfers ended up," said Smithson.

"Do we know what happened to the money after that?"

"Not yet," said Smithson. "I have a call into Commercial Crime. I don't expect I'll hear back 'til the morning."

"Good work," said Tizzard.

"Thanks," said Smithson. "I also have a phone call that I'd like you to hear. Come in the back."

Tizzard walked back to Smithson's tech area, where he'd set up a tape recorder hooked up to the computer.

Smithson touched the screen, and the time flashed. He pressed a few buttons, and then a list appeared. "It's from Rob Skinner's home phone," said Smithson. "Most of them are to and from his wife. Except for this one." He pointed to a number and clicked on it.

"That's Marguerite Slaney's number, isn't it?" asked Tizzard.

"It is indeed," said Smithson as he turned up the volume on the speakers.

They heard a woman's voice first. "We have to be careful," she said. "They are closing in. Don't tell them anything."

"I won't," said Skinner. "But I'm going to get a lawyer. I know they can't make me talk, and they can't reach Robbie either."

"Stick with your story, no matter what," said Marguerite Slaney. "You can't back out now."

"I wish I never got involved in this in the first place," said Skinner.

"Too late for that now," said the woman. "And if you implicate me in any way, you know what will happen to you."

"You can't threaten me," said Skinner. But the line had gone dead.

"Now that is very interesting, isn't it?" said Tizzard.

Smithson just nodded.

Chapter Fifty-six

Tizzard left Smithson for the overnight shift and headed home. If he'd driven up around Windflower's house, he would have seen his friend coming back in with Lady. Both man and dog were tired out from the day, and Windflower went upstairs to join Sheila, who was sitting in bed reading her book. Windflower got in bed and tried to do the same, but before he knew it, the book had fallen from his hands, and he was gone.

He woke up some time after that in another dream. He was in a large bubble again, like the one he'd been in after using Auntie Marie's pipe. But the bubble did not lift or rise up. It rolled along with him inside of it. It was a bit crazy, and at first he tried to keep his balance. But that was impossible, so he just went along with the flow and enjoyed the bubble ride until it came to a stop with him inside.

He was in his backyard, and it was summertime. Lady was running around, and the girls were trying to catch her. Sheila was sitting on the deck, and Eddie and Carrie were across from her. Hughie had grown up and was trying to get out of his mother's arms to go play with the dog. That was when Windflower realized that the girls were bigger and much older, too. Stella looked maybe ten, and Amelia Louise looked about eight, with long hair that ran down her back. She was starting to look like her mother, he thought. Beautiful.

He turned his eyes back to Sheila. When he looked closer, he could see that she had dark bags under her eyes, like she hadn't been sleeping. There was a touch of grey at the sides of her head. He could feel a deep sadness in her, and his heart sank. He tried to push his way out of the bubble, but it held tight. He cried out to her, but neither she nor the others could hear him. He tried banging on the side of the bubble, but all that did was to make the bubble start to move away. He stopped banging, but the bubble drifted off and was soon flying into the air like the last time.

Finally, it stopped in a cloud again. It opened, and he stepped out, but this time there were no people. Well, there was one person: the man with a long white beard.

"You're back," said the man.

"What's going on?' asked Windflower. "What did I just see? Why wasn't I there? That's my home, my family."

"It was," said the man. "But in that scene you had drifted away. I mean your body might have been there somewhere, but your spirit was off in another place."

"Is that real, or can I change that picture?" asked Windflower.

"We can always change," said the old man. "That's why you were given the power to choose."

"How do I know the right path?" asked Windflower.

"Follow your heart and always choose the gift that is front of you. That's why it's called the present."

The old man and the cloud and the bubble all started to dissolve into a bright white light. Windflower closed his eyes, and when he opened them, he was back in bed with Sheila. Before falling back to sleep, he gripped her even closer than usual. "Not taking any chances," he said to himself as he drifted off.

Eddie Tizzard was having a dream tonight, too. Or maybe it was a nightmare. He could hear someone calling his name, but he didn't have to see who that was because right now he was focused on running as fast as he could, chased by a very large wolf. It must be a nightmare, he thought as he kept running. But then he stumbled, and the wolf was on top of him in a flash. The animal bared his teeth, and Tizzard stepped back.

"Don't be afraid, it's me," said the wolf.

Tizzard recognized the voice. "Sid, is that you?"

"I'm smiling at you, aren't I?" said the wolf.

"It's hard for me to tell," said Tizzard. "Why were you chasing me?"

"Why were you running away?" asked the wolf. "How do you like me now, by the way? I thought I would try being a wolf because they're extinct in Newfoundland. Did you know that?"

"I did, as a matter of fact," said Tizzard. "Now that you've caught me, do you have a message for me?"

"You know what, I don't think I do," said Sid. "I just like hanging out with you."

Tizzard looked very disappointed.

"I was just joshing ya," said Sid. "There's always a message. Even if there's no message, it's a message. The truth is, young Eddie, that you are on a good path. Stick with it. Trust your instincts and keep listening to your dad and Hughie."

"Hughie can't speak," said Tizzard.

"Children and elders are our greatest teachers. Hughie asks you to create a safe place for him to learn and grow, and when you do, he reciprocates," said Sid.

"What do you mean?" asked Tizzard.

"He teaches you to trust absolutely without any hesitation. Does he cry when you throw him up in the air?"

"No," said Eddie. "He trusts that I will catch him."

"Exactly," said Sid. "But you will have to learn to trust him, too. When he starts walking and running and climbing trees, you will want to stop him to keep him safe. He will ask you to trust him and let him go."

"I think I get it," said Tizzard.

"I think you do," said Sid. "Now I gotta go. The moon will be up soon, and I've got some howling to do."

Tizzard watched as the wolf Sid waddled away into the night. He woke up in bed a little while later. He got up, crept into his son's bedroom and peeked into his crib. Little Hughie was sleeping peacefully. Tizzard didn't do anything to disturb him, but before he left, he whispered a silent "thank you" and went back to bed with Carrie.

Chapter Fifty-seven

The morning came too early for Windflower, but it came with a bang and a crash anyway. He and Sheila jumped up in bed at the noise, and Windflower was first off the mark and ran downstairs.

Stella was standing in the middle of the kitchen, crying, and Amelia Louise was doing the same under the kitchen table. He grabbed Stella, who was closest, and hugged her.

"What happened, sweetie?" he asked, although he could see from the broken cereal bowls in the middle of the floor what at least part of the problem was.

"We were tryin' to make breakfast for you and Mommy," said Stella between sobs. "But she dropped the bowls. Now we're in trouble."

"I was making brefast, too," said Amelia Louise, who had now emerged slightly from her hideout. She wasn't coming all the way out until she knew the coast was clear.

"Come here, honey," said Windflower. "Let me clean all this up, and then I'll help you make Mommy her breakfast. Why don't you go up and ask her what she wants?"

The two girls wiped away their tears and scrambled upstairs in a race to see Sheila. That gave Windflower time to sweep up the broken bowls and put the coffee on. The first one back downstairs was Amelia Louise. "Mommy wants waffles, and Mila too," she announced.

"What about your sister?" asked Windflower.

"I guess she can have some, too," said Amelia Louise. "She has to get ready for skool."

"Why don't you help me with the waffles then?" asked Windflower.

Amelia Louise and her dad happily made up the waffle batter, and when the first one was on the griddle, he sent her up to tell Sheila and her sister that breakfast was ready.

Eddie Tizzard was having toast and coffee and giggles with Hughie this morning for breakfast. The baby had jam smeared all over his face and little bits of toast strewn all beneath his highchair. Carrie offered to clean him up if Eddie would tidy up the kitchen.

"That's a fair deal," said Eddie as he cleaned up the chair and ran the Swiffer over the kitchen floor. A few minutes later, Carrie was out with her and Hughie dressed and ready to go.

"I'll drop him off at Margaret's and see you later," she said. She came closer so he could give both her and Hughie a peck on the cheek.

"Bye." He waved to Hughie as she took him out to the car. It might be his imagination, but he was sure that the baby waved back. Feeling pretty good about that, he got himself dressed and headed over to the office.

Smithson was waiting for him. "I talked to Commercial Crime again," he said. "They're sending someone down. They want to talk to Rob Skinner."

"I'm not surprised," said Tizzard. "This feels much bigger than Grand Bank."

"They're still tracing the money. It takes a while to get through the barriers the banks in Switzerland put up, but my contact says that they have seen similar operations run by the German and Dutch gangs," said Smithson. "The guy will be here tomorrow."

"Okay," said Tizzard. "Before you go home, can you make me a copy of that tape from last night and get me that small recorder? Then, pick up Rob Skinner and bring him back here."

Smithson left, and Carrie popped by to say hello on her way out to do the highway run. Tizzard called Windflower.

"Let's go see Marguerite Slaney," he said. "I'll pick you up," he added when Windflower agreed. He waited for Smithson to bring him the tape and recorder and then went to get Windflower.

"I'm going out with Eddie," said Windflower.

"Great," said Sheila. "I'm going over to the council to present my ideas today. Wish me luck."

"Good luck," said Windflower. "Where's she going today?"

"Mila goin' to Grandma Moira's to bake a cake," said Amelia Louise.

"Well, I will certainly look forward to getting a big piece of that," said Windflower. "I should be home early. Maybe I'll barbeque something."

"I'll see what they have at Warren's on the way back," said Sheila.

"Here's my ride," he said as Tizzard's Jeep pulled up in the driveway. He kissed Sheila and gave Amelia Louise a hug so tight, she started screaming. "I love you," he said.

"I love you, Daddy," said Amelia Louise.

"You're pretty happy this morning," said Tizzard as Windflower got into the car.

"Why wouldn't I be?" he asked. "'I bear a charmed life.'"

"Me, too," said Tizzard. "Me, too. Let's see if Marguerite Slaney is in as good a mood as we are."

She clearly was not by the look on her face when she saw Windflower and Tizzard standing outside.

"I'm not answering any more questions," she said.

"That's not a very good start," said Tizzard. "You don't even know what the questions might be."

"I've told you all I know," said the woman.

"Maybe not everything," said Tizzard. "Right now we want to know what your relationship is with Rob Skinner."

Marguerite Slaney opened the door and let them in.

"Things have changed, ma'am," said Tizzard. "We'd like you to listen to something and then tell us what it is all about."

He laid the recorder on the kitchen table and watched Marguerite Slaney to see if she would react to what he played. Her eyebrows raised a little at the beginning, but she remained calm. And silent.

"What do you have to say about that?" asked Tizzard.

"Are you arresting me?" she asked.

"I am," said Tizzard. "On suspicion to commit money laundering and being involved in a criminal organization. Come with us, please."

"I want my lawyer," said Marguerite Slaney.

"You can call from the detachment," said Tizzard. Marguerite Slaney got her coat and purse, and the two men escorted her to Tizzard's Jeep and drove her to the RCMP detachment.

Chapter Fifty-eight

When they arrived, Smithson and Carrie were standing at the front talking to Betsy. Windflower stopped to talk to Carrie while Tizzard walked the woman down the corridor. Along the way they passed Rob Skinner standing in one of the other cells. He and Marguerite Slaney stared at each other, but neither spoke. Tizzard took Slaney to the last cell in the row and locked the door with her standing there, holding her purse tightly.

Tizzard couldn't tell if she was defiant or afraid. Maybe a combination of both, he thought. He went back to the front. "Can you go and talk to her?" he said to Evanchuk. "She said she wanted a lawyer."

"Let's do Skinner first," he said to Windflower. "Smithson, can you set up the recording? Thanks."

Evanchuk and Smithson went off to their tasks. Betsy was busy on the phone, as usual.

"Coffee?" asked Windflower.

"Sure," said Tizzard. "Let's get a cup, and we can chat before we do Skinner."

"I actually think it will be harder to break the woman than Skinner," said Windflower after they got their coffee. They were sitting in Tizzard's office, Windflower's old office, when someone knocked on the door.

"Come in," said Tizzard.

It was Evanchuk. "She called her lawyer. Brent Butts from Marystown. He's in court this morning but will be over after lunch. Are we charging her with anything?"

"We are, but let's wait for her lawyer," said Tizzard. "But book her in with a photo and fingerprints. I want her to feel like she's really in jail." Evanchuk nodded and left.

"I think you're right," said Tizzard. "She clearly has a role, but I'm still not sure where she fits in."

"Do you know her at all?" asked Windflower.

"Not really," said Tizzard.

"You know who would know all about her?"

"Betsy," said Tizzard triumphantly. He pushed the intercom button. "I always wanted to do that," he said.

"Yes, Corporal," came Betsy's voice over the intercom.

"Betsy, can you come and see us in my office? We need your help," said Tizzard.

Those words were magic to Betsy's ears, and she was there in a flash.

"So, how can I help you today?" she asked.

"Marguerite Slaney," said Tizzard. "What can you tell us about her?"

"Well," said Betsy. "She's not from here. Her family was from Point May, and the rumour was that they were rum smugglers. Mugglers, they called them over that way. Paddy Slaney was her second husband. I heard the first just disappeared. Paddy was working away for years, and his first wife died of breast cancer. She was a Morrissey from Fortune."

"Has she ever been in trouble, Betsy?" asked Windflower.

"I don't know about trouble. She wasn't living around here for a while. Toronto or something, I heard," said Betsy. "But she always had airs. Like she was someone special. She didn't have many friends around here. You know people don't like that very much."

"Did she travel or have fancy jewellery or anything?" asked Tizzard.

"She was always gone," said Betsy. "I'm not sure where. People guessed Florida, cause she would go away and come back with a tan. She always dressed to the nines, and that was more noticeable since most don't around here. There was always a whisper that she had money, but if she did, she didn't show it off."

"What was her maiden name?" asked Windflower.

"She was a Mercer from Point May originally," said Betsy.

"What was her first husband's last name?" asked Tizzard.

"Pilgrim," said Betsy. "Roger Pilgrim."

"Thanks, Betsy, you've been very helpful," said Tizzard.

Betsy left looking very pleased with herself.

Smithson came by to tell them that the recording was set to go.

"Great," said Tizzard. "Can you run a few names through the computer? Marguerite Mercer and Marguerite Pilgrim. See if anything shows up."

"Sure," said Smithson.

"Ready to go?" Tizzard asked Windflower.

"Ready," said Windflower. "That was smart to pick up on that. I was thinking the same thing. People seldom turn bad overnight."

"Thanks," said Tizzard. "I learned from the best."

Tizzard got Skinner from his cell and brought him into the interview room. He and Windflower sat across from Skinner.

"Do I need a lawyer for this?" asked Skinner.

"We haven't charged you with anything, but you can call one if you want," said Tizzard, standing up again.

"No, no, let's see how this goes," said Skinner.

"So, we heard the call from Marguerite Slaney," said Tizzard.

Skinner looked surprised but not shocked.

"It's time to stop the games," said Tizzard. "We've arrested her, and you're next. This is your last chance to talk. Tell us what exactly was going on. What was your role, and what about your son? How is he connected to this? We can start there."

Skinner was starting to sweat now, and he wiped his brow. "I can give you everything," he said. "But I want to try to get my son back to Canada. He needs to get out of that hellhole in Florida. Can you help with that?"

"Maybe," said Tizzard. "Depends on what you have to say. Are you going to talk about Marguerite Slaney?"

"I said everything," said Skinner.

"Give us a few minutes," said Tizzard.

The two men went out into the hallway and walked towards the front.

"Can we do that?" asked Tizzard. "Get his son out of jail in Florida?"

"We can't, but Quigley might be able to," said Windflower. "Give him a call."

256

Tizzard went to his office and phoned Quigley. When Quigley heard the details, he said he would check and get back to him.

"Lunch time," said Tizzard when he came back to Windflower. "Put Skinner back in the cell," he said to Smithson as they passed him near the front, waved goodbye to Betsy and drove to the Mug-Up.

The café was crowded, so they got their sandwiches to go: turkey with dressing on whole wheat bread. They got back in Tizzard's Jeep, drove down to the wharf and parked looking out to sea. The day was bright and cold, and even the few seagulls that hovered near the fish plant seemed to shiver in the noontime sun.

"I love being by the water," said Tizzard. "It's all I know. I can't imagine not living near it."

"You still thinking about trying to get a transfer on the island?" asked Windflower.

"Yeah, I'm going to talk to Bill Ford. See what he can do. In the best-case scenario, both of us can get assigned to Marystown," said Tizzard. "I'd love to have a few more years being close to my dad. He's not getting any younger."

"You are really blessed right now," said Windflower. "You have the opportunity to learn from Hughie and your dad. My people say our best teachers are the elders and our children."

"I think you're right," said Tizzard. "Ready to go back?"

"Ready," said Windflower.

Chapter Fifty-nine

When they got back to the detachment, a man in a rumpled suit was sitting in the chair next to Betsy.

"Brent Butts," he said and stood to offer his hand to Tizzard and Windflower.

"I'm Tizzard, and this is Winston Windflower," said Tizzard. "He's assisting with this case."

"I'd like to see my client," said Butts. "Marguerite Slaney. She said she is being charged. Can you tell me the nature of those charges?"

"We haven't formally charged her yet," said Tizzard. "We want to question her first. It's in connection with possible money laundering and a criminal organization."

"Those are very serious charges," said Butts. "Do you have evidence of my client's involvement in these activities?"

"All in due course," said Tizzard. "Why don't you talk to your client, and then we'll meet with you and her. It will become much clearer after that. Let me arrange that for you." He walked to the back, found Carrie and got her to bring Marguerite Slaney to the larger boardroom.

"Right this way," he said to the lawyer as he escorted him to the room to meet with his client. As he was leaving them, his cell phone rang. It was Ron Quigley.

"Okay, we can make the transfer. But only if it's really good stuff you're getting from Skinner," said Quigley. "I had to pull in a huge favour for this."

"No pressure," said Tizzard.

"Welcome to the big leagues, Corporal," said Quigley.

"I think I'd rather play Little League," said Tizzard.

Quigley laughed. "You'll be fine. You've got Windflower to help out if you get stuck. But you can do this, Eddie."

"Thanks, Ron. I'll do my best."

"'Be not afraid of greatness: some are born great, some achieve greatness, and some have greatness thrust upon them,'" said Quigley.

"That would be me," said Tizzard. "Thrust upon me."

Quigley laughed and hung up.

"We've got a green light from Quigley," said Tizzard. "As long as I deliver the goods."

"No pressure," said Windflower.

"That's what I said," said Tizzard. "Let's get Skinner."

A minute later, they were back in the interview room with Rob Skinner.

"I have the authorization to help you out," said Tizzard. Skinner's face brightened. "As long as what you have merits it."

"So, we've got a deal?" asked Skinner. When Tizzard nodded, he looked at Windflower. "You're my witness in all this," he said.

Windflower just shrugged.

"Paddy Slaney brought me in," said Skinner. "But this has been going on for a while. Sid was up to his neck in it, and he wanted me to join him, but I resisted. It was only when Robbie got caught down South that I came in. Slaney said he could help me get Robbie off the hook and make a lot of money."

"But he didn't get your son off, did he?" asked Tizzard.

"No," said Skinner. "But he was right about the second part. There was so much money flowing through that nobody could keep track of it. Paddy said we were investors in a multinational corporation. Big shots. He was travelling all over the world. He wanted me to come along, but that's not my thing. It wasn't Sid's either."

"What happened to your brother?" asked Tizzard.

"He was trying to get out," said Skinner. "But this is not the kind of business that you can just walk away from, is it?"

Tizzard let that question sit there until Skinner was ready to talk again.

"He was killed," said Skinner. "Then dumped in the lake in St. John's. There was some baloney story about him killing himself. That wasn't Sid. He would never do that."

"So, who killed him?" asked Tizzard.

"Slaney," said Skinner. This time he hesitated.

"How do you know that?" asked Tizzard.

"She told me," said Skinner.

"Who told you?" asked Tizzard.

"Marguerite Slaney," said Skinner.

"Here's a pen and paper," said Tizzard. "I want you to write down what she said to you."

Skinner took the pen and started writing.

"Tell us everything you know about the operation. How it all worked, who was involved. Write it down," said Tizzard. "We'll be back."

He and Windflower left the room and closed the door. They didn't have time to debrief before Smithson and Evanchuk met them in the hallway. They both had papers in their hands.

"Her prints popped up this," said Evanchuk, holding up her paper.

"Marguerite Slaney, also known as Marguerite Pilgrim," said Smithson, waving his. "Four years in Millhaven for drug dealing and money laundering."

"And the OPP in Milton, Ontario, were investigating her in the drowning death of Andrew Pilgrim," said Evanchuk.

Tizzard had a look at both documents and handed them to Windflower.

"Very interesting," said Tizzard.

"Ahem," said a voice from down the hall. It was the lawyer. "We're ready for you now," said Brent Butts.

"Okay, just wait in there until we get set up," said Tizzard.

"Move Skinner back to his cell and stand in front so Slaney and her lawyer don't see him or speak to him," Tizzard said to Evanchuk. "Smithson, reset the recorder for us."

Windflower followed Tizzard back to his office. "I've never seen a case move this fast. You must have the magic touch."

"More like beginner's luck," said Tizzard. "Now that we have a truer picture of Marguerite Slaney, I can't wait to talk to her again."

"Me, too," said Windflower as Smithson knocked on his door to let him know everything was ready to go. "Bring them into the interview room."

Chapter Sixty

Marguerite Slaney looked exactly the same as before, except that she no longer had her purse to hang on to. She looked determined, thought Tizzard as he exchanged a quick glance with Windflower.

"Well, gentlemen, I hope we can finally clear things up here. Do you intend to proceed with charges?" asked Butts.

"Let's have our conversation first," said Tizzard. He looked directly at Marguerite. "Do you want to tell us anything before we start?"

The lawyer started to say something, but the woman waved him off. "I have done some bad things in my life. And I've paid a price for them," she said. "My husband is talking to your American colleagues right now, and I'm afraid I have little to add."

"What we're most interested in is what happened to two other local residents," said Tizzard. "Sid Skinner, who we now believe was murdered. And Leo Broderick, who met his demise right here in Grand Bank. What can you tell us about those two deaths?"

"Sid Skinner died in St. John's, I believe," said Slaney. "I wasn't even there."

"That's not what someone told us," said Tizzard. "They said you told them you killed Sid Skinner."

"Who?" asked Slaney. "That fool brother of his? I would be very careful about whom you choose to listen to. Especially a killer."

"What do you mean?" asked Tizzard.

"Rob Skinner," said Slaney. "He killed Broderick. I saw it myself. He had these darts with poison that he got from his drug-dealing son. He probably still has some of that poison left in his house."

Tizzard glanced at Windflower again, and when he did, the lawyer took the opportunity to jump in.

261

"What my client is saying is that she has some direct evidence to provide about a crime that she hopes will help her reach an arrangement with you," said Butts.

"She wants a deal?" asked Tizzard.

"I'm sure that we can work something out," said Butts.

"Stay put," said Tizzard. "We'll be back."

He and Windflower went to his office again.

"What now?" asked Tizzard.

"It's possible that both of them are telling part of the truth," said Windflower. "I think it might be wise to search both of the houses."

"Good idea," said Tizzard. "And talk to Ron Quigley."

"An even better idea," said Windflower. "Who do you want to work on the search warrants? Call Judge Prowse?"

"Ask Carrie to do it," said Tizzard. "I'll call Quigley."

Windflower got Carrie to call the judge, and when she came back with the okay, he went back to Tizzard. "Still waiting?" he asked.

"I've got a message in," said Tizzard. "Warrants, okay?"

"Yes," said Windflower.

"Okay," said Tizzard. "Carrie, put Slaney back in her cell. Her lawyer can stay in there, or we'll call him when we need him. When you're done, grab Smithson. I want all three of you to go together. Do one house at a time, starting with Skinner's. We're looking for weapons, including any kind of pellet gun, ammo, poison, or anything that looks like it might be, and the usual drugs and money."

Smithson, Evanchuk, and Windflower were soon on their way to Rob Skinner's house. His wife was quick to leave when they told her why they were there, muttering something under her breath; Windflower couldn't make out if they were prayers or curses. If it was prayers that they wouldn't find anything, they must have gone astray.

There was a safe in the basement that Smithson and Windflower managed to drag upstairs and into the trunk of Smithson's cruiser. They couldn't close the trunk, but Smithson tied it down while Windflower joined Evanchuk in taking a look at the shed out back. There were two rifles, which may have been perfectly legal. Almost every house around here had a gun for shooting birds or going moose hunting. But they also found a key that was marked "Self-Serve Storage," with a phone number on the side of the handle.

"Marystown?" asked Windflower.

"It's behind the mall," said Evanchuk. "You want me to go?"

"Let's talk to Eddie when we get back," said Windflower.

With the safe hanging out of the cruiser, they drove slowly back to Marguerite Slaney's house.

Eddie Tizzard was on the phone with Ron Quigley.

"Leave all the drugs and money laundering stuff for Headquarters," said Quigley. "You focus on figuring out the murders. We already have some of the pieces, and we can talk to the Americans. They have Albert Slaney, and they know where the young Skinner is."

"Okay," said Tizzard. "It sounds like they both want deals. How do I deal with that?"

"Your call," said Quigley. "But I can tell you that unless they have something extraordinary, it's hard to get a deal if they have killed somebody. Who do you think did it?"

"I dunno," said Tizzard. "They're blaming each other. It could be one or the other. Even both?"

"Follow the evidence," said Quigley. "What do you have?"

"Not much," said Tizzard. "Two dead bodies. Both likely poisoned. I guess we have a sample of the poison. The witnesses are hardly reliable."

"Go with that then," said Quigley. "See if you can find any traces of the poison or how it was delivered that is connected to either one of them."

"That's good," said Tizzard. "At least my head is not full of craziness anymore."

"There may be a method in your madness," said Quigley. "Let me know how it works out. I'm going to see about transport for your prisoners. Once you're finished with them, we can deal with them up here."

Tizzard hung up and was starting to walk to the back to look for a snack when he heard someone whispering. It was Marguerite Slaney.

Chapter Sixty-one

She said, "Listen, dope. Stick with our plan. They'll never figure out which one of us is telling the truth, so they won't charge either of us. Unless they can find that pellet gun you had."

"Nah, they'll never find that," said Skinner. "I put it in our storage unit. Safe and sound."

"Good," said the woman. "They'll cut us a deal on the other stuff. That's what Albert said when I talked to him."

"Okay," said Skinner.

Tizzard waited, but there was no more talking. He made a show of reopening his door and calling out to Betsy. She came running.

"Can you see if she needs anything? A drink or to go the bathroom or anything?" he said.

"Sure," said Betsy, a little surprised that was his urgent request.

Tizzard went back into the office and called Windflower.

"We're looking for a pellet gun of some sort," said Tizzard. "I think it may be in storage."

"You're in luck," said Windflower. "We found a key to a storage unit in Rob Skinner's house. It's from a place in Marystown."

"Did you find anything else?"

"We're bringing back a safe from Skinner's, too," said Windflower. "Maybe he'll give us the combo, so we don't have to drill it. And a shoebox of cash from Marguerite Slaney's. American one-hundred-dollar bills. We didn't count it but has to be twenty or thirty thousand."

"Okay, come on back," said Tizzard. "Evanchuk can go to Marystown to check out the storage unit, and we'll figure out the safe."

They got back to the detachment and struggled with the safe, leaving it on the floor near Betsy.

Evanchuk left for Marystown with instructions to look for the pellet gun and to make sure that the unit was registered to Rob Skinner.

The same Rob Skinner was brought to the front and asked to open the safe. He was reluctant but agreed after a little prodding from Tizzard, who swung the door open after Skinner punched the numbers in.

Tizzard and Windflower peered inside. There were stacks and stacks of bills. American. Hundred-dollar bills. "Any explanation you want to provide?" asked Tizzard.

Skinner just shook his head.

"Put all this in evidence," he said to Smithson. He turned back to Skinner. "What about Leo Broderick?"

"What about him?" asked Skinner.

"Marguerite Slaney says you killed him," said Tizzard.

"She a liar," said Skinner.

"We're looking for a gun that was used to shoot poison darts. Know anything about that?" asked Tizzard.

"Nope," said Skinner. "You were at my house. I have a couple of shotguns. Nothing like a pellet gun. I've already given you everything you need. You're still going to help Robbie get out of Florida, right?"

"That depends on how all of this works out," said Tizzard. "I'd be more worried about your own skin right now. Somebody is going to pay for murdering two people. And you're top of the list right now."

"I told you," said Skinner. "Marguerite is the one. She's the killer."

"Put him back in his cell," said Tizzard. "You should think about your next move," he said to Skinner before he left. "You've only got one left."

Smithson walked Skinner to his cell and came back to Tizzard and Windflower. "I want you to stay close to the both of them back there. See if you can hear them talking to each other."

After Smithson left, Brent Butts came out of the boardroom and walked to the front. "Is this going to take much longer? My client has given you all the information she has. Can we talk about her being released on conditions?"

"We're still following up on things," said Tizzard. "But the picture is becoming clearer."

"Good," said Butts. "I'm going out for a coffee at the café. Call me when you need me."

Tizzard and Windflower stepped inside Tizzard's office. "Now we wait," said Tizzard.

"That's what we end up doing most," said Windflower. "'To climb steep hills requires a slow pace at first.'"

"'All good things arrive unto them that wait—and don't die in the meantime,'" said Tizzard in response.

"That's good," said Windflower. "But not Shakespeare."

"My dad's favourite," said Tizzard. "Mark Twain."

The men talked about their children and life and what they were going to have for supper. "I hope Sheila gets some of those nice pork chops from Warren's," said Windflower.

"Um, my mouth is watering thinking about that," said Tizzard.

They didn't have any more time to chat because Tizzard's phone rang. It was Evanchuk. "I've got the gun," she said. "Buried under a pile of rugs in the locker. I can also confirm that the unit is registered to Rob Skinner."

"Okay," said Tizzard. "Wrap it up and bring it back. "

"That's great," said Windflower when Tizzard hung up with Evanchuk. "We can dust it for prints."

"I also thought we could get Doc Sanjay to see if there's any residue," said Tizzard.

"Like poison?" asked Windflower.

"Exactly," said Tizzard. "Listen, this is going to take a while longer. Why don't you go home and have some supper? I'll call you when there's more information."

"What about you?" asked Windflower.

"I think I'll get fish and chips for me and Carrie and Smithson," said Tizzard. "I have to get something for the people in back anyway."

"Okay, call me when you're ready for me," said Windflower.

"Do you want a ride?" asked Tizzard. "I can get Smithson to run you over."

"No worries," said Windflower. "I need the fresh air and the exercise."

Chapter Sixty-two

He did enjoy the fresh air, but there was a wind blowing, almost enough to knock you down. But this was a milder wind, and it was a bit of a respite from the bitterness of the northernmost breezes. Unfortunately, it was almost always a harbinger of worse weather to come. Snow, and lots of it, was likely on the way. The first taste of it hit him on the cheek when he reached his driveway and home.

Inside, another type of snow was brewing. Sheila was on the phone in the kitchen and Lady, with the girls' active assistance, was running around the living room with the stuffing from a pillow strewn behind her like confetti.

"We were trying to stop her," said Stella when they saw Windflower.

"She made a big mess," said Amelia Louise.

"And you girls had nothing to do with it?" asked Windflower.

The two girls shook their head empathically. "Not even a little?" asked Windflower.

"We were playing, and it broke open," said Stella.

"It bwoke, Daddy," said Amelia Louise, holding her hands up in the universal child's language for "there was absolutely nothing I could do."

"Well, let's get it cleaned up before Mommy comes back," said Windflower.

He got a large garbage bag, and he and the girls started picking up the stuffing from all over the room. Although at one point Stella "accidentally" threw a piece at Amelia Louise, who of course retaliated. Windflower got in the middle of the action and was throwing pieces himself soon after. There was a bigger mess than ever when Sheila came into the living room.

"What is going on in here?" she asked in that pretend "Mommy I'm very mad" voice.

"Nothing," said Windflower.

"Nothing," said Stella.

"Nuttin," said Amelia Louise.

The three perpetrators awaited their judgement in silence. Finally, Sheila couldn't take it anymore and started laughing. When they saw she wasn't mad, the other three joined in. "We'll clean this up if you get supper started," said Sheila. "I was hoping you'd be here soon, so I put some potatoes in the oven. The meat is on the counter.

Windflower found the pork chops on the counter, still wrapped in their brown butcher paper. He tore off the paper and inspected them. "Perfect," he pronounced when he saw the three thick pink chops. Light pink and firm, but not hard. "Perfect," he said again as he made up his rub in a stainless-steel bowl. Brown sugar, smoked paprika, black pepper, dry mustard, and a few strong shakes of cayenne pepper. He mixed it up and went outside to heat up the barbeque.

The wind was even brisker now, and it was pushing a fine, granular snow like needles against his cheeks. But he promised barbeque, and now he had to deliver. He went back in and sprinkled the rub over the chops, rubbing the remainder into the meat on both sides. He put the meat on the hottest part of the grill to sear it and seal in the juices. He left it a couple of minutes on each side. Then he took them off the direct heat and let them cook all the way through.

In between turning them, he went back inside and put some frozen peas and carrots on to boil and checked the baked potatoes. They were done, and so were the pork chops. He brought them in on a platter. Sheila and the girls were already sitting at the table.

"We're verry hungry," said Amelia Louise.

"Well, you're in luck," said Windflower.

He cut up one of the pork chops for the girls, sliced a baked potato in half and added that to their plate, along with a small scoop of vegetables. While he was waiting for that to cool, he plated a pork chop, veggies and a potato for him and Sheila as well.

"Voilà," he said as he passed around the food.

The pork chops were excellent, browned on the outside with a nicely caramelized and slightly burnt exterior. And so tender and juicy inside. Sheila was saying something to Windflower, but he didn't hear a word. He was lost in barbequed pork chop heaven. When he finally came back to earth, it was to accept her compliments.

"This is so good," said Sheila. "I think I'll keep you."

"It's the meat," said Windflower. "These pork chops are so fresh, it would be hard to screw them up."

For dessert they had ice cream with canned sliced peaches, and Windflower got to relax for a few minutes with Sheila and the girls before Tizzard called him.

"You ready?" asked Tizzard. "Evanchuk is back, and she's got prints off the pellet gun."

"Skinner?" asked Windflower.

"Yes," said Tizzard. "And Marguerite Slaney."

"Both of them," said Windflower. "So, what are you going to do?"

"I'm not sure," said Tizzard. "Carrie is dropping the gun off to Doc Sanjay. We'll see if he can find any poison residue and then get it tested. She can pick you up on the way back."

"I'll be ready," said Windflower.

The girls moaned a little when he told him he had to go back to work. Sheila looked a bit disappointed too. "I hope you won't be late," she said.

"A couple of hours, I hope," said Windflower. "Now who's my favourite girl?" Both girls screamed and ran towards him. He picked them up and realized that his wrist was now feeling just fine. Another blessing, he thought. He swung them both in the air and then dropped them on the couch. He smothered both of them with kisses and then ran to the window when he heard a car pull up. It was Evanchuk.

"I gotta go," he said as he kissed both girls and gave Sheila a hug. "See you soon."

"Did you get some supper?" Windflower asked Carrie as he got into the cruiser.

"Fish and chips," said Carrie. "Sum good, b'y."

"I hope you can stay around the island if this closure comes down," said Windflower. "You're getting the hang of this Newfie thing."

Carrie laughed. "I don't know about that, but I'd love to spend a few more years here, or close to here. We have family and support, and the pace of life is perfect for a prairie girl like me."

"Let's hope it works out," said Windflower.

"Let's hope there's not too much to this snow either," she said as they pulled into the RCMP parking lot.

Chapter Sixty-three

It looked busy inside. Betsy had gone home, but all the lights were on, and Tizzard and Smithson were playing a game of cards in the back. Brent Butts was sitting at the front near Betsy's station, looking bored out of his mind. "Do you think this will take much longer?" he asked Windflower.

"Not much longer," said Windflower, although he really had no clue. These things took as long as they took and were almost always stretched out. But he wasn't telling the lawyer anything. Maybe it would keep him on his toes. They would likely need him to play some role before this was over.

Smithson reset the recorder, and Evanchuk brought Marguerite into the boardroom to sit alongside her lawyer. Tizzard and Windflower came in shortly afterwards.

"My client has been waiting all day for you to figure out what you're doing," said Butts. "It's time to formally charge her or let her go."

"Okay," said Tizzard. "Marguerite Slaney, we are charging you in the murder of Albert Slaney and Leo Broderick." He turned to Windflower. "Could you get Constable Evanchuk to bring her back to her cell? Transport is on the way to transfer her to Marystown tonight."

Windflower stood to leave and Marguerite yelled at him to stop.

"Yes?" said Tizzard. "You have something to say?"

"Don't say anything," said Brent Butts. "It's a trick."

"It's no trick, my friend," said Tizzard. "We have your client's prints on what we believe is the murder weapon and a person who will testify against her. I have all that I need."

"I want a deal," said Slaney.

"What do you have to offer?" asked Tizzard.

"I can give you the people behind all of this," said the woman. "Let me talk to your boss. The guy in Ottawa who's calling all the shots."

"You better start talking to me. Right now," said Tizzard.

"It's the Germans," said Slaney. "They set this whole thing up. I talked to Müller when he was here."

"Okay," said Tizzard, glancing at Windflower with this surprising news. "But I still need to know who killed Skinner and Broderick."

"Albert killed Skinner," said Slaney. "His brother doesn't know that. He thinks that it was the Germans, too. But Albert did it in St. John's before he went to South America."

"What about Leo Broderick?" asked Tizzard.

"That was Rob Skinner," said the woman. "Broderick got panicky after Sid's body was found and wanted out. That couldn't happen, and Rob looked after it."

"Then why are your prints on the pellet gun?" asked Tizzard.

"I was holding the gun for Albert," said Slaney. "When Rob wanted to deal with Broderick, he asked me for it. Said that nobody would figure out how he died that way."

"You're certainly a part of this, an accessory," said Tizzard.

Marguerite smiled. "If I give up Müller and his crew, this is all going away."

"I'll make the call," said Tizzard. "But I need you to make a statement about Rob Skinner and his involvement with Leo Broderick's death."

The woman smiled again, and Tizzard and Windflower left her with her lawyer to write out her statement.

"Do you believe her?" asked Windflower when they were back in Tizzard's office.

"Doesn't really matter what I believe, does it?" asked Tizzard. "We charge Rob Skinner for Leo Broderick's murder and let Quigley figure out all the rest."

Windflower nodded as Tizzard reached for the phone to call Quigley.

Hours later, Windflower got a ride home with Smithson, who, like the rest of them, looked exhausted. Quigley had agreed with Tizzard's assessment and told them to send Slaney back to

Marystown with the escort that Bill Ford was sending over. She would be shipped to Ottawa as soon as possible so they could deal with her there.

Rob Skinner had been charged with the murder of Leo Broderick and was being represented by Brent Butts, who was already trying to arrange a deal. Windflower smiled to himself at that thought, as distasteful as it seemed. They always want a deal. He said goodnight to Smithson and was in the house and in bed with Sheila a few minutes later.

Carrie Evanchuk had stayed with Tizzard until Marguerite Slaney's ride arrived. When she was safely on her way, Carrie kissed Eddie goodnight and went to his sister's house to pick up Hughie. Tizzard was left alone with Rob Skinner in a cell down the hall, and he was super tired, too. He looked out his window at the swirling drifting snow and was almost hypnotized by it. He started to nod off in his chair, and before he knew it, he was out cold. Not long after though, he woke up and realized he was dreaming.

He knew he was dreaming because the surroundings were not at all familiar, and there was an old man peering at him as he lay on the ground.

"Are you okay?" asked the man.

"I think so," said Eddie. "Where am I, and what's going on here?"

"Good questions," said the old man. "You are in the future. What's going on here is debatable."

"Whose future?" asked Tizzard.

"Another good question," said the man. "You've gotten smarter than I remember." He started to chuckle.

"What's so funny?" asked Tizzard.

"The things we think we know when we are young are never what they really are," said the old man. "'Too bad youth is wasted on the young.'"

"That's Mark Twain," said Tizzard. "Do you know my dad?"

"I do," said the man. "Quite well, as a matter of fact."

"I think I'm supposed to ask you a question, but I don't know what to ask," said Tizzard.

"It's okay not to know what you don't know," said the old man. "'The trouble with the world is not that people know too little; it's that they know so many things that just aren't so.'"

"That's Twain again," said Tizzard. "How do you know my father?"

"Is that your final question?" asked the man.

"No, no, I mean, what is the meaning of life?" blurted out Tizzard.

"That's a very good one," said the old man. "Let me think." He stayed quiet for a minute. So long, Tizzard thought he might fall asleep. Then he spoke again. "Stay true to who you are, and you will become the person that you are supposed to be."

The old man smiled, and when he did, Tizzard saw the resemblance. Like looking into the mirror at an older version of yourself. Once he realized who the man was, he had a million more questions, but it was too late. The vision of the old man faded, and Tizzard woke with a start, almost falling out of his chair.

I can do that, he thought. "'To thine own self be true,'" he said aloud. He walked to the back, past a now-sleeping Rob Skinner, to get himself a snack.

Epilogue

One Month Later

The town of Grand Bank was much quieter now, especially around the RCMP detachment. They were still planning on closing it down, but Sheila had managed to negotiate a six-month grace period for the town to reorganize its policing needs.

Smithson had already made his request to be transferred back to the mainland and had just received word about his assignment.

He came rushing into the detachment.

Betsy was the first to see him. "You look happy," she said.

"I'm going to Steinback," he said.

"Where's that?" asked Betsy.

"It's in Manitoba, right across the border from Ontario. It's a long drive, but I can go home some weekends to see my mom," said Smithson.

"That's great news," said Betsy. "I'm happy for you." And she was. But she was still sad about the detachment downsizing and wondering what it would be like to have only one officer with her. She didn't even know who that would be.

Smithson went to see Tizzard, who was talking with Doctor Sanjay.

"Sorry, I didn't mean to interrupt," said Smithson.

"No worries," said Sanjay. "I'm just leaving. It took a while, but that report confirms the presence of batrachotoxin residue on the pellet gun."

"Perfect, and thank you," said Tizzard. "I'll make sure the Crown gets this report. Maybe they'll call you as an expert witness in Rob Skinner's trial."

"That would be a great honour for a simple Bengali like me," said Sanjay.

"You downplay your expertise," said Tizzard. "'It is very simple to be happy, but it is very difficult to be simple.'"

"That is very wise, young man," said Sanjay. "Your father is teaching you well. I shall go home and prepare myself to testify."

Tizzard laughed. "You will have plenty of time," he said. "At least a year and maybe longer with the backlog in the courts."

Sanjay left, and Smithson finally got to tell Tizzard his news.

"I'm glad for you," said Tizzard. "We're still waiting to hear back about Marystown, but whatever it is, it's going to be okay."

"You already have a great life," said Smithson.

Tizzard heartily agreed. He'd finished up his cases, and Rob Skinner was in St. John's at the penitentiary, awaiting trial. Marguerite Slaney was in some undisclosed location, but Ron Quigley had told him that she was very helpful in providing more ammunition against Müller and his crew. Little Hughie was happy, healthy, and growing every day, and it was a joy to be around him and his dad and Carrie on a daily basis.

Someone else who had a great life was Winston Windflower. He had breakfast with his kids and was now preparing his menu for the reopening of the B&B weekend dinners. This was fun. He was so busy in his task that he didn't hear Sheila come in. She'd dropped Amelia Louise at daycare and was going over to the council offices. But she was back, and she had someone else with her. It was the mayor, Jacqueline Wilson.

"Good morning, Madam Mayor. I'll get out of your way," said Windflower. "You and Sheila probably have important things to discuss."

"I actually came to see you," said the mayor. "We have something that we'd like you to consider."

Windflower looked at Sheila, and she smiled back at him.

"You know we've been working our way through how to deal with the diminished RCMP capacity," said Mayor Wilson. "But at Sheila's suggestion, we have also been trying to reimagine how we would like policing to be carried out in our community. We've also teamed up with Fortune and Garnish and Frenchman's Cove and agreed to pool our budget. What we want to have is a community police officer, and we'd like you to consider the position."

"How would that work, exactly?" asked Windflower.

Mayor Wilson laughed. "We're not sure, exactly," she said. "That's part of what we'd like you to consider."

Windflower looked puzzled.

The mayor laughed again. "Don't worry, we're not asking you to figure this out. But we think we can have a policing plan that keeps us safe and starts focusing on prevention instead of prosecution. The province is considering giving us money for a pilot project—thank you, Sheila—whereby the RCMP will look after traffic and the highway, and we take care of local policing."

"But how would one person do all the work?" asked Windflower.

"We'd have to recruit local volunteers," said Sheila, jumping into the conversation.

"Community safety officers," said Mayor Wilson. "We've put money in our proposal for training and a small honorarium. We think people would love to work in that role."

"So, why do you need me?" asked Windflower. "Why don't you just recruit and hire somebody else?"

"Well, we actually need you to help give this proposal more credibility," said the mayor. "What do we know about policing?"

Windflower looked at Sheila, but she had no clues to offer. He was on his own.

The mayor could see his hesitation. "You don't have to say anything right now except that you'll consider it."

He looked at Sheila again, but still no sign from her. He looked back at the mayor.

"I'll think about it," he said.

After the mayor left, Sheila made them a pot of tea, and they sat in the living room.

"I didn't suggest this," she said. "I only suggested that the plan would have a better chance of success if it had an expert attached to it."

"Thank you for considering me an expert," said Windflower.

"So, what do you think?" asked Sheila. "You do have to think about your future."

"Our future," said Windflower. "But I'll really have to think about this."

"Whatever decision you make, I will support you," said Sheila.

"Thank you, Sheila," said Windflower. "I love you more than words can wield the matter, dearer than eyesight, space and liberty."

"Flattery will get you everywhere," said Sheila. "We have an hour before Stella comes home."

Windflower did not have to be asked twice.

The End

About the Author

Mike Martin was born in St. John's, NL on the east coast of Canada and now lives and works in Ottawa, Ontario. He is a long-time freelance writer and his articles and essays have appeared in newspapers, magazines and online across Canada as well as in the United States and New Zealand.

He is the author of the award-winning Sgt. Windflower Mystery series set in beautiful Grand Bank. There are now 12 books in this light mystery series with the publication of *Dangerous Waters. A Tangled Web* was shortlisted in 2017 for the best light mystery of the year, and *Darkest Before the Dawn* won the 2019 Bony Blithe Light Mystery Award.

Mike has also published *Christmas in Newfoundland: Memories and Mysteries*, a Sgt. Windflower Book of Christmas past and present.

Mike is Past Chair of the Board of Crime Writers of Canada, a national organization promoting Canadian crime and mystery writers and a member of the Newfoundland Writing Guild and Ottawa Independent Writers.

You can follow the Sgt. Windflower Mysteries on Facebook.

https://www.facebook.com/TheWalkerOnTheCapeReviewsAndMore/